A NEW YEAR FOR THE SEASIDE GIRLS

TRACY BAINES

Boldwood

First published in Great Britain in 2023 by Boldwood Books Ltd.

Copyright © Tracy Baines, 2023

Cover Design by Colin Thomas

Cover Photography: Colin Thomas and Alamy

A CIP catalogue record for this book is available from the British Library.

Paperback ISBN 978-1-80426-532-1

Large Print ISBN 978-1-80426-533-8

Hardback ISBN 978-1-80426-531-4

Ebook ISBN 978-1-80426-534-5

Kindle ISBN 978-1-80426-535-2

Audio CD ISBN 978-1-80426-526-0

MP3 CD ISBN 978-1-80426-527-7

Digital audio download ISBN 978-1-80426-529-1

Boldwood Books Ltd
23 Bowerdean Street
London SW6 3TN
www.boldwoodbooks.com

For Neil
For the love and the laughter

PROLOGUE

Johnny Randolph remained on the landing between the dress circle and the gods of the Empire theatre, suspended between the two, just as the old year was about to roll into the new. Frances had asked him to wait, he had no idea why, but then he hadn't understood so many things these past few months.

Only a few hours ago he'd been on his way to meet her, a diamond ring in his pocket and a proposal on his lips. What should have been a magical moment spoiled once again by his sister, Ruby. The snow had been falling heavily when he'd set off and he couldn't explain what made him turn back – could only thank God that he had. A wraithlike figure, scantily clad and barefoot, had been walking towards the park. It had taken seconds for him to realise it was her, a pale shadow moving towards the freezing water of the lake. He'd run, slipping and sliding in the snow, and dragged her from it. She'd been wild-eyed, babbling incoherently about letters, begging for his forgiveness. It was a while before he'd understood. Letters he'd written to Frances, the love of his life, had been intercepted – as had hers to him. Ruby and his mother to blame. It was a miracle they'd even found each other again, and in a way, he had Ruby to thank for that. For if it hadn't been for her wayward and reckless behaviour they might have remained in London, might never have left America. He might never have found Frances again. A miracle.

A door opened and noises of the party in the rooms above drifted down to him, laughter, and music, and warmth. Two set of footsteps on the stairs, Frances, and a softer, lighter step. Two pairs of shoes, a woman's, a child's. A little girl of no more than three, with dark hair and dark eyes, like her mother's, like his. He couldn't take his eyes off her and when she smiled at him, he looked to Frances, his tired brain trying to make sense of it all.

'Your child?'

'Ours,' Frances corrected him, letting go of the little girl's hand. 'Imogen, Daddy's home at last.'

1

NEW YEAR'S DAY 1940

At the dawn of the new year, Ruby Randolph was involved in two wars. The first with the rest of Great Britain and its Allies, fighting Hitler – the second within herself. A battle she no longer wanted to win. She'd been smiling out to audiences since she was four years old, when she first went onstage with her parents and her elder brother, Johnny, putting on a happy face for people who had paid to see them – selling herself. Twenty years ago, she'd been afraid of the lights and the noise, but had loved the attention, the adoration. It had fed her – then consumed her. She'd been doing it so long she didn't know how else to live. And now that Johnny knew everything, there would be nothing worth living for.

She lay, eyes shut but not sleeping, on the chintz sofa in the sitting room, drowsy from the medication the doctor had given her hours ago, aware of the fire crackling in the grate and the house-keeper, Mrs Frame, talking in a low whisper to her husband, Ted. The detached house in Park Drive had been home to the Randolph siblings for the last eight weeks, while they were topping the bill at the Palace Theatre in Grimsby for the winter season. The house overlooked the park, the park with the lake that she had walked into only hours ago. The lake that her brother had rescued her from. She shivered, feeling the sudden chill of the water again and Mrs Frame came over to her, adjusted the blanket. She touched her hand, spoke softly.

'Miss Ruby?'

She didn't open her eyes, didn't want to see anything of the world. Not any more. It would have been better if Johnny had let her slip into the darkness, for she couldn't imagine a future now. Everything their mother had warned her of had come to pass.

Alice Randolph had told her that any number of girls would take her place in Johnny's affections when he fell in love. That would be difficult enough, but if that girl could sing and dance, why would he need Ruby to partner him? The seeds had been sown so easily and Ruby, already insecure, had struggled most of her life with fear – fear of being replaced, fear of being left alone. So it had been natural to do as her mother wished, hiding the letters from Frances and not delivering the ones he trustingly handed over, protecting herself, protecting them all. The Randolphs. Their father had died in an accident when Ruby was six, leaving behind a trail of debts. Mother had been left with nothing but the talent of her children and the will to succeed, and succeed she had – but at what cost?

'Ruby?' Was it her mother speaking? No, it couldn't be, she remembered now. Not her mother, but Mrs Frame. Her head was filled with cotton wool, soft and fluffy clouds that she wanted to float away on, to a place where nothing could hurt her.

'Leave her be, love,' Mr Frame said from his place by the fire. 'Sleep will heal, and the lass looks like she needs it. I've seen more flesh on a rabbit. Is she warm enough?'

A cool hand was placed on her forehead. 'Warm on the outside but I can't say as what she's like on the inside, poor lamb.' Mrs Frame cradled her head and gently raised it to adjust the pillow. It was a wonderful thing to be tended to with so much care; Ruby couldn't remember the last time she'd been held so dearly. It ended when Mrs Frame went back to her chair and once again Ruby's thoughts began to swirl and drift.

When the grandfather clock in the hall chimed twelve to herald the passing of the old into the new, Mr Frame got up. 'Shall we toast the year with a drop of sherry?' he suggested. 'I'm sure Mr Randolph won't mind.' Ruby knew Mr Randolph wouldn't mind, as long as he got what he wanted. She loathed this smelly, industrial place. Grimsby. He had tricked her, bringing her here, telling her he was thinking of the future, which he was – but of his, not hers. They had been due to open at the London Coliseum but when war was declared the theatres were closed, and Johnny had looked for opportunities elsewhere. By some strange quirk of fate, he had found Frances O'Leary, the Irish girl who had taken her place once, and was set to take it for good. It was about what *he* wanted. It had been, all along. He shouldn't have turned back last night, to save her; he should have let her go. She was of no use to him now.

There was a gentle chink of glass as Mrs Frame picked up the decanter and poured, the ring of their glasses as they made a toast. 'Well, love,' Mr Frame announced, 'to 1940 and whatever it brings. May we get through together, God willing.' She lifted her eyelids a little, enough to see Mr Frame peck his wife on the cheek and share an affectionate hug before they sat down again in the chairs either side of the fire. Together.

Four years, that's how long Johnny and Frances had been apart, and in that time the Randolphs had been making quite a name for themselves in America – the darlings of New York, the British Astaires. She'd never felt as loved as she had there. Until Johnny spoiled it. They'd been offered Broadway and he'd turned it down to come home. But where was home? She no longer knew.

The clock chimed the half hour and Mr Frame got up and went

to the window, slipping beyond the curtain, careful not to let the light escape into the darkness outside.

'Snow's stopped, Flo,' he said, tugging the curtains back into place. 'That's a blessing at least. I'll be getting off home. Will you be all right if I leave the pair of you?'

His wife tutted. 'Ted Frame, I've been managing perfectly well looking after folk for years. I'll be more worried about you walking back. Did you bring your torch?' Mrs Frame left the room and came back with his coat and hat. Ruby lifted her eyelids a little, watching her fuss over him, this man in his sixties, as if he were a small boy who might get lost in the dark.

Ruby closed her eyes again. Her mother had never cared for her like that. She couldn't remember one moment in her entire life when she'd experienced the tenderness she'd seen playing out between these two people who loved each other. Did her mother even know what love was? Alice Randolph had returned home to England to die, without a word to her adult children. Ruby would never forgive her for that. Never. She had pushed them to succeed then betrayed them both, leaving Ruby keeper of her secrets. Nothing was meant to come between brother and sister; Alice wouldn't allow it – but it had, more than Johnny had known, more than she had known. And it was her fault. He would know now of his child, for he hadn't returned as he said he would. Tonight the entire length and breadth of her deceit had been broken wide open and, just as her mother had warned her, it was the beginning of the end for the Randolphs.

2

The small party left the Empire theatre on Alexandra Road in the early hours of New Year's Day and headed for the terraced house on Barkhouse Lane where Frances O'Leary had lodgings. There had been no performance, it being Sunday, and the cast of the panto along with friends of the owner, Jack Holland, had gathered in the upper rooms of the small seaside theatre in Cleethorpes for 'Auld Lang Syne'. The snow had stopped falling more than an hour ago and the white carpet of the pavement was spattered with footprints of revellers long departed. It had been a bittersweet heralding in of the year, not knowing what lay ahead but vowing to make the best of it. The newspapers were calling it the phoney war, for none of the expected bombings had occurred, and as the coldest winter in years took hold across Europe, any advances had been stalled. Singer and Variety Girl Jessie Delaney linked arms with her fifteen-year-old brother, Eddie, the two of them keeping a watchful eye on their widowed mother, Grace, who walked in front of them, deep in conversation with their landlady, Geraldine. Jessie glanced over her shoulder at the small but new family behind her, and her friend and fellow dancer, Frances, gave her a small smile. Beside her,

Johnny Randolph carried their three-year-old daughter, Imogen. A child he'd known nothing of until a few hours ago. He had barely taken his eyes off her since.

The snow lit their way in the darkness as they weaved away from the promenade and into the backstreets. It was surprising how quickly they'd got used to the blackout restrictions and there would be more to come. Ration books had already been distributed, and rationing of bacon, butter and sugar was little more than a week away. Although there had not been any bombing on the mainland, the Germans had sunk many merchant ships, thus limiting supplies. Grace shone her torch on the keyhole as Geraldine fiddled to put the key in the lock of number 41 and opened the door. The two women stepped back to allow Johnny to enter first, the tall dark stranger who would bring them luck, and he walked ahead of them, Frances telling him to enter by the second door on the right and not the first. There was a flurry of activity as the rest of them made their way into the narrow hall and congregated in the back room, removing their hats and coats and draping them over the dining chairs to air. The fire had been backed up with slack before they left, and the embers glowed red beneath the ash. Jessie removed the guard and raked what was left of the coals to stir the heat while Johnny waited in the doorway, Imogen in his arms. Frances rubbed her hands to warm them, then reached out to him. 'I'll take her to bed.'

'Let me. Please?'

Frances turned to Geraldine, who nodded her consent, and she led the way, upstairs into the room that had been hers alone when she'd moved there a little over six months ago.

Geraldine had inherited the shabby and neglected terraced house from her late aunt earlier last year and she and Frances had worked together that first week to make it clean and habitable. The room had been made cosy with the addition of second-hand curtains, an eiderdown and a small rug. Frances hurried to the bed she shared with her daughter and lit the small lamp on the table next to it, pulled back the covers and moved the hot water bottle she'd placed there earlier. It wasn't very warm but at least it had taken the chill from sheets. Johnny gently laid their child down, removing her shoes, her hat and scarf, stopping awkwardly at her coat, unsure how to proceed. She came beside him, propping Imogen up with her hand, and between them they removed her outer clothing.

'She'll be all right in her dress. No need to pull her about any more than we have to.' Frances covered her with the blankets and tucked her in, then stepped back, allowing her father to sit by her side for the first time in her short life. Johnny placed a soft hand to Imogen's face, and Frances was suddenly overwhelmed with sadness for all the lost years. Years of struggle, years of shame, an unmarried woman with a child. Months when she had to leave her while she found work, a few weeks here and there, traipsing up and down the country, glad of a summer season and the chance to stay in one place for a few weeks, a chance to save. Performing in Cleethorpes had been a godsend with Imogen close by, living with her good friend, Patsy Dawkins, and her sons. Patsy, an ex-dancer, had been there for her from the very beginning, and if it hadn't been for her kindness and support, Frances might have had to make more difficult choices. It was only recently that Jessie and her family had learned of her child. Imogen had gone missing one night, as had Patsy's five-year-old son, Colly, wanting more of the magic the theatre had offered them. It had been the worst night of her life, a night when she'd been forced to reveal Imogen's existence. She'd braced herself for a hostile reaction but instead of damning judgement had received only compassion. Geraldine's response was perhaps the most surprising of all, for where she'd feared criticism she had only found understanding.

Johnny leaned forward, kissed Imogen's cheek and whispered close, 'Sweet dreams, darling girl.' He got up, unable to speak at first, taking Frances into his arms and holding her so tightly that she felt his pain as her own. 'Oh, Frances, Frances,' he whispered into her hair. 'I can't begin to imagine how hard it's been for both of you – but especially you.'

More than he would ever know, but it was hardly his fault. Blame could be laid firmly at his mother's feet – and latterly Ruby's. Because of them, Imogen had missed out on a father's love and care. It had been hard coping on her own, away from her family in Ireland who knew nothing of Imogen. If it hadn't been for good friends, she wouldn't have managed at all. That Johnny had come back into her life was wonderful – yet fraught with complications. They had a child, they weren't married – what stories would she have to spin now? He kissed her, his lips warm, and she couldn't think any more, her longing for him consuming her. She'd been holding back for so long, not daring to believe that he loved her still, and at last she could let go and be loved again. Eventually she pulled away, conscious that they weren't alone in the house.

'They'll be wondering where we've got to.'

He nodded, understanding her concern, reluctant to let her go.

'You'll never have to struggle again, darling. I'll make sure of that.' He placed his hand to her cheek. 'I have to meet with Jack Holland tomorrow—' he corrected himself; it was already Monday '—today, about the show at the Palace. There are still a few weeks left of the run. Ruby's in no fit state to dance, and, well...' He looked back to Imogen. '... there are more important things to consider now. Things I have to put right – and I *will* put them right, Frances.' He drew her into his arms once more, kissed her hungrily, and she wanted to submit to him, suddenly tired, overcome by the evening's events. She'd fought so hard to hide Imogen away from the harsh realities of her life but now that carefully constructed world had broken open, and she felt exhausted from years of holding it together. They pulled apart when they heard someone clamber up the stairs, and Eddie called a soft goodnight and wished them a happy new year as he went to his room. Johnny glanced towards the chest of drawers. On top of it was a shoebox containing letters she'd sent to Johnny and he to her. 'Ruby gave them to you?'

'She left them on my dressing-room table – with a note. I thought it was a Christmas present. And it was – in a way.'

He ran his hands over the top of them.

'They were unopened,' she told him.

'Does that make the damage less?'

'No. But if they'd known—'

His expression hardened. 'I doubt my mother would have acted any differently.'

She could only agree. Alice Randolph had been single-minded as far as her children were concerned. 'I don't understand why they kept them.' She took some of them out and showed him the sealed envelopes. 'I meant to sort them, return yours. I haven't had a chance what with Christmas and everything else, you and me – and Imogen.'

He flicked through them, rubbing his thumb over her writing, as if he were caressing her skin. 'You don't have to apologise. For anything,' he said, handing them back.

She replaced them and he took her in his arms again.

'I must go. Let you get some sleep.' He kissed the top of her head. 'After I've seen Jack, I'll be straight here. If that's all right with you?' She nodded, grateful that he wasn't barging into her life and taking over. Did he sense her need to take things slowly? She could have told him about Imogen weeks ago, when they'd first encountered each other again, but couldn't, afraid of being hurt, of being rejected. Had it been just the two of them it would have been easier, but Johnny and Ruby's lives were intertwined. Ruby would always be in the picture whether they liked it or not.

* * *

After Johnny left, Frances joined Geraldine, Jessie and Grace in the back room. They had been drinking cocoa and Jessie got up and pushed a mug of it in front of Frances as she joined them at the table.

'A lovely evening, considering,' Grace said softly. 'I always find New Year's Eve rather melancholy. Absent friends. More so this year.' She glanced towards Jessie and gave her an encouraging smile. Jessie's fiancé, Harry, was in the RAF and hadn't been able to get leave.

None of them knew what lay ahead of them, did they, good or bad, and it was silly of Frances to be afraid like this, but she was, and she couldn't shake off the fear that settled in the pit of her stomach. She'd thought it would be easier now that everything was out in the open, that she no longer had to worry in case someone found out and judged her, or worst of all, judged Imogen. The conversation was stilted, Frances aware they all wanted to know how things had gone with Johnny but were too polite to ask. And even Jessie, usually so forthright, had kept quiet. In the end, she saved them the trouble. 'Absent friends and those newly arrived.'

Jessie smiled. 'How did he take it? You keeping Imogen a secret?'

Grace glared at her daughter, but Frances only shrugged; she was used to Jessie blurting out what was in her head without thinking much of the consequences. They had been friends since Jessie arrived in Cleethorpes as a last-minute addition to the Variety Girls dance troupe and Frances had taken her under her wing and brought her to Barkhouse Lane.

'We didn't have much chance to talk. There was too much noise; it was a party...'

Jessie leaned forward. 'He knew, though?'

'When he saw her, he did. And I told him a little before we joined you all. Ruby had told him of the letters, of what she and their mother had done. But she kept her promise to me and didn't tell him of Imogen.'

'Why didn't she come with him?' Geraldine asked, curious.

The three of them looked at her and she wondered how much to reveal. Johnny had told her briefly of what had happened, but he had been too enamoured with his child, too bewildered by it all to want to talk about Ruby. Or his mother for that matter. 'He asked her to come. After all, she knew she would be welcome. We'd all helped her with that sordid blackmail business.' When Ruby's mother had died, her drinking had spiralled out of control – as had Ruby. So much so that Johnny had turned down a Broadway contract and headed for home, only to arrive back in England and have their London show cancelled when war was declared and theatres across the country went dark. It left Ruby free to party away her days. And party she did. She'd been an easy target for men to prey on, and one drunken night had been lured into the back room of a nightclub. Photographs had been taken of her in various states of undress, photographs that would be the ruin of her reputation. Would Ruby always be a liability? Could Frances allow that chaos into her life?

Grace and Geraldine waited for her to speak again. Jessie wasn't so patient. 'So why didn't she?'

Frances took a breath. 'He left her at home, then turned back...'

Jessie tilted her head to one side and Frances looked away, to Grace, who would understand, who wouldn't judge, would never blame.

'She walked into the lake at the park across the road from the house.'

Jessie gasped. 'Why?'

Frances felt the heat flood to her cheeks, but she wasn't to blame for Ruby's tortured mind. Even so, she felt she had contributed to it by asking her to keep secret her knowledge of Imogen for this past week. But it was nothing compared to having to keep her child's existence a secret for all of her three years. Frances had wanted to tell Johnny herself, in her own time.

'Poor girl.' Geraldine saved her from explaining any further. 'Her mother has a lot to answer for.' She placed her mug on a coaster. 'No doubt she had her reasons.'

'Or she was just cruel!' Jessie spat.

'Oh, I doubt it,' Grace interrupted. 'You thought Aunt Iris was cruel, Jessie. Life had made her bitter, but she didn't start out that way.'

Jessie shrugged. Frances sympathised with Jessie. She had only met Aunt Iris briefly, but enough to know that living with her – as Jessie and her family had done when their father died – couldn't have been a joyful experience.

'Life is hard,' Jessie's mother said. 'We have to try and not let it make us hard too. It's not as easy as it might sound.'

Frances drank back her cocoa. She was glad to have older women like Grace and Geraldine around her. Jessie had lost her father and Harry might be away, but she had been sheltered by Grace's steady presence. She was naïve and headstrong, and Frances hoped that when life's knocks did come her friend's way, as they must to everyone, that it would not let her become bitter too. Geraldine had lost her fiancé in the Great War and Grace had not had an easy life, but they were kind, and that meant a lot in a world where people were quick to judge.

Geraldine stifled a yawn. 'Well, I'm for my bed. There's been far too much excitement for one night. I'll wish you all a happy new year and goodnight.' She stood up and Grace followed suit. Jessie kissed her mother and Frances began clearing the table, taking the mugs and cups through to the kitchen and rinsing them clean.

Jessie picked up a tea towel. 'I'll miss you, you know, when you're gone.'

'I'm not going anywhere.' Frances had no plans to move, but it would be ridiculous to think that things wouldn't change in the future.

'But you will,' Jessie replied. 'And I just wanted you to know.' She dried the last mug and put it on the shelf, then hung the tea towel over the rail on the back door.

Frances pressed a hand to her shoulder. 'No matter where I am, or where I go, we'll always be friends, Jessie. Always.'

3

Johnny got out of the taxi on the main road and walked the rest of the way to the house he and Ruby were renting for the time they were appearing at the Palace. It was eerie and quiet, the snow still fresh in many places, and he could feel his socks dampen as it came over his shoes and melted. The last few hours had felt like a dream, a wonderful dream – but bitterness nibbled at the edges of his glorious delight. He'd needed time to think but the taxi driver had wanted to talk, and so they had chatted of the situation in Europe, and whether Chamberlain was up to the job. The driver's son was in the army and posted down south. He and the missus hadn't seen him since October and his mother was fretting. It would be the same story in many homes, families dreading a repeat of the Great War. Harsh as it was, he couldn't think of war, not at the moment. Whatever he had expected the new year to bring, it wasn't fatherhood; it certainly wasn't the knowledge of a child. Imogen. He had closed his eyes as the man talked, seeing her innocent face and felt such anger, such rage at the trouble his mother had caused. And then there was Ruby. He looked across the road to the park. The water wasn't deep, but if he hadn't had second thoughts, hadn't turned back...

He opened the gate and walked up the path. He had forgotten to take a torch, but the moon and the light reflected from the snow were enough to see the lump of coal on the doorstep that had been left for the first footer. He picked it up and opened the door, pulling back the blackout curtain and closing it as gently as he could, placing the coal on the small table beside the telephone. Shrugging off his coat and hat, he hung them on the hall stand, at the same time checking his reflection in the mirror at the centre of it. He ran his hand over his dark hair, loosened his tie and eased off his shoes, picked them up and carried them into the sitting room. A good fire burned in the grate, and he set his damp shoes in front of it, warmed his hands, then turned his back to it. Mrs Frame, their housekeeper, had nodded off in an armchair and she roused herself, and gave him a sleepy smile. Ruby was lying on the sofa where he had left her only hours ago when the doctor arrived to sedate her. With the help of Mrs Frame he had removed her clothes and dressed her in his flannelette pyjamas. Ruby's were silk and wouldn't keep her warm. He'd been shocked when he saw how skeletal she had become and when Mrs Frame had brought down a blanket, he sent her upstairs for more, fearing Ruby might die from the cold let alone the shock. She was pale and grey, as she had been for these past few weeks. Their mother's death two years ago had been a blow to them both, but the trouble with Ruby had started long before that. Alice Randolph had died and left them to cope with the fallout of her ambition. She had pushed Johnny and Ruby to the top, but had it been worth the price they paid in their personal lives – what there was of it? Anger surged again but he fought it, trying to understand, trying to forgive her. Their father had been a huge star in the West End, but he had been reckless with his money, and they'd been left almost destitute when he was killed in a motor accident. Fear of poverty had driven Alice and she in turn had driven them. Ruby had not coped as well as he. His sister drank, ate and made herself sick, he knew she did, although she would never admit it. And then there had been the bother with Mickey Harper, who had taken compromising photographs of Ruby and used them to blackmail her. With the help of friends, they had put an end to that. Friends, true friends – they had never had them before.

Mrs Frame got up and came beside him, saying in a low whisper, 'She hasn't stirred since you left. Let me get you a hot drink – unless you'd prefer something stronger.'

'Hot milk would be good, perhaps a nip of whisky in it?'

She indicated the chair. 'Sit yourself down and get warm. You look chilled to the bone.' Bending down to pick up his shoes, she said, 'I'll get some newspaper tucked inside. Good shoes need to be taken care of.'

He gave them a cursory glance and as she left the room he sank down into the chair, looked to Ruby then stared into the fire. Good shoes, good clothes, good surroundings. He thought back to the little house where he'd left Frances and Imogen. The women were kind, and he was glad that Frances had good people around her – but good shoes? How on earth Frances had managed these past three years he had no idea, but he was so damned proud of her that she had.

Mrs Frame brought his drink and one for herself. He made to get up from the chair, but she shook her head, placed her cup on the small table to her side and settled herself in the chair opposite him. 'You had a lovely evening?'

Her smile was warm, and he longed to talk, to unburden himself, but he only smiled and said, 'Yes, it was a good night. In the end.'

He glanced to Ruby, saw her eyelids flicker. 'Did your husband go back home?'

'He did. He saw the new year in with me and left soon after. No point us both being here, and your sister has been quite safe.'

He nodded. Glad he could trust someone. He should have been able to trust his mother. Alice had known there was something between him and Frances and she had intervened; nothing was going to get in the way of her children's success. Certainly not love.

'You must be tired, Mrs Frame. Keeping watch.' He was grateful for her steadying presence these past weeks, making the rented house feel like a real home. He'd had enough of hotels, fancy as they were.

'Oh, I didn't mind, dear.'

He smiled. Any formality between them had been surrendered in the crisis with Ruby. He'd always been 'Mr Johnny' and it was good to be called 'dear'. He looked at her with affection he hadn't felt before. They had stability here, in this out-of-the-way place that had been full of surprises – the first of them being Frances. That he had found her after all this time. He felt a surge of sourness in his stomach, in his mouth. Of all the empty years.

Mrs Frame checked the clock. 'You should get up to bed. You look all in. I can stay with Miss Ruby.'

'I've already put you to more trouble than I should, Mrs Frame.'

'Tsk. Think nothing of it. We wouldn't have done much different than we always do, new year or not. Although it's a strange one this year, being at war as such. So many without their loved ones. Makes you appreciate them more, doesn't it? When they're not with you.'

He agreed, suddenly taken by a wave of overwhelming loneliness. He stared into the fire.

'Thawed out a little?' Mrs Frame said presently. She hesitated, couching her words. 'I was thinking, with your sister so ill... about the show. That you'll be leaving soon. I couldn't help hearing the doctor...' She flushed, embarrassed, but Johnny only smiled at her.

'It's all right, Mrs Frame. I can hardly hide it all from you, can I.' He knew he didn't want to, sick of pretending everything was all right when it clearly wasn't. If only he'd paid greater attention to what Ruby was doing, what his mother had been doing – for years! He was ashamed of his stupidity, for not noticing what was going on, focusing on the work, perfecting their routines, their technique. After Frances there didn't seem any point in falling in love, and when she didn't reply to his letters, didn't take up her ticket to join him in America... what a damn fool he was.

Mrs Frame moved in her chair, and it jogged him out of his thoughts.

'We can hardly rush off. We've sublet our London flat so we've nowhere to go. We have an aunt, in Dorset...' He hadn't had time to think of what their next move would be. He looked to Mrs Frame and smiled. 'I might have need of you more than I did before. I have a meeting with one of my partners later this morning to decide which way to go. Ruby won't be able to work. We'll have to close the show. I should think the theatre will switch over to films.'

She smiled at him. 'Perhaps you'll find yourself in films before too long. Like Mr Astaire. He used to dance with his sister before he became a big star.'

He hadn't thought of a career without Ruby. Things had changed in ways he could never had known, war for one. He had vowed to enlist once he'd taken care of Ruby, but it was obvious she needed care way beyond what he could provide. Their mother had manipulated her own children to get what she wanted, set one against the other. It was cruel. He watched the shallow rise and fall of his sister's chest, the slightest of movements. He couldn't tell her of Imogen. It would make her far worse to know the consequences of carrying out their mother's instructions. Even so. Their mother had been dead long enough. She could have told him then – when he thought it was only a broken romance...

Mrs Frame disturbed him once more. 'I took the liberty of making up the bed in the spare room. Just in case you needed me to stay over now and then. Ted's agreeable. He'll come here for his meals and go home again. And he's doing his bit with the ARP so most nights he's on watch. He can sleep during the day and I'll not disturb him. If that's all right with you?'

She'd made it so easy for him and he sighed with relief. 'Mrs Frame, you're a gem.'

'Well, I don't know about that, but we all have to pull together in times of trouble. And I've grown fond of your sister and yourself.'

'As we have of you, Mrs Frame. I know I can speak for Ruby in that respect. She's been happier here than I've ever known her to be in a long time.' They'd been on the move in America, state to state, touring shows, making a name for themselves. Their mother had made sure they were seen in the right places with all the right people. It had been relentless but being here, with Mrs Frame taking care of them, had been a revelation. They had missed out on so much.

They both cast their eyes over Ruby. 'Go to bed, Mrs Frame. I'll sit with her,' he said, getting to his feet. 'It will give me time to think, to work a few things out.'

She got up, pressing her hand to his arm in small comfort as she left the room. Johnny raked over the coals. Remembering the lump in the hall, he fetched it and put it on the fire, and added a few more, watching the flames lick and die around them. They would need all the luck they could to get through this year. The age of conscription had been raised to twenty-seven and he would be included. Had he been a couple of months older, it would've bought him more time. As it was, he would be called to register for active service. He would have done so at the first inklings of war had Ruby been in better mental shape. She'd always been volatile, that was her nature, but this was more than that. She was damaged, and he doubted whether she would recover. On the mantel in front of him was a photo of Alice Randolph in a silver frame. The very thought of her made bile rise in his throat. No longer wanting a reminder, he stuffed the frame between two books on the shelves to the right of the fireplace. Ruby sighed and he went to her. Her eyes were closed. Did she know it was him? He sat down on the edge of the sofa and took her hand, clasped it in his.

'Oh, Ruby. It's been quite the night.' He took the stray strand of her dark hair and tucked it behind her ear as she was always doing herself. He thought of Imogen, of the dark hair of his child. Of Frances. 'There's so much to live for, Ruby. So much you don't know, that I didn't know. Mother made a mess of things but we're going to put it right. We're going to love and be loved.' He could turn things around, now that he knew. He slipped down onto the floor, his back to the sofa. 'It's going to get better from now on.'

He watched the flames, unaware of the tear that fell silently down Ruby's cheek, and she couldn't move her hand to brush it away.

4

Johnny was woken by Mrs Frame when she laid a cup of tea on the small table to his left. He had spent the last hours of the night in the chair and eased himself awake, watching as Mrs Frame went over to Ruby and took hold of her hand, pressing the back of her other hand to Ruby's head. Ruby did not move, didn't open her eyes, hadn't turned in the night as far as he was aware.

'Should I call the doctor again?' she asked in a low whisper.

'Not unless she's distressed.'

'She was rather... overwrought,' Mrs Frame added, choosing her words with care.

Johnny took his tea, and sipped a little. His mouth was parched and he ached all over. He shook back his shoulders and eased himself more upright. 'She hasn't been herself for a long time, Mrs Frame. We've worked too hard for too long. She needs rest. Deep rest.' Ruby had long ago lost the gaiety she once possessed. He'd thought it was losing their mother but now he knew it went much deeper than that. That she'd gone off the rails was understandable. They were living and working together, and she'd had no idea how to tell him what she'd done. If he hadn't found Frances, would she ever have told him at all? He forced himself not to be bitter, rubbed his eyes and yawned. His head felt thick with lack of sleep, of too many thoughts.

'While she's sleeping, she's mending.' Mrs Frame's smile was heavy with such sympathy that it almost undid him.

'Let's hope so,' he said, knowing it would take more than sleep for Ruby to recover. 'I need to go out, Mrs Frame, and sort a few things. I'll be at the Empire or the Palace if you need me.'

'And Miss Ruby?'

'If you're worried, call the doctor directly. I'll be back as soon as I can.'

* * *

He washed and changed into a clean shirt, drank back the second cup of tea and picked up his hat, his keys, then put them down again, realising he wouldn't need them. Mrs Frame would be here and for that small comfort he was grateful. He stepped out into the greyness of the morning and set off at a brisk pace, eschewing the bus, hoping that the walk would help him order his thoughts.

He'd arranged to meet Jack at the Empire rather than the Palace, wanting to call on Frances and Imogen and spend time with them before dealing with Ruby. She'd been in such a state when he'd brought her back into the house last night, and it had taken all his strength and will to calm her. When she'd begun babbling away about the letters, he hadn't understood, and when he did, her utter terror numbed his anger. Not so much at her, but at their mother. Had she known of the damage she was doing in her pursuit of fame for the Randolphs? Not knowing frustrated him beyond measure, but he had to keep a clear head and concentrate on the here and now. Business had to be sorted before he could even begin to hope of sorting his personal life.

He cut through the marketplace and onto Market Street, the road opening out to give a clear view of the promenade and the pier, the pavilion appearing to be almost floating in the middle of the River Humber. There wasn't much to tempt the winter traveller, the seaside lacking the gaiety and colour of its summer dressing. A cleaner from the Dolphin Hotel was emptying dirty water down the drain at the rear of the building and, seeing him, called out 'Happy new year', her bucket clattering on the ground beside her. He answered as he crossed the street and made his way to the Empire. The cast-iron canopy of the Victorian frontage overlooked the pier gardens the other side of the road. The hoarding across the top advertised the pantomime and the glass cases either side of the doors were filled with photographs from the production of *Aladdin*. Frances was Genie of the Ring. A small part, way beneath her capabilities. She'd been in a show with them in the West End when the Randolphs left for America. He'd sent a ticket for her to follow on – a ticket he now knew she'd never received. Anger surged again and he let out a long breath, hoping to dispel some of the bitter energy. Frances had put a stop to what could have been a successful solo career in order to care for Imogen, hiding away in one small seaside resort after another. While the Randolphs' star shone, Frances O'Leary's shrank. And for that he too had to take responsibility. He'd known how strong their love for each other was; why had he blithely handed his letters over to his mother and sister, trusting them to mail them, not questioning their honesty, only doubting Frances's love for him? He would never doubt it again. He'd let Frances down, but he would spend the rest of his life making it up to her.

The doors to the Empire were locked and he removed his glove and rapped on the glass, stamping his feet on the steps to dislodge the snow that clung to his shoes as he waited. Inside, to the right, a blonde girl he vaguely recognised came out from the box office and hurried to the doors to let him in.

'Mr Holland's upstairs in his office, Mr Randolph. He said to go right up.'

'Thank you...' He couldn't recall her name but knew she was a friend of Frances and the other girls.

'Dolly,' she offered.

'Of course, Dolly. Forgive me. It was quite the night. A lot to remember, so many people.'

She smiled, nodded. She knew of Imogen, as did many of the cast and theatre staff. They had protected Frances, probably thinking him a cad for abandoning her. Lord, what a shambles it was. He offered a smile in return and followed her up the stairs. She knocked on the door and opened it.

'Mr Randolph has arrived.' She stepped back to allow him to pass, and Jack Holland was already on his feet to greet him. The room was cosy, overlooking the pier gardens, empty benches and empty streets. It was only a few months ago he'd arrived here with his agent, Bernie Blackwood. The two of them – Jack and Bernie – were in partnership and had invited him to join them. They had three theatres – the Empire, The Palace and the Royal in Lincoln – hoping to add to the number and build a company to rival Moss Empires. He had been unsure then, thinking only of an investment, knowing that it was only a matter of months, perhaps weeks, before he would be called for service. The income would help Ruby and have given them something for the future; that was all he had been thinking of at the time. He'd had no knowledge of Frances then and it had been a complete shock to find her rehearsing with her friends, Jessie and Ginny, when he'd walked into the auditorium that day.

Jack Holland came from behind his desk and shook hands with Johnny. A man in his late forties, he had a slight limp and a scar one side of his face, a permanent reminder of his service in the Great War. Johnny had no qualms going into business with him and Bernie. Both men had seen action. They wouldn't be called to fight this time, but he had no doubt they would both play their part. Johnny took a seat and Jack returned to his desk. It hadn't been the time or place to enlarge on what had happened with Ruby last night, only that there had been problems – why spoil the evening? But there had been questions. After all, the Randolphs came as a pair, and it was rare that one was seen without the other. That had seemed fun at first, when they were children, but it was not a healthy way to live. It had all but destroyed Ruby. He exhaled, removed his gloves and hat, and Jack indicated for him to place them on the table at the side of him.

'How's Audrey's head this morning?' He smiled; Jack did too.

'Throbbing. She enjoyed herself for once. Although it could have been the drink that Bob was plying her with.' He grinned. It was well known that Audrey Holland disapproved of her husband's investment, but from what Johnny had seen of her there wasn't much that met with her approval. 'And Ruby?'

Johnny's smile disappeared. 'She's not good. I doubt she'll be able to perform tomorrow. That's what I need to see you about.' He paused. No point making promises he couldn't keep. 'We'll have to close the show. Or get a replacement top of the bill.'

Jack leaned forward, picked up a pencil and began a lazy doodle on his desk blotter. 'Short term? Longer?'

He might as well be frank; it made no sense to even try to cover up Ruby's state of mind. Perhaps he'd deluded himself that no one else had been aware how fragile she was. Perhaps he'd been the last to notice. How blind he'd been these last years, how absorbed in their career. There had been nothing else to be absorbed with. They were barely anywhere long enough to lay down roots. Relationships, if you could call them that, were brief, Ruby falling into one disastrous affair after another. He should have known; he should have paid more attention.

'I've no idea.' He considered how much to share with his partner. It might weaken his position. Jack was looking directly at him, and he knew how ridiculous that thought was. He'd liked him the moment he saw him. They hadn't been in England very long when Bernie had taken him up to Cleethorpes and Grimsby. At first, he'd sought only to get Ruby away from the parties and hedonists, to secure an investment for the future – hers in case anything should happen to him. He'd been ambivalent until he discovered Frances at the Empire. He'd chosen selfishly, not thinking of Ruby, not then. 'She's in a bad way.' To his horror, his voice cracked with emotion, and he coughed to clear his throat and disguise it.

Jack wasn't fooled.

'What about a replacement? I'd hate for the other acts on the bill to be out of work when there's so little about. And the takings are good. The pair of you are still pulling in the crowds – no one's bored of the Randolphs yet.'

His comment made Johnny smile. 'Well, that's good to know.' He thought for a while. 'I have no idea who's working where. My mind has been on other things.' He glanced to Jack, who knew a little of the background between him and Frances. Of Imogen. If he knew more, he didn't let on, but Jack wasn't a man to pass judgement unless he knew the ins and outs of a situation. He'd learned that much from working with him these past few months; he was hands-on, kind – and Johnny trusted him.

'I could ask about. Check with Bernie. I've been out of touch with so many of our fellow performers since we went to America. If we could find another big name to draw the crowds...'

Jack leaned back in his chair. 'I wasn't thinking of anyone to replace you. I was thinking more of someone standing in for Ruby.'

Johnny shook his head. 'It's out of the question...' He didn't know anything but being with Ruby.

'I was thinking of Frances.' Jack interlaced his fingers and rested them on his desk, allowing time for his words to sink in. 'You dance so well together. And when you surprised her—'

'That was one dance.' Once he'd found her, Johnny had bombarded Frances with letters and bouquets. She hadn't responded, and in desperation he'd made a trip to Cleethorpes and ambushed her when she was onstage with the Variety Girls. One dance, a dance they'd performed in the hit show *Lavender Lane* when Frances had stood in for Ruby, who'd been rushed to hospital with appendicitis.

'It's a temporary solution. But it would tide us – you – over until Ruby is well. A week, maybe two.'

Johnny shrugged. He had no idea how long Ruby's recuperation would take but he didn't think two weeks would cut it. 'Frances is tied up with the panto.'

'A part that can easily be filled by any number of girls. It was clear she had talent when she first came here. We all wondered why she wasn't dancing in some show in London but, well, now we know.' He paused. 'It would be a solution. After all, she's almost a Randolph.' A cautious smiled played about his lips and Johnny couldn't help but join him.

'I had every intention of proposing last night. New year. New plans—'

'What stopped you?'

Johnny hesitated. People gossiped. Word would soon get round; it would be in the newspapers and that wouldn't help their reputation. Frances would suffer most, Imogen too. The fallen woman and her child. He could almost see the headlines plastered across every newspaper from here to New York. No. He couldn't have that.

'Forgive me. I shouldn't have asked.' Jack was awkward.

Johnny batted a hand in the air. 'It's a perfectly innocent question - with a perfectly complicated answer.'

Jack nodded his head. 'Would you like a coffee?'

'That would be great.' Jack got up, opened the door to his left and stepped into the small office that his assistant used, the engine room of the Empire, leaving the door open and calling out to Johnny as he filled the kettle. 'Milk? Sugar?'

'Neither, thanks, Jack.' He got up himself and went to the window that looked out onto the gardens. The trees were bare of leaves, the flower beds empty. Winter was bleak in England. It wasn't just the cold; it was the damp, the grey endless days. Jack came back into the room and Johnny took the cup and saucer from him. The two men sat down. Johnny drank a little coffee.

'The proposal...' Johnny began.

'Mine or yours?'

Johnny grinned. It was easy here, with Jack. He seemed to understand when a man was floundering. 'Both. But mine first.'

He told Jack of setting out on New Year's Eve to meet Frances, fully intending to ask her to marry him. 'I had the ring in my pocket. Ruby didn't want to come along. I knew she was tired, exhausted. We'd been playing to packed houses, many of them lads on leave. Ruby was out front, chatting with them every night after the show. I thought she was better once that bother about the blackmail came to light. But that was only half the story.' He told of their mother's deceit and manipulation. 'I didn't realise the extent of it all.' He exhaled a long breath. 'Something made me turn back. I saw this figure, walking towards the park. The lake. I ran, slipped in the snow. I got there as she walked into the water.' Jack sipped his coffee, waiting for Johnny to go on. 'I carried her back, changed my suit, called the doctor out and left her in the care of our housekeeper. I had agreed to meet Frances. I couldn't let her down again.'

'And the ring was in your suit pocket?'

He nodded. 'That was bad enough. A feeble excuse.' They shared a smile. 'And then I discovered...' He blew out over his lip, the events of last night swimming around in his head. 'God, Jack. I have a daughter. A three-year-old daughter and I had no damned idea about it.' It was still so hard to believe. 'When Frances didn't follow me out to America, I thought she'd changed her mind, put her career first. That I'd been mistaken about what we meant to each other. Hell, that hurt.'

'It's a lot to deal with in a lifetime, let alone a night,' Jack commiserated.

Johnny shrugged. 'I don't even know where to begin to make sense of it all.'

'Does it need to make sense?'

'I don't suppose it does.' Johnny stared into his cup. 'But I need to make sensible choices on how we all go forward.'

'And Ruby?'

'I'll see how she is when I get back. There are some difficult decisions to make. I was hoping to find someone to take my place in the show, to keep her working, keep her busy. After the run at the Palace ended, it could have toured the provinces... I can't do anything like that now. She can't work.' He let out a deep sigh. 'We have money, financial security – but it's so easy to drift and, well, you already know how much trouble she can get herself into.'

Jack got up and opened the window a little. 'Then what about my proposal? If Frances agreed, it would give us time to bring a little stability to the situation. I'd hate to put the rest of the acts on the bill out of work. It would keep the theatre running, at least until the third of February as planned. I'm dammed if I'll let it go dark, but I don't want us to go to films just yet, not if we can help it.' He handed over a letter from the Ministry of Works to requisition the Empire. 'They'll take over at the end of the pantomime – so that's another theatre lost. We'll be compensated, but that's not the point.

Live entertainment is transformative. I saw how it lifted the men in the last war. It's important to see real people, not the celluloid images, no matter how wonderful they are. We all need to escape from life's tribulations from time to time.'

He needed escape too and Jack was offering it to him.

Johnny sighed. He longed to dance with Frances again but not like this, a replacement, an understudy. Would she see it that way? 'It's a lot to ask of her, but if she agreed I'm sure we could put something together...' He checked his watch. 'We'd only have a few hours to rehearse before curtain up.'

Jack got to his feet, smiling. 'Then what are you waiting for?'

5

Mr Frame smelled of the outdoors, of trees and bonfires, soil and tobacco. He'd been clearing a path in the garden, so that Mrs Frame wouldn't slip when she was tipping ashes and vegetable peelings on the compost patch behind the beech hedge. She'd called him inside for his dinner and, after he'd removed his boots, instructed him to go through to the sitting room.

'Look at your socks, Ted. Another hole that needs darning.' His big toe peeped through the gaping wool. 'You need your nails cutting.'

'I can't bend down to reach like I could.'

'You can bend down well enough when you're tuggin' out spuds,' she reprimanded. 'Slip your jacket off and sit on yon chair. I've put newspaper down to save the cushion.'

'I'd sooner sit in the kitchen. I could keep me jacket on.' He knew his plea was futile, but he made it anyway.

'I promised her brother I wouldn't leave her.'

He looked at the still, thin figure stretched out on the sofa. 'Strikes me lass isn't going anywhere.' His wife gave him a playful tap as he sank into the chair and scurried back to the kitchen with his jacket. She returned with a tray, placed a mug of tea and a sandwich on the small table to the side of him and spread a towel across his lap. 'What a ruddy fuss, woman.'

His wife ignored him, as he knew she would. She had her own ways and woe betide him if he interfered. But then so did he; her domain was the house, his was the garden. She took the seat opposite him.

'She needs someone with her. To know she's not alone.'

'Her brother tell you that?'

'No, you can sense these things.' Mrs Frame took a bite from her sandwich.

'Has the lass had a bite to eat?'

'I can't get anything down her. When she wakes, I'll try again.'

Ted slurped his tea, causing his wife to tut.

'Not in company, Ted. Manners.'

He gulped down another swig and quietly ate his sandwich. The lass would hardly notice. She looked dead to the world. 'She's awful thin, the lass. Don't she eat much?'

'You ask too many questions, Ted Frame.' He had clearly irritated his wife, so he kept his thoughts to himself.

He considered the young woman lying on the sofa while his wife gathered the plates and mugs and left the room. She was a wisp of a thing, not much meat on her bones and no healthy bloom on her cheeks as there should be. Flo had brought him here last night when the lass had been dragged from the water over the road. What would make a young, pretty lass like that want to end it all? A rum thing to happen. He'd never had much to do with the people at the house; he left that to Flo and kept to his gardening, the two of them glad of the work – and to be left alone to get on with it.

Flo stuck her head around the door. 'Stay where you are, Ted. I'm just popping out for a minute or two. I've a loaf for Mrs Green. I told her son I'd call in on her.' He knew better than to argue back.

He got up and put more coal on the fire, went to the window and opened the small casement, watching his wife disappear down the road. In the park across the way the trees were stark and black against the white of the snow-covered ground. Kids ran about, throwing snowballs, making snowmen, having fun, regardless of war, in spite of the fact their fathers, brothers and uncles might be far from home. And so they should be; childhood was brief enough as it was. He, alongside many others, had hoped that another war could be avoided but knew it was inevitable. They'd sorted things badly after the Great War, and if people felt aggrieved and hard done by, well, they'd get angry soon enough. And sure enough, they had. He'd been angry too, at the sheer waste of young life. Watching the Grimsby chums march out of town so proudly only to be slaughtered on the Somme. He'd found solace in the garden. That flowers would disappear under the ground and bloom again when the spring came about never failed to lose its magic. Nature was a wonder to behold. He turned and the girl opened her eyes, looked at him and closed them again. He knew that empty look. He'd seen it many times before. He sat back in the chair and the newspaper crackled as he moved to make himself comfortable. 'Thought a bit of fresh air would do you good, flower.' She didn't answer. Didn't open her eyes again. He hadn't thought for a minute that she would. Damaged things took time to mend. He picked up the newspaper Flo had left for him to read and settled back to wait for her return.

6

Imogen had woken early. It didn't matter to her that it was New Year's Day and they'd all been late to bed, yet Frances was still delighted to open her eyes and find her child there. There'd been many mornings over the years that she'd woken alone. They dressed quickly, hopping about in the cold room to keep warm, giggling quietly as they did so, then padded quietly downstairs only to find Grace and Geraldine already at the table.

'Morning.' Grace Delaney patted the chair next to her and Imogen climbed beside her.

Geraldine got up. 'Bread and jam on its way,' she announced before disappearing into the kitchen. Frances followed her and got herself a glass of water, and drank a little of it back. 'Happy new year, my dear. Let's hope it's full of good things.'

'Yes, let's hope so.' No need to tell her landlady that she'd lain awake for what was left of the night, wondering what this year would bring. There'd been little time to talk to Johnny, other than to tell him the bare facts. There was nothing anyone could do about what was past. It was the future that bothered her.

The kettle started its shrill whistle, jogging her out of her thoughts. Geraldine removed it, poured a little hot water into the pot, swirled it about and tossed it down the sink. While she'd been daydreaming, Geraldine had already sliced the bread and added a scraping of butter.

'What can I do to help?'

'Nothing,' she said kindly. 'Go and sit with Imogen – although you might have to fight Grace for her attention.'

Frances took the bread and a jar of jam and set it on the table. Geraldine followed with the teapot, and poured the tea.

'Will Johnny be calling?' Grace was gently probing.

Frances caught her eye. It was more than a simple question. 'I expect so. He said he would. He had things to do. With Ruby.'

Grace nodded sympathetically. 'It must be difficult for him. I can only imagine what must have gone through his head when he...' She tilted her head towards Imogen and smiled at her. They all did; her mouth was ringed with jam. Geraldine got up and fetched a damp cloth to wipe it.

'I should have done that,' Frances said guiltily.

'I imagine your thoughts are all over the place too,' Geraldine said, taking her seat again. 'You must feel you've exchanged one set of problems for another.'

Frances stared at her. 'It feels *exactly* like that.' She was glad to be here with women who understood the complications of life. Grace had been widowed over a year ago and, unable to manage, the Delaneys had moved to Norfolk to live with her cousin, Norman, and his wife, Iris. It had been a miserable existence, so unlike their days in the theatre. Jessie had found it unbearable and had struck out on her own to further her stage career until she discovered Grace was seriously ill. She'd brought her mother and brother here to Barkhouse Lane, having nowhere else to go. Eddie had soon found work as an apprentice mechanic and Grace, much recovered, was wardrobe mistress at the Empire, taking in alterations and dressmaking jobs when she was able. Things had worked out well for the Delaneys but what about the Randolphs? What about her and Imogen?

'This too shall pass,' Geraldine remarked. She was a smart woman, brisk but kind, her short grey hair always neat, her back always straight. She worked at the docks' offices, head of her own department. 'It was what I used to tell myself when days were tough. When I got news that my fiancé had died of wounds, I didn't think I could go on. A life without Charles seemed unbearable. But "this too shall pass" helped me through many a dark day.'

'It's hardly bad news, is it, Johnny coming back into our life?' Guilt swept over her. Geraldine had spent two decades alone. Grace was widowed. 'I should be thrilled to bits, and I am, but... I'm so worried about what might happen next. It's not so simple as moving on quietly, not with a man in Johnny's position. The papers will want to know the ins and outs of everything.' She couldn't bear the shame of it.

Grace reached across the table and touched her hand. 'Don't rush to please, dear.'

Frances appreciated Grace's gentle warning, but she had no intention of rushing into anything. She'd managed for years; a few more months wouldn't hurt.

They heard footsteps on the stairs and Jessie joined them. She pulled out a chair and flopped down at the table, yawned, pressed her hand to her mouth, and looked about her. 'Am I the last one up?'

'Your brother's still upstairs,' her mother answered.

Jessie wiggled her fingers to wave at Imogen and turned to Frances beside her. 'How come you look so together, and I look so bedraggled?'

'Because she has a child,' Grace replied. 'She doesn't have time to dither.'

'I don't dither!' Jessie was affronted and Frances bit back a smile at her friend's indignation. Grace was right, motherhood left little time for indecision.

Grace put her hand to the teapot. 'Do you want it stewed, Jessie?'

Frances got up and took it from her. 'I'll refill it. I could do with another one myself.'

'Use the same leaves,' Geraldine prompted. 'We'll need to wring every drop out of them in future. We won't be able to be so extravagant when we're rationed.'

Jessie groaned. 'Happy new year!'

A knock on the front door interrupted their laughter and Frances got up to answer it, knowing it would be Johnny. They shared a brief kiss in the hallway before she led him through to join the others.

'Daddy!' Imogen immediately slid from the chair, squeezing through the slender gap between Grace and the wall to him. He swooped her into his arms and kissed her, and the delight on her face made Frances's heart pinch. Whatever she wanted didn't matter; Imogen's happiness came first. The child laid her head on her daddy's shoulder and nestled into his neck, much to Grace and Geraldine's delight, let alone his own. Could she dare to believe that happiness was hers at last?

'Good morning, ladies.' Johnny looked about him. 'I'm sorry to disturb you but I really need to speak with Frances.' She sensed the discomfort to his tone. Now that he'd had time to think, was he having second thoughts? Did he doubt Imogen was his child? Her heart began to race at what he might have come here to say. And yet she looked at him with Imogen, holding her so tenderly, looking so proud and knew she was wrong to even think it.

'Use my room at the front of the house,' Grace offered kindly.

'You'll want some privacy. I left the gas fire on low. It will be warm enough but make sure to turn it up.'

'I don't want to impose.' His smile was disarming, and Frances relaxed a little. That things had gone wrong wasn't down to him, or her. It was important to remember that.

He gave Imogen another kiss before he put her down and Geraldine took hold of her hand. 'Will you help me wash the dishes?' She led her through to the kitchen, placing the small stool at the sink, and while Imogen was suitably distracted, Johnny and Frances slipped away.

Grace's room was once the best sitting room that overlooked the street. Two chairs were set in the recess of the large bay window, a single bed against one wall, a gas fire opposite with a mirror over it, a sewing machine tucked beside the chimney breast. The six of them often gathered there, in front of the fire – Jessie and Frances on the bed, her mother and Geraldine taking the chairs, Eddie, and latterly Imogen, on the floor. It was cosy but she felt like an intruder being there without Grace. She turned the fire a little until the ceramic plate glowed red and when she stood up, Johnny put his arm about her waist and pulled her close. He smelled so fresh and clean, and she didn't really want to talk at all. He kissed her, her lips, her face, her hair and when he stopped, he held on to her as if he was holding on to life itself. 'So God help me,' he whispered to her. 'I am never going to let you go again.' They stood quietly for a time, hearing only the clock and the hissing of the gas fire, each other's breath and beating hearts.

She placed her hand to his chest. 'How's Ruby?'

He frowned. 'She shouldn't be your first question.'

Frances shrugged. She'd had to ask. 'I feel I've gained so much, and she has lost.'

'It's not about winning and losing, darling. It never was.'

'Sometimes it seems that way.' Being with Johnny had always

felt like a battle, their entire relationship one of subterfuge and secrets. They'd met when the Randolphs were starring in *Lavender Lane* and she was Ruby's understudy. The show had tried out in Manchester before moving on to take the West End by storm. But Alice Randolph ruthlessly protected her children and nothing, and no one, was going to get in the way of her ambition for them. Especially not an Irish girl lower down the bill. They were young, Frances barely nineteen, Johnny four years older, and she'd been overwhelmed by her feelings for him, and knew he felt the same. It had been intense from the start. Perhaps that was what had alerted Alice Randolph in the first place – that she knew this was more than a summer fling. Alice had been cruel to all of them, Ruby included, and it seemed her daughter's suffering wasn't over. Not if she'd tried to end it all. Frances shuddered despite the warmth of the room. 'You haven't answered my question?'

His eyes were sad, his face drawn and pinched. It was obvious he hadn't slept much, if at all. 'She's in a bad way. When I left this morning she was still sleeping off the effects of the drugs the doctor gave her. I doubt she'll be fit to perform – for a long time. I thought work was the answer. If I kept her busy—' He swallowed, paused. 'I hadn't noticed. Not properly, what all this was doing to her. Mother's death – and her betrayal, even worse.' He took her hand. 'I am *so* sorry, darling.'

'It's hardly your fault.'

'It is. I've been so darned stupid. I should have known something was wrong. That you hadn't written. It's the same with Ruby. I noticed but only so much. I couldn't see beyond all the pretence.' He briefly closed his eyes. 'I only saw what I wanted to see. I thought you didn't want me – and, God, that crushed the life out of me. If only I'd known, it would have been so different, for both of us. But especially for you, darling.' He shook his head. 'Why didn't I post those letters myself? Why did I leave it to Mother and Ruby?'

She put her hand to his cheek, hoping to comfort him. 'Precisely because it *was* your mother and Ruby.'

He drew her closer. 'My mother almost ruined our lives. You. And Imogen. My God.' His rage gained strength. 'She's ruined Ruby's.'

'Ruby will get well.'

'Will she? You've not seen her like I have. It's not just since we came here. It started when we were in America. Then again, perhaps it started in London, when I met you. When Ruby went into hospital. She was never the same after that. In America it was worse.' He became agitated. 'Oh, darling, there's so much I want to say, so much I want to do – with you, for you…' His expression softened as he gazed at her. 'God, will this ever get any less complicated?'

It made her smile. It was comforting to know he felt as she did, that they were being swept along in a storm.

'I need to ask you something, and you can say no, I totally understand if you do.'

She heard Grace's words of warning – *don't rush to please* – and was about to speak when he stopped her.

'I want you to stand in for Ruby.'

She didn't know how to reply. That was not what she'd been expecting, and he looked at her, his brow furrowed, then changing, realisation dawning.

'Oh, darling. How could I be so stupid. I am going to ask you *that*.' He sighed. 'I have the ring.' He put his hand to his pocket, removed it, his hands empty, and sank down into the chair. 'Christ, what a damn mess.' He ran his hand about his jaw and looked up at her. 'I thought if I proposed first you'd feel pressured to say yes. It would be like a bribe, and it would never be that.'

He looked so troubled, so tired. They both were. 'I didn't want you to ask.' It had been an odd relief to admit it. His face fell and once again she sought to comfort. 'I don't mean *ever*. I mean not now. Today. Not in this chaos.' He'd misunderstood too and she faltered. Things had changed between them, and they were suddenly awkward, unsure. 'You said you wanted me to stand in for Ruby. When? Is it a dinner? A luncheon?' She leaned forward and pulled the net away from the window. The air was cool from the cold glass and it made the heat that had risen in her cheeks dissipate a little. She waved at a neighbour passing by, trying to be normal, trying not to let the space that had suddenly appeared between them not matter as much as it did.

'In the show.'

She let the net drop. 'Show?' Was it something they had booked in coming weeks? 'When? Where?'

'At the Palace. To finish the season.' He got up again. 'Jack and I don't want to close the show if we can avoid it – and put the other cast members out of a job. Jack's already agreed to release you. It's easier to find a replacement for the Genie of the Ring than a top of the bill for the Palace.'

So, a replacement, that's all he'd wanted, all he'd rushed here for. 'So, you and Jack have already sorted it out?' She tried not to be rattled but she was. It was just like Jack to want to keep the show going. He'd been generous when the theatre closed at the beginning of September, giving the cast and staff a week's pay to tide them over. He'd been generous since, so why did she feel so aggrieved?

Johnny was puzzled. 'I thought you'd love it. For us to dance again, like old times. The two of us. We'd be together always, onstage and off. I want that more than anything. Don't you?' He took her hand again. 'I don't know how much time we have left together, Frances. How long before I'm called to fight along with every other man in the country. It's just till the end of the season, five weeks, just to get us through. You'd want for nothing, sweetheart. You and Imogen could move to Park Drive; we have a house-keeper.' He looked about the room. 'You wouldn't have to share; you'd have—'

It was too much. He was going too fast, way too fast. 'Let me stop you right there.'

'I thought you'd be happy.'

Had anyone else offered her such an opportunity, she'd have snapped their hand off, but she felt she'd been pushed into a corner. As much as she hadn't wanted him to propose, it hurt that he hadn't put them first.

He put his hands to her shoulders. 'I said you could say no, and I meant it.'

If only things were so simple. 'And if I say yes? How's Ruby going to take that?'

He sighed. 'That's my problem, not yours.'

It didn't matter what he thought. It would be her problem too. Ruby wouldn't take kindly to being replaced. She hadn't years ago, and she wouldn't now.

Having sensed she was giving it thought, his enthusiasm grew. Johnny was urging her to say yes. 'I can change it without too much work. I'd worked part of it out on the walk here. In case you agreed,' he added quickly. 'We have a medley, a singsong; the crowd enjoy it. Some of the numbers you know.' He paused. 'It's a lot to ask, I know it is, and I wouldn't but... well, we only have this afternoon to rehearse but I think we can pull it off – the two of us.'

'I was looking forward to spending time with Imogen.' It sounded petulant but her disappointment was not wholly down to that. It seemed she had been right to worry.

'And you will have time, when the show ends, all the time in the world. I promise. I'll take care of you both. Once we've got through a few days' rehearsals, your days will be free again.'

In the end she agreed. But it didn't feel right, even though it would keep the show going, the cast in work. So much work had dried up; so many theatres hadn't bothered opening after they'd closed when war was declared. It wasn't just her future. She couldn't be so petty as to turn it down.

'I need to ask Geraldine if she'll look after Imogen.'

'Bring her to the house. Mrs Frame would love to have her.'

'Mrs Frame will be taking care of Ruby,' she reminded him. 'I think that's enough to ask of her, don't you?'

He was suitably chastened. 'You're right. I'm getting ahead of myself. I'll send a car to collect you.'

'There's no need. The buses will be running.'

'No more buses for you, not any more.' He pulled her close again, put his hand to her chin and as she looked into his eyes, she found she couldn't be mad at him. It wasn't his fault, and it wasn't hers. It was just a muddle and one they couldn't fight over, not if they ever had any hope of unravelling it.

7

When Johnny left, Frances faced a sea of expectant faces in the kitchen.

'Is everything all right?' Geraldine asked as Frances dropped onto a chair. Imogen scrambled onto her lap.

'Johnny and Jack want me to take over from Ruby to keep the show going.'

'Why, that's wonderful for you,' Grace was enthusiastic. 'What a terrific opportunity to be together. Isn't it, Jessie?' Her mother's look was enough to galvanise her daughter.

'Marvellous.' It was clear Jessie was finding it hard to be thrilled. Well, that was two of them. 'How long for?'

'Until Ruby's well enough,' Frances explained. 'Or until the season ends on the third of next month. Five weeks at most.' Jessie's smile was forced. 'There's no point pretending, is there, Jessie? Your face gives you away – every time.' Frances laughed. Grace shook her head in despair.

'I can't help it, Mum,' Jessie moaned. 'I'll miss Frances. She's my best friend.'

'I'll still be around. I'll be back after the show.'

'You're staying here?' Jessie didn't hide her surprise.

Imogen twisted to look at her mother and Frances sought to reassure her, running her hand over her daughter's head.

'Why wouldn't we? It's our home.' She wouldn't rush towards any changes. Her conversation with Johnny had left her uneasy and she'd felt manipulated. How could she say no, when he'd made it plain that the show would close without her agreement? She knew what it was like to lose a chunk of work, to have responsibilities. Johnny had only given her more.

Jessie's cheeks reddened. 'I thought Johnny might have wanted you to... stay closer?'

'I don't want to rush things. I have to think of Imogen. And while Ruby's in such a fragile state, it's better that we stay away.'

Geraldine got to her feet as Eddie came into the room. 'Very wise.'

Imogen slid from Frances's knee and hugged Eddie. His hair was tufted, his eyes puffy with sleep.

'How's my best girl?' He bent down and lifted her into his arms. Imogen was happy here; they both were. There was no rush to leave on her part.

'Geraldine. Grace. Could Imogen stay with you today? I wouldn't ask, but I don't want her to spend all day at the theatre and half the night too.'

'Of course. Don't even worry about it. She'll be fine here with us, won't you, Imogen? And Eddie will do your jigsaw with you.'

'I wanted to go in the snow, Mummy. You promised.' She pushed out her bottom lip and Frances felt a swell of irritation at Ruby, at Johnny.

Eddie put her down and stretched his arms to the ceiling, stifling a yawn. 'I'll take you, Immi. We can have a snowball fight.' Imogen's face brightened and she jumped up and down in excitement. 'Let me get washed and dressed first, though. I can't go out in my pyjamas!' Imogen smiled, disappointment forgotten as fast as it came. If only Frances could shrug it off the same.

* * *

When Frances left for the theatre and Eddie had taken Imogen out to play, Grace went into her room and Jessie followed. The two of them rolled up the rug and Jessie ran a cloth over the floorboards so that her mother could lay out a roll of blue satin. Grace laid a paper pattern on top of it and Jessie handed over pins and then sat on the bed, watching, as her mother cut into the fabric.

Grace sat back on her heels and studied her work. 'What are you thinking?'

Jessie picked at the skin around her nails. 'If I told you, you'd think I was being childish.'

Her mother looked up. 'Tell me. Then I'll decide if it's childish.'

Jessie sighed. How she wished she could be some exotic creature who kept people guessing. 'I'm happy for Frances. Truly I am.' Her mother nodded. Jessie went on. 'I suppose this is the beginning for her, isn't it. Her and Johnny.'

'And Imogen,' Grace added. 'They're a family now.'

Jessie left her nails alone and began tugging at the tufts of thread on the candlewick bedspread. When she'd first met Frances, she knew nothing of Imogen – none of them did. 'I suppose they'll go back to London with Johnny.'

'Not necessarily. We're at war. Johnny won't make the decisions he might once have done. Neither will Frances. Their priorities will have changed. They have each other to consider. It's not going to be easy for her.' Grace gazed into the distance. 'Poor Frances, I fear she has a lot of heartache still ahead of her.'

Jessie didn't understand and her mother, noticing, paused for a while, then looked at her. 'Darling, your path is straightforward. You have Harry; you have your career.'

'Only partly, Mum. Harry is in the RAF, and I see him less than I ever used to.' She didn't want to think of what the future held. They had seen very little action in the RAF so far. There had been none of the expected bombings. Troops were being sent over to France. The heaviest losses so far had been on the ships, both merchant and naval. 'I need to rethink what I'm going to do. Frances won't want to be part of the Variety Girls any more; she'll have no need.'

'You don't know that for certain. Johnny will undoubtedly be called to fight, so he won't be dancing, and Frances will want her friends about her while he's away, especially Patsy Dawkins and her boys. She might yet want to keep performing. You still have Ginny. You could be a duo – or get someone else to replace Frances.'

'Ginny's set on joining ENSA, the Entertainment National Services Association, when the panto ends. We've got a few shows booked after that but not much, not enough to keep us both in work.' Ginny had been one of four other girls in the dance troupe that appeared in the summer show. When it closed, the other girls had left but Ginny had remained, along with Frances and Jessie, Ginny finding work in a laundry, Jessie at Foster and Fox solicitor's to make ends meet. Only Frances had been happy, working with the landlady, Lil, at the Fisherman's Arms. At Jessie's suggestion, the three of them had developed an act and had been working cine-variety at the Empire, performing in the interval between films.

'Ginny sees her dancing as a means to an end, but you'll grow restless before long.' Her mother got up from her knees and Jessie jumped from the bed, took hold of her hand and helped her to her feet. 'Thank you.' She smiled. 'You know, Jessie, when you left home, you left to strike out on your own. Not as part of a trio, not as a dancer in a chorus, but as yourself, Jessie Delaney. You only have to contact Bernie Blackwood, your agent, and he'll get you something. You could be in the chorus in the West End in no time and work your way up the bill.'

Jessie was not enthused. It made her mother smile. She put an arm about her shoulder. 'You were never destined for the chorus. You'd never be satisfied just to be onstage; you have to be front and centre.' Jessie wriggled uncomfortably. 'If you want to be top of the bill then go for it, darling. Don't apologise for wanting it – not to me, not to anyone. Ever.' Grace gathered the remnants of material and pushed them into her scrap bag. 'You left me once. You can leave me again.'

That was what Jessie was afraid of. Leaving her mother. Aunt Iris's neglect had had serious consequences. She glanced at the clock on the mantel. 'The matinee's at half two. I'd better get to the Empire early. Someone will have to stand in for Frances. I suppose they'll choose one of the local girls from the chorus.'

'Exactly.' Grace opened her basket of cottons and took out some white tacking thread, then rummaged around for a needle. 'When someone moves on, someone else gets another rung on the ladder. When your time comes, make sure you're ready to step up.'

8

Frances arrived at the Palace before Johnny and had to wait at the stage door office while the stage manager phoned the Randolph house to verify Frances's story. He was full of apologies as he took her bag and led her to the Randolphs' dressing room.

'I'm a little more cautious these days. We've had a couple of unsavoury types turn up, purporting to be friends of Miss Randolph, and, well...' He opened the door, switched on the centre light and placed her bag to the left of him, on the long dressing table that ran the length of the room. 'I'll leave you to it. If you need anything, the name's Ken.' She stuck out her hand and he shook it vigorously.

'Nice to meet you, Ken.'

'Likewise. And don't forget. You know where to find me.'

When he left, she relaxed a little, and looked about the small, windowless room. It wasn't warm enough to remove her coat but once they started rehearsing, she wouldn't feel the cold of an empty theatre. A small, dusky pink plush sofa was set on an angle across the corner, opposite the door, the arms grubby with old greasepaint marks where hands had rested. Behind it was a large sink with hot and cold taps – a luxury – and along the other wall a rail of costumes. She walked over to the dressing table and switched on the bulbs around it to take the chill off the room. Two chairs were set in front of it, and it was easy to see where each Randolph sat, Johnny's area neat and tidy, Ruby's a chaotic jumble of make-up and brushes, exactly as she had left it on Saturday night. Frances touched his greasepaint sticks in turn, his comb, picked up a jar of brilliantine and read the label, removed the stopper from his cologne and smelled it, briefly closed her eyes. It calmed her. It would be all right. She could do this. Nerves had got the better of her as she sat in the back of the taxi, the first time she'd been left alone with her thoughts. She picked up her bag, wondering where to put her own things, not wanting to move Ruby's – it didn't seem right, and yet if she was going to do the shows in her place she'd have to. She removed her scarf, unfastened her coat and was changing into her practice clothes when Johnny rushed in, surprised to find her there. His smile matched her own and as he pulled her into his arms and kissed her, it was glorious to think that there was only the two of them. For the next few hours she only had to dance with Johnny, when she'd thought it would never happen again. Nerves were replaced by excitement, and as he removed his scarf and shrugged out of his coat, she took it from him and hung it up. 'That's a novelty.' It puzzled her and, seeing her expression, he laughed. 'Kissing my leading lady. And having her hang up my coat.'

She thought of Jessie and Eddie, how they worked together, how close they were. Of her own brothers and sisters in Ireland. It had been years since she'd been home. Shame kept her from travelling there. Would she dare to go now that Johnny was back on the scene? 'Sisters are different. How is she?'

He pulled her to him, let his forehead fall slightly to touch on hers. 'No different. Mrs Frame managed to get her to drink some thin soup but she hasn't spoken, won't look at anyone, just looks beyond them at something that isn't there.'

He didn't want to talk about Ruby and neither did she, but even though she wasn't there physically, Frances feared she would always be between them. She blanked away any thought of her. There was a lot to do and little time to do it. Keeping the production going meant more than a month's work for everyone involved in the show; she had to think only of that. Johnny was putting on his practice shoes. 'I've managed to get most of the orchestra in; hopefully the rest will turn up later. We'll go through the numbers.' He placed his foot on the chair and tied his lace. 'I can do a couple of solo numbers. If we rehearse each day this week then we'll be in fine shape by the end of it.' He stood up, taking her hands in his. 'I know it's a lot to spring on you, darling.' It was. An awful lot, and she still wasn't sure she was up to it. 'It's been a long time.'

She could only nod in reply, suddenly overcome by what lay behind them, what lay ahead, and not just learning routines. How could they move forward from here? He went over to the rail where his sister's costumes hung – jewel-coloured dresses in the finest silks and chiffons, some finessed with marabou feathers and sequins, each one exquisite. Each one probably cost what Frances earned in six months. Couldn't he see the irony? Of being second best.

'I don't know if Ruby's will fit. You're taller.' He pulled one from the rail. Held it up, saw her expression. 'I'm sorry, Frances. This is not what I wanted it to be like. Truth be told, I never thought it would happen, you and me. Us. Let alone dance again.' He put the dress back. 'Perhaps they have something up in Wardrobe. But we have little time to be picky.'

This was what she was so afraid of, that things would happen too fast.

He glanced at his watch. 'I can check if someone's upstairs. One of the ladies might be in doing the laundry?'

'Let's leave it for now,' she urged. The last thing she wanted was to try on Ruby's dresses when she'd been unable to move aside her make-up. 'We're better off rehearsing. And I only need one dress.'

He led her onto the stage, and she faced out to the auditorium. It was three times the size of the Empire and held over one and a half thousand people. It had been an age since she'd performed in so large a theatre and she caught her breath at the enormity of what she was taking on in so short a time. As if sensing her trepidation, he took hold of her hand, smiled encouragingly and led her towards the front. She felt the strength from his hand in hers and it lifted her. Someone was already in the band pit and Johnny called down to him. 'Dan, this is Frances O'Leary. She's going to take Ruby's place for a day or two.' He was being guarded. People would want to know what had happened to Ruby – if they didn't know already.

Johnny stepped down and leaned over the band rail, talking to Dan, the two of them going through the sheet music. Frances looked up into the gods, her hand held across her brow, and imagined the people looking down on her. The cheap seats were not much more than stone benches with the bare comfort of a thin leather-covered cushion. Would the audience filling them in a few hours be impressed? She would be carrying the show along with Johnny Randolph – was she really up to it? And when Ruby was well enough to dance again – what then?

He came to stand beside her. 'I've tried to make it as easy as I can. I know you can do it, darling. You just have to trust me.' He looked directly into her eyes and his held such certainty. 'Do you?'

How could she not? He was all she'd ever wanted and the thought of dancing with him, night after night, being so close, feeling his skin against hers was more than she'd ever dared to dream of. He gave a nod to Dan, who began to play the piano, then swept her into his arms, so certain in his movements, so assured, that it was so simple to surrender to him and go with the music. In an instant she let herself blend into him and they moved as one. Her worries slipped away, and she thought only of the moment, the music, and Johnny, as she'd always known she would.

* * *

Johnny still couldn't believe it was Frances he was dancing with. He placed his cheek to hers and from time to time had to pull back, just to check that it was her smiling back at him, and not Ruby. She danced like a dream, had such grace when she moved, such fluidity, more so than he remembered. She'd been nineteen, he almost twenty-three, children it seemed looking back, so innocent, so trusting – so in love. There was a lot of catching up to do and he didn't want to waste a single second of it. He couldn't dwell on regrets or what might have been; she was here now, and he had everything he'd ever wanted – and more. He pulled her closer and whispered in her ear. 'I love you, Frances O'Leary. I love you more than life itself.'

9

Jessie and Grace left for the Empire just before noon. There was a matinee at 2.30 but work would need to be done to fill the gap left by Frances. 'At least the Genie of the Ring's costume should fit just about anyone with a few minor alterations,' Grace mused. 'I can soon adjust the cuffs on the harem pants, and it doesn't matter if the bolero is a little loose around the arms.'

'I suppose you can't do anything too drastic in case she comes back.'

'Let's hope she does,' Grace said. 'It will mean Ruby is recovered.'

'You don't sound too hopeful, Mum.'

Grace gave a considered answer. 'It's easier to see progress from physical ailments and injures. Your father never really recovered from his own mental suffering. You know that as well as I. We all put on a brave face, but we can't ever fully know the damage behind the mask.'

The thought of going into another year without her father's guidance made her feel vulnerable and Jessie slipped her arm through her mother's, wanting to hold her closer. Her father had partially lost his hearing fighting in the trenches during the Great War and had been left with bad tremors, which affected his playing. His classical career, that had once been so promising, was lost to him. He would call out in the night, shouting and raging, and at other times would sleep for long periods, not getting up from his bed for days on end. It had been difficult for Grace, for all of them. As Jessie got older she was able to take on many of his piano students, but it was always a struggle.

It was comforting to find George waiting for them in his office at the stage door. The old man had been kindness itself to Jessie when she'd first arrived in Cleethorpes. He lived with his wife, Olive, in one of the terraced houses across the street and they had taken Jessie in until she found her feet. Their daughter, Dolly, worked at the Empire as an usherette and they had become good friends over the summer and months that followed. They were as close to family as Jessie had ever had. As soon as he saw them, he got up from his battered leather chair and went straight to the pigeonholes that held dressing-room keys and mail.

'Any for me, George darling?'

He handed Jessie three envelopes, and she flicked through them. Two from Harry, which delighted her, and one from Miss Symonds, her old boss at Uncle Norman's office. Jessie smiled. She was a lovely woman, and she'd grown fond of her. If she'd had to stick at typing boring and convoluted legal contracts, she'd rather be with Miss Symonds than with old Beaky Bird at the offices she'd worked in last autumn. 'When you write back to young Harry, say hello from me and Olive. Let him know he's welcome to stay any time. There'll always be a bed for him.'

She kissed his cheek. 'I will. You spoil him, and me.'

'You spoil all of us,' Grace added as he handed her a small tin. She removed the lid to find a generous slice of Christmas cake. 'How is Olive?'

'Her leg plays her up this cold weather but she's well enough.'

Grace replaced the lid. 'I'll pop across for a chat when the matinee's over and thank her for this.'

George smiled. 'She'd like that.' Mother and daughter parted,
Grace upstairs to Wardrobe and Jessie downstairs to the dressing
rooms.

Jack Holland was in the corridor that ran underneath the stage,
talking to the owner of the dance school whose girls made up the
chorus. Maggie Taylor was in her sixties and although she looked
formidable, with her steel-grey hair and beady black eyes, her girls
thought the world of her, and she cared for them as a hawk cared
for its young. She wanted them to fly, but only when it was safe to
do so.

'Ah, Jessie,' Jack said when he saw her. 'Miss Taylor has
suggested Peggy Marshall take Frances's place. The two of us are
going to take her to one side and have a quick chat, then we'll bring
her to you and Ginny. If you can help her with her lines, make sure
she's certain of her placings, it will reassure her – knowing she has
two professionals on her side.'

Jessie preened at his flattery. 'Yes, of course. She's bound to be a
little nervous, but we'll look after her.'

Ginny was in the dressing room, still in her coat, leaning
against the radiator for what little warmth exuded from it. Jessie
pulled out her chair, put her bag on it and went over to her
friend, placing her bare hands on the radiator. 'You'll get
chilblains,' Ginny cautioned, as Jessie twisted to stand beside her.
Frances's place had already been cleared of her make-up and
belongings and the space at the end of the dressing table was
bare, awaiting the arrival of Peggy Marshall. Ginny looked expectantly at Jessie.

'So, what's happened? Why has Frances *really* gone to the
Palace? Jack just said she was standing in. Is Ruby ill?'

Jessie filled Ginny in with the details – those she had knowledge of. 'I think everything got too much for her.'

'Poor woman.'

'And poor Johnny. Sad to think their own mother was the cause of it all.' Feeling warmer, Jessie removed her coat and hung it on the rail, then pulled on her thick dressing gown.

'Do you think they'll get married quickly, Johnny and Frances, now that they've found each other again? Be a proper family?'

'I haven't a clue. You know how private Frances is at the best of times. I daren't ask. She might snap my head off.'

Ginny sank down into her chair beside Jessie, picked up her brush and began sweeping it through her long red hair. 'I wouldn't want to be in her shoes. It's a lot to cope with, isn't it. First Johnny coming back into her life, then letting everyone know about Imogen – and now she's got to step into Ruby's shoes.' She flicked her hair about her shoulder, peered into the mirror and examined a spot on her chin. 'I suppose you'll know more when she comes back. If she comes back...'

Jessie had spent the entire morning wondering the same thing. She settled down to open her letters. Miss Symonds wrote of how quiet it was without her and Harry. There was a little news of Iris and Norman – not that she welcomed it. She checked the postmarks on the ones from Harry and opened the earliest. She was still reading when someone rapped briskly on their door, and it was Ginny who called out, 'Come in.'

Jack Holland stuck his head around the door. 'Girls.' He opened it wider, taking a step back to allow one of the juvenile troupe to come forward, then pressed his hands to her shoulders. Jessie recognised her from the line-up. Not they had much to do with them. Their chaperone kept them on a tight rein and they were ushered in and out of their dressing room and not allowed to get in the way of the performers higher up the bill.

'Peggy here is going to take over from Frances for the time being. Jessie, Ginny.'

They shook hands in turn and Ginny pulled out the chair where Frances usually sat. 'Do you want to put your things here, Peggy.'

The girl placed a small paper bag on the table. 'Ta very much.'

Jessie gave her a warm smile, hoping to reassure the girl, recalling how anxious she'd been when she first started out on her own. 'If you need anything just ask and we'll do what we can to help. Nervous?'

'Not really,' the girl said and Jessie bit back a smile.

'Could you give Peggy Frances's costumes and take her up to your mother, Jessie? Then Mrs Delaney can work her magic, Peggy. Once that's sorted, the girls will go over the lines with you.'

The girl nodded enthusiastically, and Jack left Jessie to take Peggy up to Wardrobe.

She came back alone, laughing. 'Lord, that girl can talk for England. She never shut her mouth the whole time. Poor Mum.'

'Poor us, you mean. We'll be cooped up in here with her for hours. Do you think it's nerves?'

'I'd love to think so, but I think that's just Peggy.'

She took out her greasepaint sticks and began applying her make-up, the two of them talking to each other's reflection in the long mirror that ran the length of the wall.

'Did you leave with Joe last night?' Jessie asked cautiously. Joe Taplow was playing the part of Abanazar. He was a magician who'd never had an acting part before and had been bullied into the role of Aladdin's wicked uncle by the producer. Gangly and awkward, it was not Joe's nature to be forceful, and as such his attentions towards Ginny had been slow coming to light.

'He walked me home. Hardly a marathon.' Ginny had been lodging with George and Olive across the road. 'It must have taken us all of three minutes. We're just friends. It's nothing more than that.'

Jessie was not convinced. 'I think he'd like it to be more. I think you would too.'

'I've told you. I'm not ready for another relationship. Not after last time.' Ginny had had a brief fling with the comedian in the summer show. She'd thought it something more, but Billy Lane had left abruptly, and when the show ended Ginny found herself pregnant. Mercifully, she'd lost the baby, and although a traumatic experience, it meant that she could move on with her life. Jessie was convinced Ginny and Joe were perfect for each other. Joe Taplow was kind and had not one ounce of the brashness Billy Lane had in bucketloads.

'You ought to give him a chance—'

Peggy waltzed in and they fell quiet.

'Don't mind me,' she chirped. 'Pretend I'm not here.'

'If only,' Jessie muttered under her breath and Ginny laughed.

Peggy pulled out the chair and opened her paper bag, taking out squat stubs of greasepaint. 'Are you and Abanazar courting, then? I told the other girls you was.'

Jessie and Ginny exchanged a look. They would have to curb their conversations while Peggy was around.

'Peggy.'

'Yes?' She slapped on her foundation colour with a heavy hand, rubbing it briskly, then added red to her cheeks and attacked her face again. Jessie glanced at Ginny, who shrugged, and they continued watching her, mesmerised by her technique – or lack of it.

'The things is,' Jessie continued, afraid to watch any longer yet unable to tear her eyes away, 'you've moved up a step now. You're part of the cast. Not the wines and spirits.'

Peggy frowned at her, not understanding.

'The bits on the bottom of the bill,' Jessie explained. 'You're playing a part. Haven't you noticed how the band stick together, you girls and boys from the dancing school?' It had been the same in the summer show, always the division, unspoken but there nonetheless.

Peggy nodded as Jessie explained further. 'You have to decide where you belong. With us, or with the dancers down the hall. What is spoken about in here is just between us. Do you understand? You're not one of the juveniles any more.'

Peggy picked up her eyeliner and Jessie was already dreading the results. 'So we're all in it together. But not really.'

'Sort of,' Ginny added as confirmation. 'You have to decide which side you're on, in a way.'

'Like the Allies and the Nazis?'

Ginny rolled her eyes and Jessie wanted to giggle.

'Not that extreme, but yes. We don't want Miss Taylor and everyone else knowing our business. We keep it private.'

Peggy went back to her make-up and drew a black line on the edge of her eyelids with a steady hand. The girls were impressed. She dropped the black eyeliner into her bag and sat back, admiring her handiwork. 'But I was right.'

'Right about what?' Ginny asked.

'You and Abanazar.'

Ginny's cheeks reddened and Jessie changed the subject, handing Peggy a sheet of paper.

She barely glanced at it. 'What's that for?'

'We've written your lines down for you. We'll cover for you where we can if you forget, but I'm sure you'll be fine.'

'Oh, I will,' she said, brimming with confidence. 'I know everyone's lines. I could stand in for any of you.'

Jessie didn't know whether to laugh or cry.

Peggy ran a red stick over her lips. 'Will I do?' She smiled triumphantly at them, looking more like the dame than the genie.

'Not bad.' Ginny's eyes pleaded for help.

'For a first attempt.' Jessie indicated to her cheeks. 'Perhaps a little less red. May I?' She picked up a rag and began removing as much as she could. Between them they created a more subtle face that enhanced her features and gave her an exotic look. When they'd finished Peggy peered closer to the mirror.

'Is that me? Is that really me?' She moved her head, turning this way and that, staring at her reflection. 'Well, ta for that. You two aren't bad at all. The other girls thought you was a bit stuck-up, Jessie, but I don't think you are.'

For a moment Jessie was lost for words until Ginny began to giggle and then she too began to laugh. 'I see it's going to be lively with you here and no mistake!'

10

Johnny and Frances rehearsed until the stage manager brought down the safety curtain and the audience were allowed to enter. Only then did the nerves begin to kick in again, and she felt her stomach tighten. She couldn't remember when she'd last eaten anything more than an apple and now she couldn't eat anything if she tried. Johnny went over the sequence of the show, Frances fixing it into her head as the stage crew began to move the scenery about them.

'You'll be terrific, I know you will,' he reassured her. 'It will be a blast. The audience are going to love you, almost as much as I do.' She inhaled deeply and let it go, wishing she could let go of the knots in her head just as easily. As he led the way back to the dressing room, a slim, dark-haired man with a thin moustache came towards them, checking out Frances, then smiling at Johnny.

'Toni, this is an old friend of mine, Frances O'Leary, from the Empire in Cleethorpes. She's standing in for Ruby for a couple of nights.'

An old friend? She raised her eyebrows. He caught her gaze and shot her an apologetic look. She held out her hand and Toni took it, bent forward and kissed it.

'Enchanted.' He smiled and she relaxed a little. He turned his attention to Johnny. 'And Ruby is not well?' He looked concerned and appeared to go along with Johnny's explanation that his sister was suffering from complete exhaustion. Frances watched the two men while they talked. He might not have asked any awkward questions but she knew damn well gossip about Ruby would be rife around the theatre, backstage *and* front of house. Idle hours between performances left plenty of time to swap juicy titbits about what everyone was up to – or what they thought they were up to. The truth wouldn't get in the way of a good rumour and Frances had already prepared herself to be the topic of conversation alongside Ruby.

A neat woman with a tiny waist joined them, slipping her arm through Toni's.

'Ah, my partner, Juanita,' he explained for Frances's benefit.

'June,' the woman corrected him in a broad Yorkshire accent. 'We heard Ruby was unwell; good of you to step in. Keep the show going.' She was petite but sturdy and although she had the most disarming smile, she looked as if she would give anyone who messed her about short shrift. Frances immediately warmed to her.

'We'll talk later.' Johnny placed his hand on the small of Frances's back and gently guided her forward. 'I'd like Frances to get a little rest. I've worked her hard all afternoon.'

June opened her mouth to say something and thought better of it. She winked at Frances. 'We'll catch up later, love. Plenty of time for a natter.' She slapped Toni on the bottom. 'You need to get your gear on. The half's been called.'

Johnny followed Frances into the dressing room. She sank on the sofa and removed her shoes, rubbing at her feet, which ached with effort. She looked up at him.

'Before you say anything...'

'An old friend?' She wasn't sure what hurt more – her feet, or his words.

'I don't know why I said it. I could have bitten off my tongue. I suddenly felt like I would have to explain too much. And I can't, not yet.'

She couldn't be angry with him. There was too much to explain – and where would he start? He pulled the chair away from the dressing table and turned it to face her. He was tired, they both were, but for the moment his life was far more complicated than hers, and she felt the need to keep a little distance between them while he attempted to sort it out.

'Let me tell everyone, please. In my own time.' She could hardly refuse him. After all, hadn't she asked the same of Ruby when she'd discovered Imogen's existence?

'What will you say about Ruby?'

'I've only said that she's ill. People in show business are used to extremes. You couldn't do this job unless you were a little nuts – going out night after night, hoping people will love you, picking yourself up and doing it again when they don't.' He came and sat beside her on the sofa, threw his head back and closed his eyes. She reached across for his hand.

'It'll get easier.' She hated always being the one to reassure, longing for a time when all she had to think of was herself. Perhaps that time would never come.

'I wish I could be so certain.' He stretched out his arm and she nestled into him, rested her head on his chest, put her hand inside his shirt. 'Funny isn't it, how things work out. Me and you here. Imogen. It still feels like a dream. A wonderful dream. I'd given up on love when you didn't—' he paused '—when I thought you'd changed your mind. I reckoned you'd found someone else. I scoured the newspapers for news of you. Couldn't find a thing.' He put his hand gently to her chin, tilted her head. 'For all Mother's conniving, it didn't work, did it? We were meant to be together, darling. Fate has reunited us.'

'It could have done it sooner,' she said wryly. It would have saved them all so much heartache. 'Even a year would have made so much difference, Johnny. How long before we're parted, and I'll have to miss you all over again?'

11

Mrs Frame moved the small table to beside the sofa and disappeared again. Her husband, Ted, had come and gone. Ruby had heard them whispering about her, their voices thick with pity – all that money and no happiness, what a waste it all was. She'd spent most of the day listening to the clock and the crackle of the fire, the sound of doors opening and closing as Mrs Frame went about the house. It was hard to think, her head full of her badness with no idea how to right her wrongs. She'd made a start, but it wasn't enough. Frances had asked her not to tell Johnny of Imogen's existence and she'd kept her word. Each day had been unbearable, knowing he wasn't with his child, hadn't been with his child for years. She thought of her own mother, hating her, loving her, and hating her again. What Ruby had done, she'd done to make her happy; she only ever wanted to make Mother happy. They couldn't let Johnny leave. It would all fall apart if he did. She thought of the boys she'd hurt, the men she'd used, and who'd used her in turn. It had all felt like a game, but it was a game she'd lost.

Mrs Frame came back and ran a duster over the furniture, caught Ruby looking at her through the mirror.

'You're awake. Feeling better?' she said kindly.

Ruby didn't answer. Couldn't open her mouth or find the words. The inside of her head felt like it was filled with fog.

The housekeeper turned to her and smiled. 'I've got a lovely bit of chicken soup on the go. Now you're awake, I'll bring some through.'

Ruby forced herself to shake her head. The effort exhausted her.

Mrs Frame tucked her duster into her apron pocket. 'You must eat something, Miss Ruby, or you're not going to get well.' She tutted. 'Your mother wouldn't want to see you like this, now, would she.'

Ruby felt chilled and closed her eyes again. She didn't want to think of her mother. Mrs Frame left the room and a few minutes later Ruby smelled chicken soup. She heard the tray placed beside her. Mrs Frame lifted her forward and placed another pillow behind her back. Ruby opened her eyes.

'Now. I don't know what went on before you came here – or since for that matter – and it's none of my business, but you can't carry on like this, Ruby Randolph. I wouldn't let a child of mine get away with it and I'm not going to let you.' She picked up the spoon. 'Open wide.'

Mrs Frame held the spoon in front of her mouth and eyeballed Ruby, her face stern. Ruby opened her mouth like a bird and Mrs Frame pushed the spoon gently into it, tilted it so that Ruby took every drop and then dabbed at the side of her mouth with a cloth. Ruby closed her mouth and swallowed. It felt like a stone dropping into her stomach. Mrs Frame smiled her approval, put the spoon in the bowl again and held it up. Ruby didn't want to eat any more. But Mrs Frame was stubborn. 'I've had three girls, each one of them like chalk and cheese – but a broken heart is a broken heart; we're all the same on that score.' Ruby took another mouthful. 'I've got them through their ups and downs, and I can get you through yours, if you'll let me.' She put the spoon into the bowl and let Ruby rest a little.

'I can tell how much your brother means to you and you to him. My lot fight like cats and dogs but let anyone else upset 'em and they'll soon know about it. Now then. Let's finish what's left. Your brother will be back soon enough and no doubt he'll need something nourishing too.' Ruby looked at her, at the bowl. She picked up the spoon, took up some soup, paused. Mrs Frame watched her. She put the spoon to her mouth and drank a little. 'That's the ticket. Good girl.' It took a long while to empty the bowl; each time the spoon went into her mouth, Ruby wanted to retch, but Mrs Frame was watching and she forced herself to keep it down. When Mrs Frame took the bowl back into the kitchen, Ruby struggled to the lavatory, holding on to the wall for support. Sweat beaded on her head with the exertion and she kneeled down at the toilet bowl and brought it all back, then lay on the floor, the cold tiles a relief.

12

For the first time in many months, Frances arrived home alone to Barkhouse Lane. The taxi pulled up outside the house and she waited while the driver stepped out to open the door for her. He asked her what time she'd like to be collected tomorrow and wished her goodnight. In less than twenty-four hours, her life had been transformed and it was hard to imagine that this was the way it would continue. Inside the hall, she pulled back the blackout curtain as quickly as she could, closed it again, balancing her torch on the small table beneath the coat hooks, and removed her coat. The door to the back room opened.

'How did it go?' Jessie whispered.

Frances paused on the bottom stair. 'Let me go to Imogen then I'll tell you all about it.'

The bedside lamp was on in her room and beneath its glow lay Imogen, her cheek on her pressed hands. Her gas mask stuck out from underneath the bed. It had been fashioned to look like Mickey Mouse and meant to be more fun for the children, but there was nothing fun about it. She hoped she never had cause to use it.

Frances kneeled beside her, touched her face and kissed her. 'Mummy's home, sweetheart. I'll be up soon.'

When she went back downstairs, she was surprised to find Grace and Geraldine sitting around the table with Jessie. Grace had already poured her a cup and they pushed a sandwich in front of her. 'There's a little ham left over from dinner.'

She was ravenous; she'd eaten very little that day, rehearsing, then too nervous to eat – and she never ate before a show; none of the performers did. 'I thought you'd all be in bed.'

'We wanted to know how it went.' Jessie's eyes glittered. 'You tell me about your night then I'll tell you about Peggy.'

'Peggy?'

'The girl who's taken your place. What a caution she is.'

Frances sipped her tea. 'You go first.'

'Mum and Geraldine have already heard it.'

'But Frances hasn't,' Geraldine interrupted, 'and it will give her chance to eat something.'

Frances took a bite from the sandwich, grateful for their thoughtfulness. 'How has Imogen been?'

'An angel. Eddie kept her occupied until bedtime then he read her a story.'

Jessie regaled her with tales of how Peggy had told her she knew everyone's lines, how she said the girls thought Jessie was stuck-up.

Frances laughed. 'I wonder what they think of me?'

'Oh, don't worry, she told us.' Jessie grinned. 'Believe me, no one escaped. You're the bee's knees. They *love* your hair, your nail polish and matching lipstick. Aladdin is brash and hard, the Grand Vizier is boring, Joe's a bit gormless...'

'That must have gone down well with Ginny?'

'She didn't give anything away. Although Peggy was watching for her reaction.' Jessie shrugged. 'I don't know why she keeps insisting they're just good friends. He's clearly besotted with her.'

Frances thought of Johnny introducing her as an old friend. It wasn't so simple, but then neither was Ginny's relationship. They all had more complications in their life than they needed. 'Ginny is wise,' Grace interrupted. 'It's as well not to rush into these things.'

The same could be said for her own situation. Frances finished her sandwich. Geraldine topped up her cup.

'Would you like a piece of fruit cake, Frances?' Geraldine had got used to their upside-down ways of eating late, sleeping late.

'That would be lovely.'

She left, taking the teapot with her and Frances waited for her to return, kicked off her shoes and rubbed at her feet. The relief was wonderful. She smiled to Grace and Geraldine. 'It's been a long day.' It would be the same again tomorrow and each day until they got the routines tight – she supposed exactly as Ruby danced them. Jessie sat down again, eager for her to begin.

'It all went well, really well. It's a great show and the cast were friendly enough.' It had been awkward, and she'd mostly kept out of the way, not wanting to be asked questions, not wanting to answer them. Johnny was right; there was too much to explain and it just wasn't the right time.

'What was the audience like?' Jessie asked.

'A full house.' It had been wonderful walking onstage to stand beside him. Johnny had gone out and given a little spiel about his sister, and what a trouper Frances had been to step into her dancing shoes. It wasn't her shoes, only her beautiful dresses, but she had got over that by thinking only of the other performers, that they would have work. It had helped to concentrate on that, not on how scared she was, and when she stepped out onto the stage, into the spotlight, Johnny waiting for her, his arm outstretched to take her hand in his, her fear melted away. She was welcomed with rapturous applause, the warmth and goodwill of the audience washing over the footlights. It was the last moment she'd been aware of them until they finished their routine, for in the darkness they disappeared, and she only saw Johnny, felt him close, leading her, wanting her to be loved. She would savour the moment again when she was alone. 'How about the Empire?'

'Same,' Jessie said quickly, eager to hear more from Frances. She told them of the other acts. Of Juanita, who was June, and her Spanish husband, Toni.

Geraldine came back to the table with Frances's cake. 'It makes me laugh how these acts invent themselves names.'

'But it makes sense,' Jessie interrupted. 'Better than going to see Tony and June Smith. People expect something out of the ordinary in variety.'

'As long as they live up to it,' Geraldine said dryly.

'Oh, they do,' Frances countered. 'They're very good but then they've been in the business years. Toni's in his late forties, I imagine, perhaps older. He looks the part, very dashing.'

'And you and Johnny?' Jessie asked.

'It was an absolute joy.' The years and the sorrow had fallen away as they danced. It was good to have a larger orchestra, and the rounded sound filled the auditorium. He was light on his feet, and she felt as if she'd merely floated by his side. The audience had been appreciative, so much so that she'd forgotten the complications of their situation, glad to be doing something that made her forget.

'It sounds like you had a wonderful night.' Grace reached across and squeezed Frances's hand. 'It's a generous thing you've done. It can't be easy for you but I'm certain the rest of the acts on the bill appreciate it.' She'd known Grace out of everyone would understand. It hadn't been easy at all, but she'd done it, hopefully for all the right reasons. Grace got up and pulled her dressing gown about her. 'I'm to my bed. Don't stay up too late, you two; you need your beauty sleep.'

'Some of us more than others, according to Peggy,' Jessie quipped.

Frances laughed. 'I hope I get the chance to meet her.'

'If she gives you your job back, you might. Although I think you'll have to fight her for it. That's if you're coming back?' Frances didn't comment and Grace placed herself in between them as she reached across to gather the cups. Jessie stopped her. 'Leave it, Mum. I can do that.'

Jessie kissed her mother and they both said goodnight to Geraldine. Jessie began clearing the table, telling Frances to sit down when she got up to help. 'You've had a longer day than me. I didn't have to rehearse all afternoon.'

'It was worth it.'

'What did Johnny say about Ruby?'

'Nothing much, simply told everyone that she was ill and I'm taking her place for a while.'

'And they believed him?'

'Who knows. Would you?'

Jessie shook her head. 'I shouldn't think any of them did either.' She ran the hot water and began washing the dishes. Frances came beside her and picked up the tea towel. 'Anything else happen?'

'No.'

'He didn't *ask* you anything?'

'No.'

'But he will,' Jessie said confidently.

Frances turned her back, placing the dry cups on the shelf. Jessie put the last plate on the draining board, shook the water from her hands and dried them on the bottom of the tea towel Frances was holding. 'Is something wrong?'

Frances managed to smile. 'Nothing.' She dried the plate and placed it on the shelf, then hung the tea towel over the sink. 'Let's get to bed. I've another long day again tomorrow.' Talking to Jessie had only reignited the doubts she had tried to squash while she concentrated on getting her steps right, but now that the first show was over, they came roaring up to taunt her as the high of the performance dissipated. Old friend. Was he letting her down gently, or was she simply there because the show had to go on?

13

The following morning, Ginny and Dolly were in the back sitting room of the terraced house in Dolphin Street, knitting socks from a pattern distributed by the WVS under the watchful eye of Dolly's mother. While the girls kept a steady pace, Olive's needles clicked along at lightning speed. She was seated in one of the two armchairs either side of the coal fire, Ginny in the other, and Dolly on a dining chair that she'd turned away from the table that was tucked neatly into the bay window.

Ginny had come to lodge there when Imogen came to live at Barkhouse Lane with her mother. George and Olive had welcomed her with open arms and instantly made her feel at home, making sure she was comfortable and at her ease. And yet it was better than home, for when her mother died three years ago, she felt she no longer had one. Her four brothers had signed up to fight long before war was declared. One by one they'd escaped their father's fists and he'd expected his only daughter to remain as his unpaid skivvy. Over the years Jane Thompson had scraped together every penny she had to ensure her child kept at her dancing classes, knowing it was a way out of their miserable existence, and Ginny took it at the first opportunity.

'Did your mother knit?' Olive asked, laying down one thick sock and reaching over to the table at her side. She picked up a bag of sweets and offered them to the girls. They stopped their own poor efforts and helped themselves, tossing the papers onto the fire.

'Nothing fancy. Pullovers. She darned, she washed.' It had been nothing like this. Her mother's life had not been cosy; her father drank what he earned. But she didn't want to talk of that here, not wanting it to mar the peace of her life any more than it had to. Her memories were not happy ones.

'Will you go back to Sheffield when the panto ends?' Dolly asked.

Ginny hadn't thought too far ahead, finding it easier to cope that way. Her friends had helped her through the darkest of times: an unwanted pregnancy, a miscarriage that only the women of Barkhouse Lane knew about. It was doubtful whether she would ever come across such kindness again, but it was time to move on and leave her grubby past behind her.

'I'm going down to London to sign up for ENSA, the forces entertainments arm. I'll need to audition. If I don't get in, and I can't find anything else, I'll join one of the forces. Or one of the factories.' That was bottom of her list. She'd worked in a laundry for a time when the theatres were closed at the outbreak of war, bitterly aware of the irony. Her mother had wanted her to break away from the drudgery of doing other people's dirty washing.

Olive looked up as the front door opened and George came in, closely followed by Joe Taplow. The young magician quickly removed his woollen hat, frantically pushing down at his hair, which was sticking up at all angles, and glanced awkwardly at Ginny.

'I found this young man on the doorstep. Come in, Joe,' he

encouraged, aware of the young man's reticence. 'He wanted a word with you, Ginny.'

She put down her knitting and got up. 'Is everything all right, Joe?'

He nodded. 'I came to ask if... if you wouldn't mind... if you could...'

'Would it be better if we went outside?' she suggested, knowing how shy he was.

George gave him a gentle slap on the back. 'Go in the best room. It's blasted cold outside.'

'I didn't want to intrude,' he stammered. 'It will only take a minute.' Ginny took him by the elbow and led him back outside onto the front step, knowing he would feel less awkward, less like he was imposing. It was still bitterly cold, and she shivered a little, wrapping her arms about herself. Noticing, he hurriedly removed his scarf and handed it over. She wound it around her neck, puzzled as to what could be so important that he couldn't ask her in front of the Harveys.

'What is it, Joe?'

It took him a minute to form his words. At twenty-two he had none of the confidence of Billy Lane, none of the swagger. It was possibly why she felt so comfortable with him.

'I have a booking, for Sunday, the fourteenth. At the wireless base in New Waltham. A children's show. I... I wondered if you would be my assistant. I need someone to hand me my props.'

The relief that it was nothing untoward made her smile. 'Of course I will. It's not as if I'm inundated with offers.'

He moved the weight to his other foot, awkward again.

'Oh, I didn't mean it to sound like...'

She touched his arm. 'You could've asked me inside,' she told him gently. 'Save us standing out here in the cold.'

He rubbed his hands to warm them. 'I thought you might say no.'

The thought amused her. 'Come inside.' She tilted her head towards the door. 'George and Olive won't mind. Then you can tell me what you need me to do.'

He followed her into the house, down the slim hallway and into the back room. George had added more coal to the fire and was washing his hands at the sink, and Dolly and Olive had resumed their knitting. They looked to her and Joe and welcomed him as they did everyone who crossed their threshold.

'You look perished, young man,' Olive said kindly. 'Get yourself by that fire.' Ginny bent forward and picked up the knitting she had left on the chair and put it on the table behind Dolly. 'Take off your coat, or you won't feel the benefit when you go out again.'

It all happened so seamlessly, and in no time at all Joe was seated in front of the fire. Ginny removed his scarf from her neck and handed it back to him. He placed it by the cushion on the chair. 'Joe has a booking. A show for the kiddies at the wireless station. I'm to be his assistant.'

He perched on the edge of the chair, his unease evident and Ginny half regretted asking him in. Never in her life had she met someone so unsure of himself in company. How he ever came to be on the stage was a mystery.

'Stay and have a brew with us, lad.' George checked his pocket watch, moving his glasses further down the bridge of his nose to see better. 'You've a while yet afore you need to be back at the theatre. Sit back and make yourself comfy.'

Dolly put down her knitting and took over making the tea, urging her dad to sit down on the chair she'd vacated. Olive was already reaching behind her for her stick, then on her feet, instructing Dolly to reach down the biscuit tin. She offered round a plate of bourbons. Joe declined but she insisted. 'Plenty more. Take one while you can, ducky. They won't keep for ever and neither will we.'

'So, what is it you want Ginny to do?' she asked as he helped himself.

'It's a children's party. A week on Sunday, in the afternoon. I need an assistant.'

'Ooh, that's nice, isn't it, Ginny?' She gave her a sly wink. 'We all need a little bit of magic.'

It made Ginny smile, but Joe had either not noticed or, more likely, was blissfully unaware of their playful teasing.

'What do you want me to wear, Joe? I could wear the red dress I use when I sing with Jessie and Frances. Or just a nice frock. My green wool?'

'Oh. No, wear the red,' Dolly chipped in before he could answer. 'The children will love it, won't they, Mum?' They smiled encouragingly at Joe. He sipped at his tea, shot Ginny a look and the two of them listened as Dolly and Olive chattered on about children's parties they had been to over the years. Joe drained his cup and held it on his lap.

George shook his head. 'You'll not get a word in now.'

There was laughter as they chattered on and they included Joe, drawing him into the conversation, about the theatre, about the war. George tapped his fingers on the table. 'What's next for you, son?'

'I've applied to the army. Twice.' He checked his watch and got up, holding on to his cup and saucer, looking for the best place to put it. As Ginny stepped forward to take it from him, he said quietly, 'We didn't really get a chance to talk about the show.'

'We can talk about it later, at the theatre.'

Dolly was quick to apologise. 'That's mine and Mum's fault, talking about the parties.'

'I've enjoyed it,' he said, putting his coat on to leave. There was more fussing from Olive, telling him to take care and that he must come back again soon.

Ginny saw him out. When she returned, Dolly held up his scarf that had been tucked down between the cushions. Ginny took it from her. 'I'll give it to him at the theatre.'

Olive had taken up her knitting again and she smiled at her as she folded the scarf. 'A lovely young man. He doesn't talk much.'

'He couldn't get a word in, Mother,' George teased. He winked at Ginny. 'But yes, I agree. He is a lovely young man.'

14

Johnny returned to the house in Park Drive only to wash and change his clothing. He had checked in on Ruby, who had been asleep in a chair in the sitting room – or pretending to be. He thought it the latter. Ruby didn't like facing up to her responsibilities, but he had no time to play her games, not when he was making Frances work so hard. They had been rehearsing since 8.30 that Tuesday morning, and he'd sent her home in a taxi so she could spend a couple of hours with Imogen. They'd both had to call in favours – from the Frames, who had now both moved in to take care of Ruby, and Grace and Geraldine to look after Imogen. On his way back to the house, he'd picked up an early edition of the *Grimsby Telegraph* and when he got in had spread it over the kitchen table to read while Mrs Frame pressed his best suit. He turned to page four to make sure the advert had been amended and quickly scanned the competition. Most were showing films, but the Tivoli was still going with variety. He was glad to have the healthy competition and it hadn't affected their audience numbers. News had quickly spread of changes to the bill at the Palace and curiosity had filled the seats despite the foul weather. Last night's performance had gone tremendously well, the support from the audience lifting them as they performed the hastily put-together routines. Any relief he'd experienced had been supplanted by the joy he felt that Frances had been received so well. She deserved any accolades that came her way. What a trouper she'd been. He checked the heavy black box of the Palace advert that announced the New Randolphs, that the small print correctly stated Miss Frances O'Leary would be taking the place of Miss Ruby Randolph while she was indisposed. He hoped Frances would be pleased with it. It was a small gesture, but he could build on that. The shops had reopened and he'd had flowers delivered to the dressing room, taking all the stock the florist had. He couldn't wait to see her face when she opened the door and saw them. It thrilled him to be able to spoil her, to give her such moments. It would never make up for what she had lived through these last few years, but it might go some way to showing her how he felt.

'How's Ruby been today, Mrs Frame? Has she eaten anything?'

'A bit of this and that, not much to speak of. I took her up some breakfast after you left. She didn't touch the toast, but she ate a little of the eggs. I gave her soup.' He was well aware that 'gave' meant 'fed', but Mrs Frame was too polite to say. Even so, he was glad she had persevered. 'I brought her down after eleven. I didn't want her to be lonely up there on her own. And Ted thought it better she has people around her.'

He placed a hand on her shoulder. 'Thank you. Ted's right. Ruby doesn't like to be alone. She never has. Did the doctor call?'

'He did. He left some more tablets in case she might need them.' She patted her apron pocket. 'I thought I'd keep them on me.'

'Yes. Thank you for that, Mrs Frame. Much safer.' He didn't need to enlarge on why, grateful that the Frames were on the ball as far as Ruby's mental state was concerned. He wouldn't want a repeat of New Year's Eve.

Ted Frame came in from the garden when he heard the whistle of the kettle and groaned as he bent down to untie his laces, leaving his boots on the doorstep. Johnny saw Mrs Frame's eyes flick to check for any holes in his socks and smiled to himself. She was a stickler for propriety.

'Afternoon, Ted. I see you've got another good bonfire going out there.'

'Last of the leaves, bit of rubbish I found here and there.' He washed his hands at the sink and looked about for the towel, not noticing that his wife was holding it out to him. He rubbed them dry, then draped it over the rail on the range. 'All going as it should be, Mr Randolph?'

'Dare I say better than could be expected – in the circumstances, fraught as they are.'

Ted dragged out a chair and sat down. 'Well, sometimes we never know what we're capable of until we're pushed.' His wife placed a mug in front of him, and handed a cup and saucer to Johnny. The two men sipped. 'Same as war, same as everything. What are they reporting today, then? Anything change?' He indicated to the newspaper.

'I didn't have time to look. To tell the truth, I didn't buy it for the news.' He put down his cup; he'd barely drunk the tea. Mrs Frame handed over his suit. 'Help yourself, Ted. I'm done with it. There'll be other copies at the theatre.'

Ted folded over the pages. 'I'll enjoy that later, in front of the fire. Happen, I'll sit with your sister a while.'

'Make sure you put your feet up, Ted. You too, Mrs Frame. And help yourself to whatever you want in the line of food and drink. I'm only too grateful that you've stepped in like this.'

'Well,' Ted said, 'times like this we have to pull together.' He slipped off his jacket and hung it over the chair. 'Don't you worry about a thing. Me and Flo have got it all under control.' Mrs Frame tutted loudly, and Johnny could only smile. If anyone had things under control, that was purely down to his wife.

Before he left, he went into the sitting room to see Ruby and found her staring vacantly at the fire. 'Feeling a little better?' She nodded without turning to look at him. He went closer. 'I can't stop, Ruby; I've things to do, to keep things running smoothly.' She didn't react; he hadn't expected her to. They'd have to talk about what had happened before too long, but he wasn't ready for what might follow when Ruby unburdened herself. Would it make her worse or better? And sad as it was to see her so shattered, he wanted to be with Frances, with his child. Wanted to grab a little happiness while he could. 'It will be easier next week. I'll have more time. We can talk then. Okay?' He put his hat on, and bent to kiss her cheek. There was no response but he couldn't wait any longer. He had waited long enough already.

15

Jessie was putting the final touches to Peggy's make-up, this time teaching her how to apply shadow and contour, make her eyes larger, the whites whiter. She stepped back, checked her, leaned forward and rubbed at a mark on Peggy's cheek.

'There.' Jessie dropped the greasepaint stick onto the table and watched as Peggy scrutinised her work in the mirror. 'I hope you paid attention. Now you'll look dark and mysterious and not like you've got two black eyes.'

'Thanks, Jessie.' She gave her a gap-toothed grin. 'You've been really kind to me.' Ginny walked in, put her bag under her chair and hung her gas mask on one of the hooks that ran along the wall facing the mirrors. 'You both have. Afternoon, Ginny.'

Ginny put her hand to Peggy's chin and moved her face from side to side, checking Jessie's handiwork. 'It looks great.' Peggy grew a little at the compliment.

Jessie handed her a rag. 'Now wipe it off and you have a go.'

Peggy sagged. 'Do I have to?'

'How else will you learn?' Jessie glanced at her wristwatch.

'Plenty of time before curtain up. And don't rush at it like a bull in a china shop.'

Peggy took the rag and rubbed at her face.

'New scarf?' Jessie said as Ginny unwound it from her neck.

'It's Joe's. I didn't want to forget it.'

Jessie raised her eyebrows.

'It's nothing like that. He called in at Dolly's. He's got a gig, a week on Sunday, a kids' party. He wants me to go along and help.'

'That's practically a marriage proposal from Joe!' Jessie teased.

'I'm handing him props. Twirling about a bit. That's all. Stop reading more into it than it is.' She pulled a face as a warning that little ears were listening.

Jessie stopped teasing. 'Where is it and how did he get it, do you know?'

Ginny shrugged. 'I can ask. It's at the wireless station.'

Jessie stopped to monitor her protégé's progress. 'That's right, Peggy. A lighter touch will make all the difference.' She gave her another grin. Jessie went over to the rail and checked her costumes were back from the laundry, then began to take off her outdoor clothes and put on her dressing gown.

'Has he got it through a local agent?'

'I've no idea. Why?'

'I'm being practical. There aren't any shows advertised after the panto, which can only mean that Jack Holland hasn't been able to stop the ministry requisitioning the Empire. If I can get a local agent, it might be easier to get work around here. Smaller gigs that mean I can stay in the area instead of travelling too far – for when the panto ends.' Bernie's contacts were concentrated in London. He could get her a tour easily enough but she didn't want that, not yet. She couldn't keep moving her mum and Eddie about. Once had been enough, and she knew her mum was happy here. It had been a harsh winter and she'd been warned that Grace would be vulnerable, her chest weakened from her awful illness last summer. Wherever Jessie went she would have to go on her own, and she wasn't sure she wanted to. She enjoyed being part of the Variety Girls. It had been an unexpected joy to perform with Ginny and Frances. 'I've heard there's a few concert parties getting set up to work the army bases. If we find out who's organising them, that would keep us busy.'

'Jessie, I've already made plans, you know that.'

'But what about our act?'

'That was only ever a stopgap, something to fill in while...' Ginny was cautious, choosing her words carefully. 'I really want to move on. Too many memories here...' She stopped talking. Jessie followed her gaze and saw that Peggy hadn't progressed her make-up. Seeing them, she quickly slapped beige greasepaint on her cheeks and vigorously rubbed it in.

'I couldn't help hearing,' Peggy said, as she wiped her hands on a rag. 'I bet Frankie Pankie—' she corrected herself '—Frank Parker, has something to do with the concert parties. He's a local agent. I'm going to sign for him in a few weeks, when I'm sixteen.'

'Hmm, that won't be long, will it?' Jessie said.

Peggy paused, her eyes wide. They knew she was fourteen; she'd told them herself. A night onstage and how quickly she'd grown up – or so she thought.

'No. No, it won't.' Peggy swiftly moved back to her make-up and the two girls exchanged glances.

'Perhaps I need to get Frankie Pankie's number,' Jessie said, 'although perhaps I don't, with a name like that.'

'He's got an office in the marketplace,' Peggy interrupted, 'by the bus station, above the club there. I'm surprised you ain't heard of him already.'

'Maybe it's a good job we haven't,' Ginny said.

'Suit yourselves,' Peggy replied haughtily. 'I was only trying to help. One good turn and all that.' She wiggled the make-up stick.

'And it's appreciated.' Jessie stood behind her, her hands on the younger girl's shoulders. 'That's so much better. You're a quick learner.'

Instead of the words encouraging her, Peggy's shoulders dropped. 'If only I could learn everything quick.' Jessie was puzzled and, noticing, Peggy perked up and started to sing a line or two from 'Wish Me Luck as You Wave Me Goodbye', mimicking Gracie Fields.

Ginny applauded. 'When you *are* sixteen, Frankie Pankie is going to snap you up. Can't you get some shows now? Won't your parents go with you as a chaperone?'

She slouched in her seat. 'I can't...'

'Can't?' Jessie asked.

She seemed relieved when Joe stuck his head around the door.

'Looking for your scarf?' Jessie shot Ginny a cheeky look.

'Take no notice, Joe,' Ginny said, handing it over. 'You left it behind at Dolly's. Did you want to talk about Sunday?'

'If you've got time.'

Ginny followed him into the corridor.

'What did you mean by "can't", Peggy?' asked Jessie.

'I need a parent to give their permission and me dad's at sea and me stepmother won't sign it just to spite me.' She carried on with her make-up. 'He's soft on 'er, in't he, that Joe. Dun't she like him?'

They could hear Joe explaining to Ginny where they would meet and what he wanted her to do. The two of them would be good together but Joe was painfully shy, and Ginny was still bruised from her encounter with Billy Lane.

'She does like him,' Peggy whispered, 'but the show will be over if he don't get a move on.'

Jessie agreed but she didn't want to discuss Ginny's business with Peggy. She sat down and picked up her black eyeliner. 'You need to darken your left cheekbone more to match the right,' she instructed, and leaned into the mirror to shape her own eyebrows.

Ginny returned a few minutes later and picked up a brush, pulling long strokes through her wavy red hair. 'You look like Rita Hayworth,' Peggy said, 'with your hair like that.'

'Do you think so?' Ginny smiled at the compliment.

'The spit,' Peggy said, leaning back in her chair on two legs. 'I'm right, aren't I?' She looked at Jessie through the mirror.

Jessie put her hand on the back of Peggy's chair and made her upright. 'Ginny's far prettier.'

'Ginny's not pretty,' Peggy said, disgusted. 'Ginny's beautiful.'

Ginny laughed. 'For one second I was about to give you a wallop, Peggy Marshall.'

'Don't do that. I get enough of them at home.' She suddenly sprang to her feet. 'I'm going to look through the peephole, check on the house. I hope the snow ha'nt kept 'em away.'

'She's a funny kid, isn't she?' Ginny said when they were alone. 'I can't quite make her out.'

'Neither can I.' Jessie put her elbow on the table. 'But then I can't understand most people.'

Ginny changed the subject. 'What news of Harry?'

Jessie rested her chin in her hand. 'I got a letter this morning. He asked to meet me halfway between his barracks and here. I can get the early bus on Sunday and meet him in Lincoln. A few hours is better than nothing.'

'And *you* have plans to make,' Ginny said, deflecting the attention back to Jessie.

'Yes.' Plans that had kept her awake at night. They'd got engaged three weeks before Christmas but just lately she'd got cold feet – and it was nothing to do with the weather. Once she was married to Harry, she'd never have a chance to follow her dreams. And she wasn't sure she was ready to let go of them, not yet.

16

Twice Ruby had spoiled the moment – and Johnny wouldn't allow her to do it a third. When he'd first managed to have dinner with Frances after finding her again, Ruby had staggered into the hotel, drunk, disturbing them when they'd barely had a chance to talk. Would Frances have told him about Imogen then? He would never know, for Ruby had drawn the attention fully in her direction as she always did. No wonder Frances had been reticent. The second time was when he had set off to meet her on New Year's Eve, the ring in his pocket. It was in his pocket now. This time he would succeed – but would she say yes? He was nervous, ridiculously so. Frances didn't need him, he wasn't fool enough to think that, but hopefully she wanted him, longed for him as he did her.

There'd been little opportunity to arrange anything special. He wanted to be alone, away from anything – or anyone – that might interrupt them. It was too early to book for dinner and too late for them to eat before a show. There was no privacy at Barkhouse Lane, and he didn't want Ruby to be anywhere close when he proposed. The blackout had rendered so many romantic places unsafe and so he had arranged to meet her on Corporation Bridge, around the corner from the Palace Theatre. Small slivers of light appeared along the wharf, the soft hush of water as the tugs moved in the semi-darkness, a squeak of a bicycle wheel that he could barely make out on the other side of the road. The dock was crowded with ships, moving wood, flour, and jam from Tickler's factory back and forth. If an army marched on its stomach then Britain had to be sure it kept its fighting men well fed. There had already been too many losses, of merchant ships and minesweepers, of men – already too many widows, too many children fatherless. They were all too well aware of it in Grimsby and other ports around the country. The war might not have come to the land, but it had certainly come to the sea.

It had been strange, coming home and yet having no home to speak of. Had he known then what waited for him in England, he would have left America at the first opportunity. All too soon they would be parted again. He'd be called up and then who knew where he'd be posted, or how long he'd be away. He touched his pocket, took out the ring, opened the blue and gold box and closed it again. He was desperate to make an occasion of it, the best he could in the circumstances. There was an urgency now. He wanted them to be together, a family.

A few minutes later he saw her walking towards him, wrapped up against the cold, her head held high, her familiar red beret tilted on her head just so and he felt a surge of longing. He had always loved her. Always.

Although he wanted to rush towards her, he held back, wanting to hold on to the image of her walking towards him, lit by the crescent moon, the slits of light from oncoming cars shining like small diamonds. She deserved diamonds, and silks and satins, not the shabby second-hand things she'd had to make do with. He felt a sweep of anger, his mother looming up unbidden, forced the thought away. It was just the two of them. It should have happened long ago.

She hunched forward, her hands in her pockets, her bag and the cardboard box that held her gas mask over her shoulder. Her scarf was wrapped about her face, covering her nose, her mouth, but as she came closer he could tell by her eyes that she was smiling, bemused. She pulled down her scarf and her breath clouded before her.

'Why meet here?'

'It's private.'

She looked about her, at the cyclists, the occasional lorry, the odd passer-by, and laughed. Her breath clouded again, drifted on the cold air. She thrust her hands back into her pockets. She was as different to his sister as she could be, independent and self-contained, and he didn't think he could love her more.

He leaned forward to kiss her, got caught on her bag, her gas mask, and she grinned, adjusting them to one side. She touched his face, and he leaned into it, then took her hand in his and removed her glove, loving the softness of her skin. He held it for a while, the warmth of their bodies connecting them.

'Close your eyes,' he told her. She frowned but did as he asked, and he put his arms about her waist. 'Imagine we're in London. Not here.' She opened one eye. 'Humour me. Please?' She closed it again and he pulled her closer. 'Remember that night on Waterloo Bridge, when we stood watching the boats go down the Thames?' She nodded, smiling now and he knew she was with him in that other place, that other time. 'We can see Big Ben to one side, the dome of St Paul's the other. There's not much traffic; it's long after the show has ended. We went to celebrate with the cast in the American Bar.'

'My first glass of champagne.'

'You'd been so nervous, but there was no need. You were everything I knew you'd be, and more.'

She opened her eyes, gazed at him and he kissed her, told her to close them again. The clock in the tower opposite the theatre chimed the hour.

'Ah, Big Ben.'

She giggled.

He put his fingers to her lips. 'We slipped away, the two of us, out of the river entrance from The Savoy and onto the bridge.'

'It was a fine night,' she said. 'There were so many stars. Millions of them.'

'There were, and you were the newest and brightest of them all.' That night was seared in his memory, not because Frances took Ruby's place, or because she'd been triumphant, but because he knew then that he wanted to spend the rest of his life with her. He kissed her, full and hard on the mouth, and the years that had separated them fell away.

'Marry me, Frances?'

She opened her eyes and he took the box from his pocket and opened it, revealing the diamond cluster.

'Oh, darling, not the safest place to propose, on a bridge.' She was laughing at him, her eyes glittering with tears of happiness, but she still hadn't answered him. He moved to drop to one knee, and she stopped him. 'People will stare.'

'Let them.'

'No, I don't want them to. The answer's yes. It was yes the first time you asked me all those years ago. Nothing has changed.' She held out her hand and he placed the ring on her finger, pulled her to him and kissed her, then swept her into his arms, loving her more than he ever thought he could. There was nothing they could do to change the past, only look to the future – and hope that it was better.

'I don't want another day to pass without you by my side,' he told her. 'I'll move heaven and earth to make that happen, and I'll spend the rest of my life making it up to you, and Imogen.'

She placed her hand to the back of his head, his neck. 'Isn't life so sweet and so cruel, darling. That we should find each other again, when being together is out of our control. Yours and mine. And there's nothing we can do about it.'

He didn't want to think that far ahead, knowing he would have to leave her again, and Imogen. Please, God, they would have a little time to be a family. He looked up at the sky, at the stars above and prayed that God was listening.

17

Johnny placed a gentle arm about her shoulder as they walked down to the theatre. The door of the Palace Buffet on the corner opened and noise drifted out into the street. A queue for the performance was already forming and snaked past the flour mill and the offices of Albert Gait's. Johnny pulled back the door and as it closed, took hold of her hand. Such a small, discreet gesture, but one that let people know they belonged together. They stopped and said hello to the front of house staff then made their way through the pass door to backstage, and Frances doubted whether she'd ever felt so at peace and yet so excited.

The stage manager handed Johnny his mail and they waited for the key. 'Miss Randolph is already in.' She saw Johnny's cheek sink as he clenched his jaw.

'Thanks, Ken.' His voice betrayed nothing of his feelings one way or another, but Frances felt her heart flutter. He glanced at her, his smile reassuring, and they walked towards the number one dressing room nearest the stage. They could hear other voices from open doors but theirs was firmly closed.

She took a deep breath. 'Do you want me to leave, give you a moment?'

'No,' he said tersely, as he gripped the handle. 'Stay by my side.' He squeezed her hand to reassure her.

Ruby was in her silk robe, sitting at the dressing table, her hair pushed back from her face with an Alice band, a powder puff in her hand. Every light was on, the bright, bare bulbs enhancing the hollows of her pinched face. Her dresses, each and every one of them, had been removed from the rail and were draped across the sofa, her shoes a jumble beneath them, as if she had been checking everything was still there. There were flowers everywhere, great bouquets of roses and exotic blooms, of lilies and hyacinths, the air heavy with their rich perfume. Johnny closed the door. Frances, not knowing where to stand, or where to sit, went over to the sink and washed her hands to distract herself, the diamonds of her ring glittering in the light.

'Ruby, what are you doing?' Johnny said calmly, although it was clear he was anything but. 'You should be at home, resting.'

She smiled sweetly at him. 'I'm fine.' She continued patting her face, clouds of powder floating about her shoulders as she pressed too hard. She moved closer to the mirror so she could see Frances. 'Hello, darling. How's Imogen?'

Johnny stared at her. 'You knew?'

She gave a small laugh. 'Of course I knew. I saw her in the theatre with Frances on Christmas Day. She asked me not to say anything.' She twisted to face Frances. 'You wanted to tell Johnny yourself, didn't you, darling. And I kept my promise. I wanted to put things right. For Mother. For me.'

He glanced to Frances for affirmation, the hurt clear in his dark eyes.

'I wanted to tell you. I tried to – but you left with Ruby, for the show for the troops. I didn't want to run down the street...'

'To cause a scene? No, you would never do that, would you?' Ruby stood up and reached for her dress. 'I went and said hello to everyone, wished them a belated happy new year. June told me you'd changed the show, some of the routine.' Another withering smile for her brother. 'You'd better get me up to speed.' She began removing her robe.

Johnny moved to stop her. 'You can't dance. You're not well enough.'

Ruby's face darkened, her body suddenly rigid. She shrugged Johnny's hand away. There was a knock on their door. Frances tensed. 'Your half-hour call, Mr Randolph, Miss O'Leary.'

Ruby stepped towards the door, opened her mouth, but Johnny barred her way, called out, 'Thank you,' and pushed Ruby into the chair. Her eyes were wild and she glared at Frances. Frances moved away from the basin, wanting to be anywhere but in this small room, with no windows, and no air.

'Get dressed, Ruby,' Johnny demanded. 'I'll get Ken to call a taxi and take you home. Does Mrs Frame know you've come here?'

'I am *not* a child,' she snapped. 'I'm a *Randolph*. We are *billed* as *the Randolphs*. We dance as *the Randolphs*.' She shot a look to Frances. 'Shouldn't you be at home, looking after your child?'

Frances was incensed – she wasn't going to stand in a corner and have Ruby Randolph tell her what she should and should not be doing. How dare she after all the trouble she and her mother had caused. She stepped forward, out of the shadow.

'I should, Ruby. It's what I've wanted to do since the day she was born but because—'

Johnny took hold of her hands. 'Don't. Please don't.'

'Sweet,' Ruby said. 'Go home. People have come to see the Randolphs – and you're not a Randolph.'

'But she will be, Ruby. You'd better get used to it.'

Ruby got up, and tripped over one of the shoes she'd left so carelessly about the room. Frances dashed forward to catch her but Ruby fell awkwardly, dragging Frances down with her. Johnny reached to help Frances up, only to have Ruby hit his hand away as she got to her feet. She lashed out again, her long nails catching Frances, who cried out and put her hand to her cheek. Ruby began to laugh hysterically, and Johnny moved quickly, drawing back his hand and slapping her face. It shocked her to silence, and she staggered away from him, catching her heel on her dress, falling over a vase of roses. She lost her footing and fell backwards, catching her head on the rail as she went down. Frances rushed to her, and raised her head from the floor.

Someone knocked on the door; they heard Ken's voice. 'Is everything all right?'

Johnny lifted Ruby onto the sofa, Frances hurriedly moving the clothes strewn about them and turned away from the door as Johnny opened it.

'Ken, can you see if there's a doctor in the house.' He loosened his tie. 'Ruby's... she needs help.'

After he'd closed the door, Johnny took hold of Frances's chin, assessing the damage to her face. 'Your cheek.'

'It's nothing. I can cover it with make-up.'

She was shocked and knew that he was too. He went over to the sofa where Ruby lay and put his hand to her forehead. 'She's out cold. It must have been when she banged her head. She's not well.'

That much was evident but if Johnny thought it was no more than a simple illness, he was deluding himself. 'It's more than that, Johnny. You've got to admit to yourself how ill she is before you can have any hope of helping her.'

He took hold of his sister's hand. 'I should have got her into a clinic months ago. I could have done that in London. I've left it all far too long.'

She kneeled beside him. 'Seems we both left things too long. I wanted to tell you, about Imogen.'

He shook his head. 'Don't apologise. It's not your fault. None of it is. I was surprised, that's all.'

'Ruby had to keep that secret for almost a week. It was cruel of me. I should have come to you, but...' She sighed. 'I was so afraid you'd reject me – and I could bear that – but I had to protect Imogen.' It was a pitiful excuse, but it *was* the truth. It didn't matter how much she had to tolerate as long as Imogen was safe.

Ken came back with a doctor who had been in the audience, and he checked Ruby over. 'She was overwrought,' Johnny explained. 'She's been ill.'

Frances pressed her hand to his arm. He needed to acknowledge that this was far more complicated than a bout of exhaustion. He must have understood because the tension in his arm slackened, and he said quietly, 'She needs professional help.'

The doctor understood. 'Is there a telephone I can use? I think we should get her to hospital as soon as we can.'

When the ambulance left, Frances began to clear up the mess, and hung the dresses on the rail, checking them for damage. Water from one of the vases had spilled onto an emerald-green gown, leaving a dark patch, and some of the threads were torn. Johnny bent down next to her and handed her the roses from the floor. 'It was meant to be a surprise. The flowers—'

'And they are,' she consoled, smelling each bloom as she returned them to the vase. 'They're quite beautiful.' When some semblance of order was restored, the two of them sat quietly in the dressing room, unable to process what had just happened. The stage doorman brought them both a nip of brandy.

'You all right, Miss O'Leary?' he asked.

She gave him a warm smile. 'I'm absolutely fine.'

They managed to get through the show, putting their own troubles aside to allow others to forget theirs, and the special moment on the bridge had been tainted by what came after. Would it always be like this?

He dropped into his chair when they came offstage, his body leaking with sweat, and when he undressed, she hung up his suit and handed him a towel to wash. Afterwards they signed autographs and chatted with the troops as they always did but as time went on and the adrenalin rush had lessened, Frances's cheek began to sting. Johnny was concerned for her.

'Come with me, back to the house. I can telephone the hospital from there, in private. I want to spend time with you, to talk, not to work, or dance, or please anyone else. Just us.'

They chose to walk, wrapped up against the cold, the stars bright in the sky. They were used to the darkness now, always carried a torch. There had been attacks, muggings; it paid to be on your guard. War did not bring out the best in everyone and the blackout carried its own dangers. He clasped her hand in his. She wanted to be with him, wanted them to be a family, but how on earth could she bring Imogen into such chaos?

18

Mrs Frame was in the sitting room, full of apologies when they arrived at the house. 'I only left her to put the hot water bottles in. Ted's on ARP duty tonight. He sat with Miss Ruby for a while and she seemed to perk up, took an interest when he showed her the newspaper.' She wrung her hands on her pinny. 'I called the theatre. I thought she might have gone there.'

'It's not your fault, Mrs Frame,' Johnny comforted. 'It was selfish of me to ask so much of you.'

'But I shouldn't have left her.' She avoided looking at Frances and Johnny must have noticed because he took her by the elbow.

'Mrs Frame, this is Frances O'Leary, my fiancée.'

It was odd, hearing him say it out loud, after all this time. He was no longer guarded, her acceptance of marriage releasing any hesitancy he might have had. She should be happy, deliriously so, but as it was, she only felt unsettled.

'Pleased to meet you, Miss O'Leary,' Mrs Frame said, holding out her hand. She glanced to Frances's cheek but didn't comment. 'Should I get you a bite to eat? A drink?'

'We can do that, Mrs Frame. You must be tired,' Johnny said kindly.

'I can't say I'm not. It's been very upsetting. You say Miss Ruby's in the hospital?'

Johnny nodded. 'The best place for her, Mrs Frame.' He rested a gentle hand on her shoulder. 'Why don't you get off to bed, get some rest. I'll telephone the hospital in the morning, and we'll find out what's what.'

'Well, if you're sure...' She was hesitant and Frances felt it was because of her, but after a few words of reassurance she said goodnight and went upstairs.

Johnny raked the coals to stir up the flames then led the way to the kitchen, and indicated for Frances to sit down at the table that had been covered with a light blue cloth. He filled the kettle, got bread and opened the larder, placed ham and butter in front of her and found plates, a couple of knives. 'Sorry it's not much of a celebration. I'd planned dinner at the Royal when the show finished. The chef was staying late. There was champagne on ice...' She sensed his bitterness that once again Ruby had blighted their special moment.

'This is much nicer,' she said, hoping to cheer him, to cheer herself. They had both struggled through the remainder of the evening, but the drama was over, for the time being, and she wanted to forget and have something that was normal, something that would make her feel anchored. 'You're very domesticated.'

'Habit. When you're on the road all the time.'

'I thought you might have had people to do things for you – like Mrs Frame.'

'We do sometimes, but not always. Mostly it was just me and Ruby.'

'It must be hard for her. You've been so close.' She thought of her own siblings. How long since she'd last seen them. If anyone was to blame, it wasn't Ruby. And what sense was blame anyway? It wouldn't change anything. What time they had lost together could never be regained. She got up and sliced the bread and buttered it, sliced the ham. He put two mugs on the table, and filled the teapot.

'New Year's Eve supper,' he said as she made them into a sandwich. 'I don't think Ruby ate any of it.'

'She's very undernourished,' Frances said. 'Perhaps when she begins to eat properly she'll recover quickly.' He didn't look convinced. They both knew Ruby was way past the cure of a few good meals. Johnny returned the ham and butter to the pantry, and they took the sandwiches into the sitting room. The fire had taken hold, and it was warm and more luxurious than Frances had ever known. The generous damask curtains were edged with heavy braid, the pelmets deep. There were easy chairs, a sofa, and heavy mahogany furniture polished to sheen. He made her sit down in the armchair by the fire and pushed an occasional table to her side.

'Kick off your shoes, relax.' It was hard to relax in such surroundings, but he was easy; he was used to it. A door above them closed.

'Does Mrs Frame live here?'

'Almost. She and Mr Frame, Ted, have been here the last couple days, to care for Ruby. I should have made the doctor call for an ambulance on New Year's Eve, but it didn't seem right.' He let out a long sigh. 'I didn't want to admit to myself that she was that bad – and that I couldn't do something to fix it.'

'It must be difficult.'

He looked at her. 'No more difficult than your life has been. Because of us – Mother, and to a lesser extent, Ruby.'

She stared into the flames. She didn't want to be bitter. She'd seen it eat away at people. 'They couldn't have known.' Would it have made a difference if they had? Alice Randolph was not protective of her children; she was controlling. There was a huge difference.

'I need to make sure they keep her in the hospital – for her own safety, as well as ours.'

Frances didn't reply. He came to sit opposite her and they ate and drank in silence.

When they'd finished, he got up and went to a table that held glass decanters, which glittered in the firelight. 'Sherry? Whisky? Brandy?'

She remembered the kick of the brandy Ken had given her. 'A small whisky would be wonderful.' He poured two glasses, added a splash of water, handed her one and raised his to her.

'To us.'

She got up and clinked her glass to his. 'To us.' She sipped at the whisky, felt the fire of it bite in her throat. Her head was spinning but it was nothing to do with the alcohol. She had been frightened by Ruby, more than she cared to admit. Johnny took a mouthful of whisky, placed his glass on the table and took hold of her about the waist. 'I was so afraid you'd say no – on the bridge.'

'Why ever would you think that?'

'It felt like tempting fate. That I could be this happy. That after everything – finding you, Imogen. Oh, God, Imogen.' He gently touched her face round the scratch, and shook his head. 'I don't want to wait, Frances. I want to get married. As soon as possible. You can live here with Imogen. You'll have everything. I'll make certain of it. Mrs Frame will take care of you both.'

'And you?'

He smiled sadly. 'Our timing is dreadful, isn't it?'

'Only offstage.'

'But if I hadn't come back at all...'

'I would have managed.' She would have been lonely, but she was used to loneliness.

'I have no doubt about that.' He took another sip from his glass. 'What about Ruby?'

'Let's not talk about her, not tonight; let it be just the two of us.'

If only it was that easy. 'But we need to talk about her. We can't forget about her, no more than I can forget about Imogen.'

He sat down on the sofa, and she joined him. 'I'll know more when I go to the hospital. I doubt they'll let her out for a while.' He drank back his whisky, drained the glass. 'When they do, I'll see if she can stay with our aunt Hetty in Dorset, Mother's sister. She's the only one who can handle her. She never had children so dotes on the two of us as if we were her own. But she has a full life and... there's no one else.'

'No other family?'

'No. Father was an orphan. Mother only had Hetty. That's it. Not like you, with your mammy and daddy.' He mimicked her accent, and she nudged him, smiling. 'Will they come over for the wedding? And your brothers and sisters?'

'I don't think so. It could take too long to organise. It might be too dangerous for them at the moment.' Here she was, making excuses, just as she always did, afraid of being disappointed.

'Tell me what you want and it's yours.' He put his arm about her shoulder and drew her to him. She could hear his heart beating, so strong and steady, and it made her feel steady too. Together they would get through whatever lay ahead. She sat up and kissed him.

'I don't *want* anything. Truly. Let's keep things quiet, and simple. No announcements in the *Times*.'

'Oh, and I had wanted to tell the world.' He was only half teasing. Johnny would want everyone to know, but that was the easiest way to lose control of their story and she wasn't prepared to reveal it, not without thinking things through.

'Please don't, darling. I'm not ready for the world to know yet.'

He nodded, understanding. 'Your wish is my command.' He

took her hand in his, kissed her fingers, and for a while they simply watched the fire, their thoughts their own.

Frances tried to stifle a yawn but failed. 'It's very warm.'

'You're very tired.'

She nodded.

'You could stay the night—'

'I couldn't.'

'I don't mean my bed. You could have Ruby's.'

That was the last thing she wanted. She had taken her place in the show, worn her costume... she already felt like she was being swept along in a storm, that a strong wind was propelling her where she didn't want to go. It was important to be steadfast, to keep her feet on the ground.

'I wouldn't want to embarrass Mrs Frame; she seems a nice sort.'

'She is.'

Frances pushed on her shoes and got up. 'I should go.'

He stood beside her. 'I'll call a taxi.'

'I could be hours waiting for one.'

'You can't walk, not at this hour.' He thought for a moment. 'There's a couple of bicycles in the garage. If you wanted...'

'That would be perfect.' She wasn't used to taxis, to housekeepers, to someone taking care of her. If felt strange, like a pair of shoes that didn't fit. He helped her on with her coat, put on his own, picked up a torch and she followed him outside. He checked the tyres and the brakes before handing it over, then began checking the second bike. 'What are you doing?'

'You don't think I'd let you go home alone, did you?'

'I'll be perfectly fine. I'm used to looking after myself.'

He wheeled the bike out to hers. 'I know you will, but I'm here to look after you now. Please let me.'

They walked down the drive and onto the street and he got

astride the bike, wobbled, missed his footing on the pedal, and tried again.

She giggled. 'When did you last ride a bike?'

'When I was eight, maybe nine.' He smiled at her. 'It'll be fun.'

Their lives were worlds apart. It was fun when you had a choice. She got on her own bicycle and lagged behind, smiling to herself as he struggled to find his stride. When he did, she pedalled alongside him – and suddenly riding a bike was fun after all.

19

When Johnny left her safely at her front door, Frances gently balanced the bike against the inside of the front wall and entered the house as quietly as she could. There were no sounds this time, no one wanting to know her business and for that she was glad. Johnny's proposal seemed like it belonged to another day. She wished it had. She touched her face. It had stopped stinging, but her skin had raised protectively around the mark left by Ruby's nails.

She went through the small back room to the kitchen and poured herself a glass of water, drank it back, and almost jumped out of her skin when Grace came into the room, squinting against the light. 'Everything all right? Oh, your face.' She hurried towards Frances to take a better look. 'Were you attacked?'

'No. Yes... but not like that.' She drank more water, and refilled her glass. 'Johnny made sure I was safe. I seem to be safe from everyone except his sister. I'm sorry I disturbed you.'

'I was awake, drifting in and out of sleep. I couldn't settle. Would you like some cocoa?'

'If there's enough milk.'

Grace looked in the small pantry. 'I'll do half and half.'

While Grace moved silently about the kitchen, she whispered of events at the theatre. They took their mugs and sat down at the table.

'How has Imogen been?'

'A poppet.'

Frances was overcome with misery. 'I thought my life would be less problematic once my secret was out. Who'd have thought it would be worse.'

'It only seems that way,' Grace counselled. 'It's always darkest before the dawn.'

Frances rested her mug on the table. 'There's been a lot of darkness.'

'I know, my lovely girl. You must have hoped that when Johnny came back into your life things would improve.'

Hope, that's all it was. 'I wasn't so stupid as to think it would be easy. He loves Imogen. He loves me.' She removed her gloves and showed Grace her engagement ring. 'He asked me to marry him.'

Grace took hold of her hand, admiring it. 'Oh, Frances. It's beautiful.' She opened her arms and hugged her, and while Frances welcomed their closeness, a small part of her wished she'd been telling her own mother, sharing her excitement with the woman who'd given birth to her, nurtured her, then let her fly. How she longed for her once familiar embrace, for whispered words that never failed to comfort, or to soothe. Grace gripped her shoulders. 'I'm so happy for you, sweetheart. It's good news when we have so little. Have you set a date?'

'Johnny's going to get a special licence. He doesn't want to wait.'

'And you do?' Grace was concerned.

'I don't know what I want. Yes, I want to be with Johnny, I want to be a family, for Imogen to have her mummy *and* her daddy but —' Frances withdrew her hand, rubbing her finger over the diamonds. 'I fear that we will go through life with Ruby firmly between us.'

'From what you say, she sounds very ill.'

'"Tormented" would be a better word.' She couldn't get Ruby's face out of her head, her contorted features, the pure hatred in her eyes. And the smell of fear, primal fear. She touched her cheek.

'Hardly surprising, is it?' Grace considered. 'It must have been a terrible burden to keep that secret from her brother when she relies on him so much.'

Frances had tried to be forgiving. She felt only pity for Ruby in her present state but doubted she would ever find it in her heart to forgive Alice Randolph. 'What kind of mother does that to her children?' She wanted only happiness for her child and was prepared to sacrifice her own for it.

'Someone who's afraid,' Grace offered. 'We all do our best with what we have. And she was grieving – not that that's an excuse – but sometimes, blinded by grief, we make bad choices.'

'Did I make bad choices?'

Grace shook her head. 'You made the best choice you could at the time. As do we all.' She drank back her cocoa. 'We have to keep going forward in the darkness. You perhaps know that, more than most. Ruby will no doubt feel shame and guilt, afraid of what she has done, afraid of being on her own. Perhaps the example of your strength will help her.'

Frances briefly closed her eyes. 'I'm tired of being strong.' It would be easy to move to the house in Park Drive, easy to hand responsibility over to Johnny, but she couldn't; it wasn't her way.

'Think of the alternative,' Grace suggested. 'Would you want to be weak and simpering?'

'It might be nice, occasionally.' Many times she'd wanted to give up and hand over her worries for someone else to take care of. And she hadn't been without opportunity. Over the last few years men had made advances, but she'd never let anyone get close, fearing the consequences more than she feared finding enough money to live on. Grace pressed her arm, and she looked at her.

'One day you'll be glad of the choices you've made. We can only see the wisdom of it when we look back on our lives. God willing, that's a long way in the future for you yet.'

20

Frances couldn't sleep, her mind too busy, her body too restless. She heard the front door open and close as Geraldine left for work and she eased herself away from Imogen, dressed quietly and quickly, and went downstairs.

Jessie was in the back room, the airer wound down from its position in front of the fire. She was draping her blouse and underwear over it and gasped when she saw Frances's cheek.

'What on earth happened to you?' Jessie pulled the airer to the ceiling, fastened it in position by looping the rope round the hasp on the wall and listened while Frances told her of the night's events.

'Do you think Ruby will stay in hospital?'

'She needs to. Whether she will or not is another matter.'

'Surely they won't let her out in that state.'

'I have no idea.' Johnny had thought he might have to sign papers to keep her in. 'Oh, and this happened.' She held out her hand for Jessie to admire her engagement ring, but wasn't quite prepared when Jessie threw her arms about her, squealing with delight, and almost knocked her off her feet.

'At last! I'm so thrilled for you. How wonderful. Have you set a date?'

Jessie's excitement was exactly what she needed to give her a boost. 'Johnny wants to get married as soon as we can...'

'And?'

Frances sucked her cheeks. 'I don't think rushing is a good idea.'

Jessie ducked under the clothes that dangled above her and warmed herself in front of the fire. 'You don't know how much time you've got.'

'That's rather morbid.'

'I didn't mean it like that. Things as they are. With the war and everything. It'll be his turn soon enough. You can't hold back any more, Frances. Won't Imogen want to be with her daddy?'

'Of course she will, and so do I, but things need to be sorted out first. We can't live in a house where Ruby's so volatile. It might not be safe.'

'What might not be safe?' Grace said as she joined them. She examined Frances's cheek. 'That's gone down nicely. It should heal well; you have good skin.'

'Have you already told Mum?' Jessie asked.

'We spoke last night,' her mother told her. 'Move away from the fire, Jessie, you're hogging all the heat.' Jessie had no sooner moved than the door opened and Eddie came in and took her place. She glared at him.

'What have I done now?'

She saw her mother's bemused expression and could only sigh. 'Nothing. Won't you be late for work?'

He pushed aside her blouse and slip and checked the clock on the wall opposite. 'No, I've got plenty of time.'

Jessie helped her mother in the kitchen while Eddie chatted to Frances. If he'd seen the mark on her cheek, he didn't mention it and instead asked her how the show had gone at the Palace.

Jessie returned and placed bread and butter on the table. 'I might see you later, Ed. I'm going to the social club near the bus station. There's an agent there. Frank Parker.'

'Frankie Pankie,' Eddie said.

'That's what Peggy called him.'

Eddie nodded. 'Everyone calls him that.'

'Surely not to his face?' Grace interjected.

Eddie shrugged. 'I don't, Mum, but I've heard others.'

Grace tutted. 'I don't like the sound of that. I ought to come with you, Jessie.'

Jessie shot Eddie a look and he dipped his head and carried on eating. Having her mother worry was the last thing she wanted. 'I'll be fine, Mum. I need work when the panto ends and I haven't got enough bookings at the moment.'

'What about Bernie?'

'I'm thinking of staying closer to home while the weather's this bad. No good if the buses and trains are out of action – and there are plenty of clubs and places around here. I've relied on Jack Holland too much.'

'There's the Palace,' Frances suggested. 'Although they usually book in an entire show and not individual acts. I can ask Johnny.'

Imogen came downstairs and climbed onto her mother's lap, staring at the scratch on her cheek, frowning as she did so. Frances took hold of her hand and kissed her fingers.

'What happened to your face, Mummy?'

'I scratched myself. Isn't Mummy silly? I shall have to cut my nails.' She spread her fingers and Imogen nodded, easily satisfied. How long would it be before her innocent questions weren't so easy to answer?

21

Jessie left her mother working in her room, the rhythm of the sewing machine treadle a steady beat as she made her way out of the front door. It was icy cold and she tucked her scarf about her ears and face, cutting through the alleyways and side streets to avoid the harsh wind that blasted off from the seafront. As she reached the marketplace, one bus was moving off and another idled as passengers boarded, exhaust fumes pluming and swirling in the air.

At the entrance to the social club, she pulled at one of the double doors and walked in, stopping for a moment while her eyes adjusted to the dim light. It smelled of stale ale and cigarette smoke. At the end of the room was a raised platform, and on it a piano, a drum kit set centre stage. It was much like any other social club she had been in with her father. She closed her eyes, hoping to sense him beside her but the images that caught her attention were not happy ones. He would take her along to sing with him when he was feeling too frail, or too ill to carry the show alone, not wanting to lose the booking or the income. Word soon got round the club owners and he began to lose what little work he'd had. She'd been unaware of it to begin with, but as she got older the desperateness of their situation came to full focus. He had asked her to take care of Mum and Eddie, and she was determined to keep her promise.

A couple of men huddled in a dark corner and they gave her a cursory glance before returning to their whispered conversation. A bald man in his fifties was behind the bar, polishing glasses, and only looked at her when she was stood in front of him. It made her feel uneasy, but she took a deep breath and said, 'I'm here to see Mr Parker.'

The man set the glass down, picked up another, and pushed the tea towel inside it. 'Does he know you're coming?'

'I didn't know I needed an appointment. I'm looking for work. As a singer.'

'Tek a seat.' He called over his shoulder. 'Julie, tell Frank there's a turn wants to see him.'

A girl appeared from a door behind him and scurried off to another door at the side of the stage. She emerged a few seconds later and went back behind the bar. Jessie waited, making herself tall in the hopes of appearing more confident than she felt. After a couple of minutes that seemed like twenty, a portly man with oiled hair came towards her, his chin tilted forward, assessing her. She got to her feet and held out her hand. His limp grip belied his large frame, and she was reminded again of her father's instructions. *Shake hands like you mean it*. He asked her to take a seat and she did so, relieved she hadn't had to go into an office alone with him. That had been one of her mother's instructions.

'Well, now. Miss Delaney, isn't it? From the Empire.'

She was flattered. 'It is.'

He smiled. 'Saw you in the summer show. I was there on the last night. Hoped to chat with Vernon Leroy but...' He splayed his hands. 'Hard to get close to people like that.'

Jessie blushed. It hadn't been difficult for her, not with one of his stars, Madeleine Moore, paving the way. 'I was lucky enough to audition for him. I was going to be in his next production but then—'

'War broke out.' He finished her sentence. She nodded. 'Shame.' He pulled out a cigarette, put it in his mouth, took a lighter, inhaled, then turned to his side and blew the smoke away from her. It still caught in her throat, and she suddenly remembered the haze of smoke that hung in the air when she sang with her father, how their clothes reeked of it and her mother would hang their stage outfits in the yard to rid them of the smell. 'Lost opportunities, eh?'

'Yes,' she said, not wanting to dwell on what might have been, 'but hopefully only temporarily.'

'That depends, doesn't it? Life's changed for us all. And if it's the same as the last time, we won't be getting good news anytime soon.'

She didn't want to think about it. It was a delay, that was all it was. 'But the theatres reopened soon enough.'

'Aye. And some of 'em are closing again just as quick. It's only going to get worse, believe you me.' He flicked his ash on the floor. 'Going to be a struggle to keep going before too long, but places like this, well, less overheads than the West End. We'll be all right.' He took a drag on his cigarette. 'Now then, what can I do for you?' He sat back in the chair, which seemed far too small for him. It creaked under his weight.

'I was told you were putting out concert parties. I thought you might have a place for me?'

He smiled broadly, revealing nicotine-stained teeth. 'A girl like you I can find work for anytime. For you on your own, is it? Not with the other two girls – what d'ya call yourselves. Variety Girls?'

'No. Just me. They have other plans.' That seemed to please him. She knew not to be overly enthusiastic, but her relief must have been evident on her face. It was work, work she loved – and it would save her from the torture of another office job. Once Grace was through the worst of the winter months, it would be different; only then would she feel more relaxed about striking out further from home. There was Bernie, and Madeleine Moore had kept in touch with Grace; she only had to ask either of them. He screwed his cigarette in the ashtray and got up.

'Give me a minute, love. I'll check my diary for openings.'

She sat back, taking in her surroundings. There were no windows to speak of, only two to the front of the building that had been painted with black paint, and the ceiling discoloured by nicotine. It was dingy and dark, but it was work; if Frank Parker paid well enough, she could put money aside to keep her going when she eventually did go to London, because, sitting here, she knew she would. She wanted a bigger stage, and she wanted to earn enough to keep her mother in comfort without passing her responsibilities on to Harry.

Frank Parker came back, pushed a document in front of her and took a seat opposite. From his inside pocket he withdrew a pen, unscrewed the top and held it out to her. 'Sign that and we can be in business this weekend. I've got exclusive contracts with most of the clubs in the area – any that's worth having. When that panto ends, your feet won't touch the ground.' He shoved the pen towards her and, hesitantly, she took it from him. She peered down at the contract, turning the page. She'd seen contracts like this before – but Bernie had put them before her having already gone through them. There was no contract between her and Bernie, just a long-standing friendship with her father that bound them together. She trusted Bernie Blackwood but she knew nothing about the man in front of her. She shifted uneasily on her chair. Frank Parker had not mentioned a contract.

'There's a lot to read.'

He flicked his hand. 'Standard contact. You don't need to do nothing but sign on the line there.' He reached across, turned the page and indicated the place with his finger. His nails were neatly manicured, his cuffs white, his wristwatch expensive.

'I don't have a contract with my London agent.' She'd never needed one. 'The only contracts I've ever signed have been for a production – for the summer season and for the panto.' Truth be told they were the only contracts she'd ever signed. Her father and Bernie had taken care of everything else.

He ran his hand about his chin and pulled at it. 'That doesn't sound very professional. You want the security of a contract.' He sat back in his chair, and took out another cigarette. She was beginning to wish she'd let her mum come with her after all. Over his shoulder she saw the girl move around, wiping tables and occasionally looking in her direction. Jessie caught her eye and she looked away. Something didn't feel right. She turned to the front of the contract and began to read.

He leaned towards her. 'Listen, love. I'm a busy man and I haven't time to sit here while you read through all that wording. You either want the work or you don't.' He was still smiling but his voice had a hint of irritation. She tried not to rush.

'I need to read it before I sign anything.' She'd typed enough contracts for Uncle Norman to know to read the small print. To read everything, and most of all, to understand it before you signed. She thought of Harry at his desk, poring over the minute details of charts and plans, knowing even the tiniest mistake could cost a client hundreds, if not thousands of pounds; Uncle Norman would have him out on his ear if he made one.

'That's not a good start for our relationship, is it, if you don't trust me.'

He leaned close. He smelled of cologne and stale smoke. Something niggled at her. She opened the contract; the print was smaller and the light was too low to see it clearly. Was that his intention? Her heart began to beat faster and her palms became sweaty.

'I'd like to take it with me. Take my time.' Someone at the solicitor's she'd worked at last year would help her.

He didn't like that. He shook his head. 'Take it or leave it. None of my contracts leave the premises.' He snatched it from the table and put it back into his pocket. It gave her the jolt she needed. She could hear Harry's voice, telling her to slow down, to think before she acted, and it gave her the courage to stand her ground.

'Then I'm afraid I will.' She returned his pen and got up. 'Thank you for giving me your time, Mr Parker.'

He remained seated. So, he was bad-mannered as well as sulky; it strengthened her resolve. He leaned further back in his seat. 'You're making a big mistake, little girl. One you'll regret.'

'Maybe I will. But I don't want to be pressured into something when I haven't had time to think.' He'd rattled her, with his 'little girl' comment, but she knew that had been his intention. She picked up her bag and coat and slipped it over her arm, walking out as steadily as she could, though her legs were shaking. He called out to her.

'When you can't get work, you know where to find me.'

She was careful not to let the door slam as she left.

Outside, she was relieved to see Eddie leaning over a bus engine. She walked over and stood beside him. He looked up, grinning, then was serious. 'How did it go?'

She told him.

'Good job you worked at Uncle Norman's. You might have signed it otherwise.'

She'd thought the same herself. Even though she'd felt trapped at her desk, day in and day out, it had clearly had its benefits. 'It might have all been above board.'

He shrugged. 'If it was, why didn't he let you take it to read? Sounds dodgy to me.'

A truck pulled up and a group of squaddies piled out from the back. They looked in her direction and one of them shouted out. 'Isn't he a bit young for you, gorgeous?'

'He's my brother,' she answered, turning her back to them.

Another fancied his chances with her. 'Move aside and let a man in.' Jessie twisted, furious. He didn't look like a man, just a boy, not much older than Eddie. None of them did really and she hoped that war would be over long before Eddie was old enough to enlist. The culprit received a good-natured thump in the arm from his colleague, who called an apology and the group headed off towards the promenade. She and Eddie watched them walk away.

'I suppose I'd better go and see if there are vacancies at the solicitor's.'

'Something will turn up, Jess. Frank Parker can't be the only agent in town.'

'He seems to have all the clubs in his pocket. I'll not get work in them if he has anything to do with it.'

'What about Bernie?' Eddie took a rag from his back pocket and rubbed it over his hands.

'Not yet. I want to be on hand in case Mum gets ill again.' It still scared her, the thought that her mother could relapse, sink back into the walking pneumonia she'd had last summer. It wouldn't take much for her to go downhill.

'But I'm here. I can take care of her.' She had no doubt that he would do his best, but he was only just fifteen, still a boy when all was said and done.

'I know you would, Ed.' It was sweet of him to offer. 'It's just not the right time for me. Something else will turn up.' She couldn't leave, not yet, and, resigning herself to the fact, she turned on her heel and headed towards St Peter's Avenue to make a plea to beaky Miss Bird.

22

Johnny stepped out of Foster and Fox solicitor's office and checked the clock on the tower of St Peter's Church. Almost 11.30. It had taken less than an hour to set his house in order. The sands of time were running through the hourglass far too fast for his liking. It was already 9 January and an entire week since he'd proposed to Frances. Their routines were bedding in nicely and they'd taken a day off from rehearsing. The pair of them needed a rest, not that he'd had one. He'd called at Cleethorpes town hall to set the ball rolling for a special marriage licence and set up an account for Frances at a department store in Victoria Street. From today she could walk in and order whatever she wanted for herself and Imogen – clothes, shoes, anything that took her eye if she so wished. They had gone without long enough and it eased his conscience somewhat to think he could make life a little easier for his two girls. But there was still much to do. Before he'd left the house that morning, he'd telephoned the hospital to check on Ruby's progress but hadn't visited, knowing she was safe enough where she was, being well cared for by professionals who knew how to help her best. They'd do a far better job than he had. They'd diagnosed nervous exhaustion and ordered complete bed rest until she recovered a little and would then reassess. He might as well leave it to them and concentrate on the things he could do, while he had time to do them.

Jack Holland came to his side. 'Not an easy bit of business but a necessary one.' Johnny tucked his scarf into his coat, and pulled out his gloves. He was glad he'd asked Jack to be his executor. Should anything happen, he knew the man would follow his instructions to the letter. He'd asked him to be his best man too, and for the first time in many months he sensed his life had begun to gain a little stability.

'In the circumstances it would be foolish not to. I'm only glad that it's set down in writing. It will give Frances and Imogen security should anything happen to me.' He had left his half share of the Randolphs' business to his soon-to-be wife and daughter. It had been a sobering morning, but he hadn't wanted to leave anything to chance. His own father had died young, leaving his mother in dire straits. It had ruined his mother's joyous nature.

'Your mother was a shrewd businesswoman. She made some excellent investments.' He should be grateful but his anger at what she had done had tarnished things. The Randolphs owned a fair few rental properties dotted about London and Dorset, which brought in a steady income. She'd left everything in order before she died, with detailed instructions as to where the money and paperwork were lodged, and what was secured and where. Johnny had taken charge of it all, had made further investments in theatres with Jack and Bernie Blackwood. In time he would make more. If things worked out as he hoped.

Jack patted him across the shoulders. 'It won't be needed but you can relax a little, knowing you've done your best by them. Have you heard anything from the war office?'

He shook his head. 'I've held back on registering, trying to buy myself time, with Frances, with Imogen. I'll wait for them to call on me.'

'Damn awful timing,' Jack said as they crossed the street and made their way down Albert Road.

'I sound like an ass. Not wanting to stand up and be counted.' It wasn't that he didn't want to. Had Ruby been well, they'd still be in America. He might have come back alone to fight for his country – but then he might never have found Frances. Even though he wished things could be otherwise, at least there was one positive outcome to Ruby's wild behaviour. It had brought them here, and for that he was grateful.

'Not at all,' Jack reassured him. 'You sound like a man who has a lot of catching-up to do.'

They walked side by side.

'And Ruby? How is she?'

'Not good, not good at all.' He was glad to have another man to talk to. It had been lacking in his life so far, having someone he could trust. It was a cut-throat business, and he'd never felt at ease in it. Perhaps that had hardened his mother as much as widowhood.

'It's early days. Time will heal.' Jack's breath curled in a cloud as he spoke. It was bitterly cold now that they were headed towards the seafront and a heavy mist concealed the end of the road.

'Will it?'

Jack nodded. 'She's traumatised.' He considered his words before speaking again. 'Forgive me if I speak out of turn but—'

'Listen, Jack, you seem to be one of the few people who tell it like it is and I can't tell you how extraordinary that is.' He was sick to death of the phoneys, of men with power who held the purse strings, who manipulated and schmoozed, who offered the world and withdrew it when the next shiny thing came along. Ruby had fallen prey to too many of them, believing their syrupy compliments, wanting to be loved.

'I've seen a lot of things in my time. Shell shock. Trauma. Your sister is fighting a battle within herself – perhaps the hardest battle of all. But she's tough. And she has you.'

'I don't think it's enough.'

They stopped at the end of the street and Jack rested a hand on his shoulder. 'You can get through this, son.'

The words landed like a pillow and a lump rose in his throat. He'd been a boy when his father died. No man had called him 'son' since. 'I don't know if I can help her. Or forgive her.'

'But you will. And when you do, perhaps she'll be able to forgive herself.' He put his hand into his pocket. 'I'm going to the theatre. I have a nice bottle of Scotch in my filing cabinet. Fancy a nip to keep the cold out?'

'That's a fine offer, Jack, but I need to see Frances. And Imogen.'

'Of course you do. Well, you know where I am if you need me.'

'I do indeed.' At the end of the road, they went their separate ways, Jack turning left for the Empire and Johnny right, towards Barkhouse Lane.

23

A cheery face had been drawn in the steamed glass of the bay window of Barkhouse Lane. The artist grinned when she saw him and disappeared beneath the net curtain. By the time he'd lifted his hand to knock on the door, the handle wiggled, and Imogen opened it and ran into his arms.

'Daddy!'

There would never be a day when he would tire of that word, of seeing her face, of feeling her small arms about his legs as she clambered to be held by him. He wanted to savour each moment to carry him through the days to come, days when he would be without her again. Sweeping her into his arms, he felt in his pocket for the sweets he'd bought earlier. Frances came into the narrow hall and he set Imogen at her feet, left her to her sweets to embrace Frances, then followed her through to the room at the back of the house. There was an oak table and four chairs, a dresser filled with china, a wad of papers wedged behind plates. A writing pad and envelope were on the table.

'Where is everyone?' He removed his hat, placing it on the table next to them, unbuttoned his coat and took a seat. Imogen climbed onto his lap.

'Geraldine and Eddie are at work. Grace is at her post with the WVS and Jessie... here, there and everywhere.' She sat opposite him. A small fire burned in the grate, taking the chill from the air but not really adding heat to the room. He wanted them both to have more and it gladdened him that he could provide it. 'You look pleased with yourself.'

'Do I?' Imogen slipped from his knee, disappeared through the door and scrambled upstairs. Frances ran her hand over the table-cloth, smoothing out small creases and he rested his hand over hers. 'That's because I am. I've requested a special licence. We can marry without having to wait for the banns.'

'Oh.' She withdrew her hand.

'We didn't want to wait. We agreed.'

She was curt. 'Did we?'

He couldn't remember if they'd talked it over or not, but what did it matter? She'd said yes. 'I thought you'd be delighted.'

She didn't answer and her silence made him uneasy. Imogen returned with her doll and began peeling off her cardigan. There was a struggle as she tried to remove the sleeve and, frustrated, she handed it to her mother, who finished the job and gave it back. 'It's all a bit rushed, isn't it?'

It made him laugh. 'When we've waited so long? I was thinking of you, of Imogen. *Our* family.' He reached for her hand again, irritated that the table was between them. 'I don't want us to be apart any longer than we have to be.'

'Did they give you a date?'

'The twenty-seventh.'

She raised her eyebrows. 'The last night of the panto.'

'Is that okay?'

'It will have to be.' He saw her parents' address on the envelope, and realised why she was so tetchy.

'Have you told them about us? Imogen?'

She shook her head. 'That's my third attempt. I don't know where to begin.'

He put his arm out to touch hers. It was clearly distressing her and there was nothing he could suggest that would soften the blow that her news would no doubt be to her parents.

'Would you like them to be here? For the wedding. I could organise a flight to bring them over.'

She sighed. 'That won't be necessary. They'll need time to make sense of everything.' She gave a small laugh. 'If it could ever make sense. It will be quite the shock.' She stared at Imogen, who was kneeling before the fire, talking to her doll. No wonder she didn't know where to begin; neither did he. What a bloody mess it all was. He'd thought her to be thrilled but he should have known Frances would want to go at her own pace. She'd never been a girl to be rushed. Except she wasn't a girl any more, not the girl he'd left behind four years ago. She was a woman, a mother. He patted his hand on the table.

'I extended the lease on the house at Park Drive. You did say you wanted to stay here if I get...' He looked to Imogen. '... get called away.' She nodded. 'And I know it's early days, and we don't know how long this damn war's going to continue but I put Imogen's name down at the private school close to Park Drive. There's a waiting list and I thought—'

She twisted to face him. 'You did what?'

'I thought...'

She put up her hand to stop him speaking. 'That's just it. You thought. You thought... about what you wanted. Without discussing it with me.'

'No, it's not like that—'

'Then what is it like?'

Imogen turned at their raised voices and they stopped their quarrel, smiled at her. Reassured, she went back to fussing over her doll. Frances walked through to the kitchen, leaned against the sink and stared out of the window. He went over to her, pressing his hands to her shoulders.

'Frances.' He could hear Imogen chattering to her doll, the chime of the clock as it struck the hour. Time was marching on and soon, too soon, he would be marching as well. He let his hands drop.

'Frances,' he said again. This time she turned to face him, her fists clenched by her side.

'These are things we should discuss together, Johnny. You can't make all the arrangements and just expect me to go along with it. I'm not Ruby. I can think for myself. I've had to.'

It was a fair reminder. He would not forget again. Their mother had organised everything when they were children and he'd simply taken over. He chose the music, choreographed their routines, booked the hotels and trains – everything. Ruby went wherever he told her, just as she'd done as a child. He took hold of her hands and she unclenched her fists. 'I'm sorry, darling. Forgive me. I wanted to make you happy, to spoil you. And Imogen.' She looked down at her feet and he knew she was blinking back the tears that had pooled. When she raised her head, he put his thumb and forefinger to her chin, and gazed into her eyes. 'Forgive me?'

She smiled and his relief was instant.

'I know you did it for all the right reasons.' She put her arms about his neck. 'I don't want to fight; I'm done fighting.'

He kissed her again. He was willing to fight, but not with Frances. 'Me too, darling. Me too.'

* * *

The house was quiet when Jessie returned from the shops. She plonked the basket and the box containing her gas mask on the table, peeled off her hat and gloves, tossing them beside the basket, and warmed her hands in front of the fire. Frances had placed two chairs next to each other and Imogen was asleep across them, covered with the blanket Geraldine had knitted for her.

'It's freezing out there.' She unravelled her scarf and flung it on the chair, pulled the ration cards from her coat pocket and tucked them behind a plate on the dresser. 'I thought you were going out with Johnny?'

'He left a while ago,' Frances said sheepishly, causing Jessie to wonder what had gone on. Feeling a little thawed, Jessie took off her coat and hung it up in the hall along with her hat and scarf, pushing the box containing her gas mask on the floor below it. When she returned, Frances was deep in thought.

'Has Johnny upset you?'

'Oh, Jessie. You do ask such impertinent questions.'

Jessie shrugged. 'It's not impertinent. It's being caring.'

It made Frances smile. 'Or plain nosey.'

'Caring,' Jessie insisted. 'So, did he upset you?'

Frances peered into the basket, and took out the carrots and potatoes Jessie had queued so long for.

'Yes. And no.'

'He either did or he didn't.'

Frances carried the basket through to the kitchen, spread a sheet of newspaper over the draining board and rubbed the soil from the vegetables onto it. 'Johnny's got a special marriage licence.'

'Oh, that's terrific!'

Frances didn't look too happy.

'Isn't it?'

Frances picked up a knife and started scraping the carrots. Jessie put her hand on her arm to still her. 'What's wrong?'

'I'm being ridiculous.'

Jessie took the knife from her hand. 'You!' She began chopping the carrots, the slices uneven and haphazard. She caught Frances pulling a face. 'It all tastes the same, no matter what size the slices are.'

'But it doesn't look so nice on the plate.'

'Stop distracting me. Why are you being ridiculous?'

'He offered to pay for my parents to come over for the wedding.'

'Oh, how lovely.' She saw Frances's expression. 'Not lovely?'

'And he's put Imogen's name down at a private school.'

'Cripes. He hasn't wasted any time.' She looked at her friend, at a loss as to what there was to be upset about.

'No. That's the problem.'

Jessie was confused. 'Surely it's wonderful to have him take care of things for you.'

'He can't just take over, making decisions on my behalf. Or Imogen's.'

'But he *is* her father.'

'And I'm her mother. How would you feel if Harry started making your decisions for you – where you'll live, what you'll do all day, where you can or cannot work.'

She'd thought of it often. He'd wanted to hurry things along last summer, but she wasn't ready to settle down. She wasn't even nineteen until the middle of April and a long engagement was beginning to appear more sensible. Many a time she'd thought to take a leaf from Frances's book and be more cautious. Her meeting with Frank Parker had proved she could do it when she needed to.

'See what I mean now? What about London? Could you give it all up?'

'Could you?'

'That's not an answer. Anyway, enough of me, nosey. How did you get on?'

Jessie stopped chopping. 'I tried the solicitor's I was at before, Foster and Fox. I can't say old Beaky was thrilled to see me but they're short-staffed so she's got as much choice as I have. I start on the 29th, the Monday after the panto ends. Happy new year.'

'Happy new year,' Imogen echoed, sitting up on the chair and pushing off the blanket. It made them both laugh, and the intensity of their individual problems dilute.

24

A band of light moved across the bed linen as the sun began to set and Ruby watched its progress. She could hear the click of footsteps in the corridor outside her room and had come to know the staff by their gait. The heavy, lumpen amble of the orderly, the steady light step of Lucy, the young nurse, the brisk no-nonsense stride of the matron. It was how she measured the progress of the day, listening, and watching the light, the shadow. There was a painting on the wall in front of her, a landscape of a cornfield, and a high window to the right where she could see the tops of trees, their bare branches bending on blustery days. There had been snow. She remembered the snow, the light, the water. And Johnny, she remembered Johnny. She closed her eyes. She mustn't think of him. Mustn't think of anything.

A mop slapped on the lino, clattered as it hit a metal bucket, water dripping as it was wrung out, then slapped the lino again. Then music, someone humming. She strained to recognise the tune. It was a song her mother loved, a song she'd sung herself so many times. What was it? The title escaped her. So many things she couldn't quite grasp.

The door opened slowly. From the corner of her eye she saw the old woman check for visitors before bringing the mop and bucket into the room, starting in the corner, the continuous swish, swish as she moved back towards the door, pushing the bucket with her foot. She smiled at Ruby.

'All right, dearie. How are we today?'

She didn't wait for Ruby's answer. Ruby never answered – but that didn't stop the woman.

'Good job you're tucked up nice an' warm in 'ere. It's brass monkey weather out there. I was only saying to our Terry this morning how raw it is.' Ruby listened to her steady commentary. It was the same every day, the woman mopping and talking, wiping the surfaces, the table, the picture on the wall. Then her 'Cheerio' as she moved on to the next room, the muffled sounds of her conversation with the patient in there, the clatter of the bucket, the swish of the mop. Ruby drifted in and out of sleep most days, glad of her empty head, ignoring the procession of people looking at her as if she was a specimen in a laboratory. The trolley would be next, bringing food she couldn't eat. Would it be the one with the squeaky wheel? Would it be the nurse who kicked it, what was her name? The one with the lovely smile and the cold hands. She heard voices. One she recognised as Johnny's. Footsteps again, outside the door. She closed her eyes. She couldn't look at him. Not any more.

Two men came in. She sensed Johnny walking over to the window. The other man was at the foot of her bed, picking up the clipboard that hung at the rail. She could hear the pages being turned before he returned it.

'How are we today, Miss Randolph? Feeling more rested?'

She didn't respond. It was too much effort. Johnny sighed heavily, tugging at his cuffs. He always did that when he was uncomfortable. She knew the signs, even with her eyes closed.

The doctor waited, then he moved to Johnny at the window,

blocking out the sunlight. They spoke in low voices and when the doctor left Johnny drew the chair close to the bed and sat down.

'How are you, Ruby? Do you feel any better?' He always began with the same words, as if he was reading from a script, finding his way into the story. He spoke of the show, of the weather. He never mentioned Frances – or Imogen. She felt him lean close to her, his breath as it landed on her cheek. She wanted to reach out and catch hold of it. If she could find the words, she could tell him, but it felt like she was in the bottom of a pit, unable to reach hold of his hand – and he didn't take hold of hers. He had no need to, not now. Before they'd only had each other but now he had Frances. Imogen. A family. Her mother had warned her. A long time ago. She'd been in hospital then, Mother at her side. Frances had been her understudy. Taken her place. She'd been a success. They'd had to get rid of her before she got rid of Ruby.

'I know you can hear me.' He leaned closer, his cologne so familiar. It was good to have familiar things when everything else was so strange. 'It doesn't matter whether you respond or not.' He paused. 'They've called up all the men to the age of twenty-seven. It's only a matter of time before I get my marching orders and I want you to know that you'll be taken care of. You don't need to worry about anything. Just… Get well, Ruby. Get well.' He patted her hand, rested it and she felt the strength of it flow into her, just as it did when they were dancing. She wanted his strength to seep into her until she could find her own, but he took his hand away too quickly. He didn't say anything else and after a while he got up, said goodbye and quietly closed the door behind him when he left.

25

The bus was full and Joe and Ginny stood side by side in the aisle, holding on to the rail above them, the bags containing his props at their feet. From time to time she felt his eyes on her, but when she turned, he always looked away. She leaned forward a little as the driver headed further into the countryside. Through the window she could see fields and trees blanketed in white. In all the time she'd been in Cleethorpes she hadn't even known how close this all was. She would have enjoyed a day out in the countryside, but Billy Lane hadn't been the kind of man to enjoy the fields for anything but rolling around in with a girl. And she knew any girl would do. It galled her to think how easily she'd been taken in by him. When she'd discovered she was pregnant, Jessie had urged her to contact him, knowing she could find him via her agent, Bernie. Billy had broken his contract and left the summer show before the end of the run as soon as Bernie Blackwood mentioned he had contacts with the BBC. They'd heard nothing from him since, and she knew if he could abandon the show, he'd think nothing of doing the same to her.

'Almost there,' the driver called out to them and a few minutes later the metal towers of the wireless station came into view. As he had promised them when they boarded, he stopped the bus a yard or so from the entrance.

'Have you been here before?' Ginny asked as they gathered the bags between them and stepped gingerly along the grass verge. The path had been cleared, which was a huge relief as her galoshes only just covered her ankles.

'No. Someone from my old village is stationed here. He came to the panto with his children and asked if I'd do a party. I used to do a lot of them back home.'

'Where is home, Joe?'

It seemed odd to her now that she hadn't asked before, but then they knew very little about each other.

'Boston. Although I gave up the house. Mother went to be with her sister in Preston the moment war was announced.' He alerted her to a patch of ice and she stepped around it.

'Is that where you'll go too?'

He shook his head. 'I have no idea. I'll have to force myself on the army again.'

'Force yourself?'

'Once I'd seen Mother off, I gave up my job at the bank. I went to enlist but they wouldn't have me.'

Ginny stopped walking. 'I don't understand.'

He smiled ruefully. 'I didn't either. I wanted to do my bit but they rejected me outright. Said they didn't want just any Tom, Dick or Harry coming forward.' He adjusted his grip on the battered case he was carrying. 'I suppose I don't look like fighting material.'

She remembered how awkward he had been in rehearsals, trying to be the pantomime baddie. 'What do fighters look like? None of us know what we're capable of, do we? Not until we're up against it.'

'No,' he agreed. 'They told me to try again another time.' Ahead of them was a sentry post and he put down his bag, reached into his deep pocket, pulled out a letter and handed it over to the guard, who read it and gave them directions.

She trudged behind him, her cheeks burning with the cold, her eyes running. At the huge front door they were greeted by a woman who told them to take a seat, then went behind a reception desk and picked up the phone. They waited, glad to be in the warmth, and Ginny removed her gloves and unwound her scarf. Further along the corridor a door opened, and she heard heels clicking along at a brisk pace and then a man appeared. Joe got to his feet.

'Good to see you, Joe. How are you?' They shook hands. 'And this must be...?'

Ginny put out her hand. 'Ginny Thompson. I'm working with Joe at the panto. I came along to be his assistant.'

The man winked at Joe. 'Going up in the world, eh. Needing an assistant.' Ginny picked up a bag. 'Here let me.' He took it from her. 'Brian Grainger.' He bared his teeth in a smile. 'Don't suppose you've got your rabbit, Joe?'

Joe shook his head. 'No, had to give him away when I left.' Grainger was clearly mocking him, but Joe didn't seem to notice.

'And how's Mother?'

'Well, thank you. With her sister.'

Grainger was talking to Joe but shooting Ginny sly glances. She turned away, watched the comings and goings at the reception.

'Better let you get set up, then, old man, with your lovely assistant. If you want to follow me.' He stood back, stretching out his arm to indicate the way and as Ginny moved past he placed his hand on her back, keeping it there as they walked, talking all the while to Joe. For all his plummy voice, he was the same as any other bloke who fancied his chances. She moved to one side to let someone pass and slipped beside Joe, hoping it wasn't too obvious, and when the chap opened the door to a large room, she made sure Joe was behind her.

He led them to a small, curtained-off area.

'Not what you theatricals are used to but all we could rustle up for a dressing room, I'm afraid. Not much space. We didn't allow for an *assistant*.'

His manner irritated her, and she was glad when he left. She quickly slipped into her red dress. It was bright and colourful, and she hoped the children would like it. She smiled when Joe turned his back while she undressed, and she gave him the same courtesy. They had gone over what he wanted to do at the theatre and again on the bus journey. It wasn't more than handing him his props and adding a little drama to the proceedings. The girls had teased her mercilessly about it.

'He's asking you out, Ginny.'

'Don't be silly,' she'd replied, feeling the need to defend both Joe and herself.

'He needs a little encouragement,' Jessie countered. 'He's a bit backward about coming forward.'

Ginny had ignored her. 'I don't want to encourage anyone. In a couple of weeks the panto will be over and we'll probably never see each other again.' A couple of weeks. That's all it was. It would be bittersweet to leave. She'd made good friends these last few months, but she longed to leave the bad memories behind.

Now, Joe looked uneasy.

'Nervous?'

'Not of the magic.' He fumbled with his bow tie, looking about for a mirror and she offered to do it for him. When they were ready, he pulled back the curtain and they began to set up his props, the small table with the false bottom, various boxes that needed to be in place before the audience came in. Back behind the curtain, she handed him a pack of cards and folded the coloured silks in the way he had instructed her.

'What made you choose magic?' she asked as he placed them carefully in his pockets and about his person.

'I was given a magic box for Christmas. My uncle Rex did a few party tricks, not professionally, just for family. Friends. There was just Mother and me. Father died in the Great War before I was born. I was a solitary child. I practised and perfected simple tricks at first.' He tucked the silks into his inner pocket. 'Uncle Rex got me a couple of parties when I was eleven.' He stopped. 'Am I boring you?'

'No, not at all. It's fascinating.' It was the most she'd ever heard him say.

'I joined the Magic Circle as soon as I could. I wanted to work in the theatres and, well, with Mother safely out of the way, and having handed in my notice, I thought I'd give it a go. I didn't want to go off to war and think I hadn't tried.'

They were interrupted by the sounds of children coming into the room. 'And so to war!' He grinned. 'They sound a lively lot.'

* * *

It was a lovely afternoon. The children were well behaved but not shy and Joe encouraged them to join in. He had a small prop, a wooden house with two doors, and made a white wooden rabbit go between them. He asked the children to shout out which door they thought the rabbit was in. They were wrong every time, and there were whoops and shouts of delight as Joe whipped them up. Ginny chose a little girl to join them on stage. Joe handed her a magic wand, got her to repeat the word 'abracadabra' a couple of times, and gently teased and joked with her as she helped him perform a trick. He was so supremely confident that Ginny found it hard to believe this was the same Joe Taplow who usually remained firmly in the background.

Afterwards, when they were packing up and the room was empty, Brian Grainger came over to them. Joe was fumbling with a tricky clasp on his case. 'Excellent, old man. You haven't lost your touch.' He leered at Ginny. 'Shall I pay the lady – or is that what you do? Pay her. Couldn't see you with a gorgeous girl any other way.' Ginny didn't flinch. He obviously hadn't taken to her giving him a wide berth when she arrived.

Joe abandoned the case, shot upright and stepped so close to the man that he had to lean away. 'Ginny *is* my assistant. And my friend. I'd ask you to choose your words more wisely, Grainger.'

He backed off, his hands in the air, surprised by Joe's outburst, as was she. It couldn't happen very often, and she got the impression that Joe had tolerated the man longer than he should. He apologised as he handed over the envelope. Joe slipped it into his pocket. 'We'll see ourselves out.'

It was dark when they left and an icy wind gusted as they waited for the bus to take them home. The pair of them stood with their hands thrust deep in their pockets, scarves high above their noses and ears, stamping their feet to keep warm. Joe hadn't spoken a word. Eventually, he pulled down his scarf and said, 'I feel I must apologise again for that man's rudeness, Ginny. I'm so sorry you were subjected to it.' He could barely look at her.

'Oh, I meet men like him all the time in this business. It's not your fault.'

He let go of a little of his anger. 'He's always been a prig. I didn't do the show for his benefit. I did it for the children. Trying to keep a bit of magic going when there's so little of it left.' He smiled at her. 'Thanks for coming with me. It made it a little bit magic for me too.'

He warmed her heart, this gentle man – his kindness, his awkwardness. She had wanted to protect him, but it seemed he could take care of himself when he needed to. They heard the bus labour up the road and could make out the small slits of the head lights as it came closer, and picked up the bags, ready to get on board.

'Perhaps there's a fighting man inside me after all,' he said quietly as the doors opened. 'When I have something worth fighting for.'

26

Frances was standing on a dining chair in the middle of the room and Grace was kneeling at her feet, her mouth full of pins as she altered the hem of the dark navy wool skirt. Imogen was beside her, measuring her doll, and pretending to write down measurements on the back of an old envelope as she'd seen Grace do many times. The gas fire was on low but the room was warm with so many of them in it. It was Geraldine's half-day and she was sitting in one of the easy chairs reading the local newspaper, her spectacles gradually slipping to the end of her nose.

'Anything of note?' Frances asked, standing erect and gazing into the mirror over the mantelpiece. Through it she could see Jessie stretched out on her mother's bed, reading a copy of *The Stage* newspaper. Although she ringed adverts and wrote for auditions, Frances felt it was all a pretence for her mother's sake. She was loath to leave her; she'd admitted as much. She'd managed to get a few bookings locally, but Frances knew from her own experience that ambition would gnaw away at her until she took a chance again. How long would Jessie last at the solicitor's?

'Someone was fined for repeatedly breaking the blackout. A

premises off Chantry Lane was raided by the police.' She flicked the page. 'More cold weather expected. Some of the trawlers have been frozen in the Humber, unable to move.' She put the paper down. 'I've never known a winter like it. This year's already beginning to bite us without the weather adding to it.'

'It's miserable queueing for everything,' Jessie chipped in. 'I'm beginning to hate shopping.'

'Then thank goodness there are still things to look forward to,' Grace said, pressing one hand to her knee to steady herself as she got to her feet. 'That'll do, Frances. If you slip the skirt off, I'll get it sorted. How does the jacket feel?'

'Perfect.' Johnny had wanted her to buy something special for her wedding day, but nothing would fit her as well as the outfit Grace had tailored for her. Besides which, there would be too many questions if she went elsewhere and she couldn't bear spinning any more lies, no matter how small. They had taken Imogen to a department store and bought her a 'party' dress for the occasion, not wanting their child to know it was for her parents' wedding – and then he had spoiled them, his girls. There had been too many parcels to carry, and Frances had chosen to have them delivered to Park Drive, for in little more than a week that was where she'd be. A respectable woman at last.

'You look wonderful, my dear,' Geraldine said admiringly. 'Mr Randolph is a very lucky man.' Grace was a superb seamstress and had saved many of them a fair few pounds with her skills. Not that that was her only talent. She too had once been on the stage, and Frances often wondered if it had been hard for her to give up a promising career to care for her family. It was a future she faced herself and she wasn't sure she was prepared for it. Once she and Johnny were married, life would be more settled – or as settled as it could be with the country at war. She would no longer have to worry about bills, where she was going to find work, how long she'd be apart from Imogen. It would take some getting used to. What on earth would she do with all that free time?

'Mummy, you look beautiful.' Imogen beamed. 'Is it my turn now, Auntie Grace?' The women grinned to each other. There were no alterations necessary, but Imogen loved her special dress so much that she jumped at any excuse to put it on. It was the prettiest, and the most expensive, dress she'd ever had: pale blue with a navy sash about the waist, a white lace collar and lots of petticoats, which the child loved most of all. Johnny had bought her a navy coat and hat to go with it, but it was the dress Imogen was enamoured with.

'Yes, let me hang Mummy's suit up,' Grace told her. 'Jessie will help you put your dress on.' The beloved dress was hanging on the back of the door and while Jessie reached for it, Imogen pulled off her cardigan, hopping from foot to foot in excitement.

Smiling, Frances removed her skirt and stood in her slip, then gave it to Grace, who draped it over her sewing machine and fastened the jacket on the tailor's dummy. Then it was Imogen's turn on the chair. The women made sounds of appreciation while Imogen preened and ran her hands over the petticoats.

'Do I look beautiful too, Mummy?'

'You look pretty as a picture. Just like a princess.'

Grace took the tape measure from around her neck and began measuring Imogen, the child standing to attention like a doll. Geraldine folded the paper and tucked it by her side. 'How are preparations going along, Frances?'

'Smoothly, thank goodness. There's not really much to organise. It's all very simple. And quiet.' They hadn't wanted to draw any attention to themselves, create any publicity that might highlight the fact that Johnny Randolph was marrying a dancer who already had a child. How long would it be before some newshound discovered the child was his? Jack Holland had helped keep things low-key and it would all be very discreet at the town hall. 'Lil's having a little bit of a do for us afterwards. It's only a short walk from the town hall to the Fisherman's Arms.'

'That's very good of her.'

'It is,' Frances agreed. 'We've invited the Harveys – George and Olive, Dolly of course. Joyce from the café, Mr and Mrs Frame. A few from the Empire, the Palace, but not everyone. My friend, Patsy, is going to come along with her two boys, Colly and Bobby—'

'They're my bestest friends in the whole world, Auntie Geraldine.'

'Are they now? Then I look forward to meeting them.'

'Lil thinks a lot of you,' Grace commented. 'I bet she misses you working there.'

'I miss it too; she's been very kind to me.' For a time, Lil had been the only one in Cleethorpes to know of Imogen. It helped, having someone to talk to, who wouldn't judge. Lil was as tough as they came, brash and blonde, married – and widowed – three times but when she walked out behind her bar, no one would hear a whisper of her own worries and troubles. Frances thought her more family than friend.

'Are your parents making the journey?' Geraldine ventured. They all knew Frances had not told them of her dilemma until recently, and although they were full of sympathy for her predicament, there was nothing they could do to help.

'No. The weather is too bad.' It was a fair excuse. Her mother had written of how shocked they'd been at their news, more so that she'd kept it from them so long. Rose O'Leary had been understanding but her father wouldn't even consider giving them his blessing. Her mother had said to give him time to get used to the idea. Frances wasn't sure he ever would. 'I didn't expect them to. Not at such short notice. It's a long way for them, things being as they are.' Did they believe her? She sensed that Grace did not.

Grace hugged her. 'They'll come round, darling. It's all very new, and a lot to digest for them.'

Geraldine tapped the newspaper at her side. 'Perhaps it's just as well. These are dangerous times, what with the mines and submarines. It wouldn't be safe. And I'm sure you would rather they be safe.'

'Yes. Of course.' It was meant to comfort her, but it didn't. Nothing was as she had hoped it would be, not since she fell in love with Johnny. She was used to being alone, without her family, sharing only letters. People moved to the other side of the world and that was all they had. She was too practical to yearn for things to be otherwise, and yet she couldn't help dreaming. Had things been different there would have been announcements in the press, a white wedding, wonderful photographs as keepsakes; but it was not to be.

'Has Johnny no family to speak of?' Geraldine asked.

'Only an aunt. But she's in Dorset, and it's the same thing. The weather, and time, is against us.' Aunt Hetty had sent her the most beautiful card and a letter that she would treasure always. They had never met, but Frances knew she would like her the moment she did, for the woman was full of apologies for her late sister's behaviour and wished them every happiness, and to make sure to take it whenever they could.

'It will still be wonderful,' Jessie said, aware of her disappointment. 'You'll look divine, and Johnny absolutely adores the bones of you. Honestly, it's like a film, really, isn't it, Johnny coming back and finding you.' She clutched a cushion to her chest. 'Soooo romantic.' Grace shook her head at her daughter and Frances laughed.

'The fates have been kind,' Frances said. 'At long last.'

'Good will conquer in the end.' Geraldine got up, and patted her shoulder. 'It's going to be a wonderful day.' Grace helped Imogen off the chair and Jessie picked it up and returned to the back room.

'Any progress with Ruby?' Grace ventured.

'Still the same. But no worse. For a good part of the time she's been sedated. Johnny said they're thinking of reducing her medication in a couple of days.'

'Such a shame she won't make the wedding,' Geraldine commented. 'It might have helped her come to terms with things.'

Frances had thought the same herself, but Johnny wouldn't entertain the idea, even if she had been well enough to attend. She was too unpredictable and there'd already been enough upset along the way. There was no point mentioning that Johnny was still struggling, his anger against his sister and mother sometimes overpowering. They'd had plenty of time to talk it over in the dressing room as they waited to go on. She wasn't sure if it helped, but it was far better than to ignore what had happened to them.

'Johnny doesn't want her to know,' Frances told them. 'The doctor thinks it might set her back.'

Grace pushed her lips forward and looked directly at Frances. 'Doctor knows best.' It was clear she didn't agree, and Frances didn't think so either but knew better than to interfere. It was a pitiful situation for them all.

27

Harry Newman was in the NAAFI recreation building nursing a beer, Ginger Stevens to one side of him and Pete Baxter the other. Behind them, a matronly singer murdered a Cole Porter song, the strangulated notes enough to shatter the glass in his hand. Ginger cupped his hands over his ears and Pete stared into his beer.

'What a ruddy row. I'd rather hear a dog howl than hear another song from that screechy piece.'

Harry grinned. 'I've heard worse.'

'Impossible.' Ginger picked up his empty glass. 'Fancy another?'

Harry drained his glass. 'Can you bear to stick around?'

'Another pint might dull the pain. Same for you, Pete?' Pete was the new man in their room. Jimbo had failed his last exam and been sent elsewhere; nothing was ever said, and the beds were never empty for long, no matter how or why the former occupant had left. It felt odd at first, but Harry had been getting used to it. Since enlisting in August, he'd already seen a fair few men move on. He never got to hear of their disappointment and supposed that was the way the top brass wanted it. Keeping morale high, the men positive. This wasn't a place that held any store in looking back.

And then there were the accidents – men who never got their chance to defend the country they had sworn allegiance to when they'd first signed up. Pilot error could be fatal and it only made him more determined to focus on the job. But he wasn't working now; this was R and R, rest and relaxation, although when the singer went into yet another song he thought that idea blown out of the water. There was nothing relaxing about her voice.

It was a fitting end to what had been a boring but intense week. He hadn't been able to add to his flying hours due to the weather being so bad, which was a blow, but had given him more time to swot for his next set of test papers. He wasn't far off the requirement and if he passed these finals, he would get his wings and be posted to an operational training unit. Word was going around that North Coates was opening up next month and he hoped to be transferred there as part of coastal command. There had been a sense of urgency from the beginning, bracing themselves for bombardments that didn't happen. The Brits were vastly outnumbered, their airpower no match for the Germans. Chamberlain had done his best, but Hitler didn't understand honour and decency and the country had been ill prepared for war. Government negotiations had bought them time, ramping up production of their machinery and trained men. Although there had not been land battles, and the British Expeditionary Force in France had resumed leave, the war at sea was already having an effect, not just in lives lost, but in the volume of shipping tonnage destroyed and lack of supplies. The bad weather had slowed things down on both sides, but ships off the east coast were still being attacked, the losses heavy.

Ginger returned with the drinks just as the singer finished and the comedian came on. 'Thank Christ for that. I can drink this pint a little slower.'

The comedian wasn't half bad and they turned to face the stage, leaning back against the bar. It was a simple affair, nothing of the theatre Jessie was playing, with its red plush seats and velvet curtains, just a simple wooden platform that served as the stage. One of the chaps in ground crew had painted a backdrop of Piccadilly Circus. In civvies he was an accountant but he definitely had a strong artistic streak that he'd been able to give free rein. Quite a few of them had mucked in to stave off the boredom and it was a pretty good set-up. The musicians among them had got a band together and they were already making their own entertainment. Pete could strike up a fair tune on the piano and it made him wish he too had the talent to entertain, for it certainly passed the long hours. They had begun to get the odd ENSA concert but none of the big stars had made an appearance as yet.

'We need to get that girl of yours down here,' Ginger suggested, when the show was over. 'And her lovely friends.'

'Is she a singer?' Pete didn't know much about either of them – or they him.

'Sings, plays piano, dances.' Harry took Jessie's photo from his inside breast pocket and handed it over.

'A looker too. Has she got any friends?'

Harry grinned. 'As a matter of fact...'

Pete returned the photo and Harry put it back in his pocket. 'Is she close?'

'Close enough.' He wished she was closer. 'She's in Cleethorpes, not too far.'

The three of them stared at the two middle-aged women serving behind the counter. Ginger gave him a nudge. 'When can you get her here?'

'And her friends,' Pete added. 'We want first dibs.'

There was no need to tell them that Frances was spoken for, and even if she wasn't he knew she would soon enlighten Pete and Ginger as to what she thought of them. 'I'm at her friend's wedding next week. I'll see what I can do.'

28

Grace climbed into the passenger seat of the WVS van. 'Will you drop me at the hospital?' she asked her companion, who was driving back to the depot. 'There's someone I need to visit.' She unfastened the collar of her greatcoat. Even though it was classed as uniform, everyone in the WVS had to buy their own, and she was glad to have it, glad to have her children, for they'd insisted she have one and had paid the majority of the cost. She'd been able to contribute from her own small savings, the first time she'd had any in many a year.

When Davey had died, she'd been at her wits' end, wondering how she would ever manage. Living with her cousin, Norman, and his wife had been her salvation in many ways but it made her shudder to think how shrunken and withered she had become there. The wrong environment could soon stifle any brave spirit. Eddie had rolled along happily enough, but that was his nature, whereas Jessie had been like a genie forced into a bottle with no way of escape, until she had found her own. And now here she was, about to settle for another bottle at the solicitor's, and this time of her own choice.

She soon found the reception, enquired of Miss Randolph's whereabouts and followed the directions given to her by the woman at the desk. It was long before the evening visiting hours but wearing her uniform granted access to all manner of places. It was much warmer in the hospital building and she unbuttoned her coat as she walked, acknowledging nurses and orderlies with a smile as they strode efficiently down the linoleum corridor.

Ruby was lying on the top of her bed, fully clothed, a film magazine laid across her chest. She opened her eyes as Grace came into the room but didn't turn her head. Grace removed her coat and laid it across the chair to the side of the bed. The room was filled with cards and flowers and for a split second Grace felt she should have brought something too, but one look at Ruby and she knew it wouldn't have made the slightest difference. There was nothing Ruby was in want of, not materially. Grace knew that deadened feeling.

'Hello, Ruby,' she said gently. 'Remember me? Jessie's mother, Grace. We met at a theatre function, a little before Christmas. I was passing and thought I'd call in and see how you were.' Ruby did not respond but then Grace hadn't thought for one minute that she would. She was much thinner than when Grace had seen her last and even then she hadn't been a healthy weight. There were other girls Grace had known in her dancing days, who didn't eat to avoid a bloated stomach, aware of every line and sinew of their bodies – and not in a healthy way. It was damage to the mind that then transferred to the body, and Ruby was no different. The heady scent of lilies assailed her and she went over to the windowsill, bent to the flowers in one of the vases set upon it and inhaled the richness of them. 'Your flowers are glorious. Isn't it wonderful to have such colour in the deepest of winter?' They must have cost someone a small fortune. Such a shame they would not be appreciated.

Grace moved her coat to one side and took a seat beside the

bed. There was the slightest flicker of interest as she did so. She took the magazine. 'May I?' She turned the pages, looked at the images. 'I see Tyrone Power is to star in a new movie. I loved him in *Alexander's Ragtime Band* with Alice Faye. Did you see it?'

Ruby ignored her.

'The panto ends this week. Jessie is thinking of going back to work in a solicitor's office. I don't know how long that will last.' She smiled to herself. 'You know what it's like, don't you, Ruby. You can't give it up so easily, can you, once you've felt the love from the audience, when you know you've given your very best and the audience know it too. There's nothing quite like it, is there?' Ruby clenched her fists. So, she was listening. Grace perused the magazine again, choosing the articles to comment on with care. 'Mr Astaire has made another picture, *Broadway Melody of 1940*. Have you ever thought about going into films, Ruby? I think you'd be rather good at it; you have those fine features the camera loves.'

Ruby slapped her hands over her ears.

'It's no good, my dear, trying to block out the world. It won't work. You have to—'

'Shut up! Shut up! Shut up!' Ruby shouted. Grace heard someone pounding down the corridor and a stout nurse burst into the room. Grace remained where she was.

The nurse stopped when she saw her, her expression quickly switching from one of irritation at her patient to concern for Grace. 'Are you quite all right?'

'I'm absolutely fine. My fault entirely.' It was not what the nurse had expected, and Grace got the feeling that Ruby had, perhaps, pushed them all to their limit. 'I obviously said something to upset Miss Randolph.'

The nurse checked Ruby, who had turned her face to the wall, then left, leaving the door ajar and Grace sat back and waited. As dusk fell, she got up and drew the curtains against the blackout. A while later she heard a trolley coming down the corridor. A tray was brought in and put in front of Ruby. The stout nurse adjusted the back rest and plumped the pillows, then held out the spoon to Ruby, who would not take it. She let out a long sigh.

'I've told her, it'll be the tube if she doesn't eat. And we don't want that, do we?' There was no kindness in her words or her manner as she stood beside her patient, and Grace well understood that Ruby's suffering would be considered self-indulgent by those who were looking after the sick and the dying. But it was suffering all the same.

Grace intervened. 'Please, allow me. You must have so many other things pressing on your time.' The nurse was quick to agree and left her to it. Grace closed the door after her, then removed the cover from the tray and picked up the spoon.

Ruby stared past her. Grace had seen it all before – the refusal, the apathy. She pushed the table forward and sat on the side of the bed. 'Now then, my dear, I know how hard it is to swallow so we will take it one spoonful at a time.'

Tenderly taking hold of Ruby's chin, she dipped the spoon into the liquidised food and held it at Ruby's lips. 'Slowly, slowly, Ruby.' It was a while before she conceded but as her lips parted, Grace smiled. 'That's it, darling girl, that's it.'

Grace offered gentle words of encouragement each time Ruby took from the spoon. It was how she'd cared for Davey when he'd returned from the convalescent home. He would thrash around, awoken from nightmares, shouting and flailing, sweating and shaking. At first she'd been afraid, but less afraid than he, and she had soothed and calmed with lullabies and soft words. Ruby approached each spoonful with distaste, her lips barely parting, but Grace knew not to give in. Her own stubbornness was a match for

Ruby's. When the bowl was empty, Grace moved the tray under the bed and out of sight.

'I want to be sick.'

'I know you do. I'll stay with you until that feeling passes, because that's all it is, a feeling.' And the girl had to learn to feel again. She took Ruby's hand in hers and they waited together.

29

Harry arrived at the Empire in time to catch the last half of the panto. He left his bag at the stage door and slipped inside the auditorium as a wave of hissing and booing greeted Abanazar's entrance. Joe shook his fists at the kids. A few boiled sweets were aimed his way and he dodged them like bullets before he exited, stage right. Laughter followed as the dame put Wishee Washee through the mangle, the oversized foam rollers contracting as the comedian waggled his arms and legs in exaggerated movements to milk it for laughs. Harry leaned on the brass rail that ran along the back of the stalls, enjoying the show, but when Jessie walked out onstage, the exotic backdrops of old Peking, the rickshaws, the Chinese lanterns and the gaily coloured costumes of the chorus faded into the background. He only saw her, his girl, and he longed for the time when it would just be the two of them.

When the song sheet came down and the end of the show was near, he collected his bag and walked around to the stage door. He said a quick hello to George and walked up into the wings as the rest of the cast took their places for the finale. When Jessie saw him, her face broke into the biggest smile and she squeezed her way forward, threw her arms about his neck and kissed him, oblivious of who was around them. It was worth the damn rotten journey for that alone. He had forty-eight hours with her, and he didn't want to waste one minute of them.

He waited in prompt corner with the stage manager as first the dancers, then the rest of the performers, made their way from the back of the stage to the front, the applause rising as those higher up the bill came forward – rousing cheers for the dame and Wishee Washee, boos for Abanazar. He moved further down the wings as it became less crowded, watching as Jessie waited at the top of the temple steps, hand in hand with the girl who was playing Aladdin, both dressed in their wedding finery. A happy ending. Would he and Jessie get theirs? She saw him in the shadows and her smile widened, her eyes sparkling in the light. She never looked happier than she did when she was onstage.

When the curtain came down for the last time the performers hurried off to the dressing rooms and Harry waited at the stage door with George while Jessie changed from her costume. 'Olive's aired your bed, Harry lad, and there'll be a little bit of supper put to one side for you.' He handed over a key. 'Just in case we've gone to bed.' Harry put it in his pocket, once again appreciating their kindness. The Harveys insisted he stay with them when he came to see Jessie and wouldn't have him forking out for a boarding house. Their quiet generosity was much appreciated. They were still chatting when Jessie came up behind him and put her hands over his eyes.

'Guess who.'

He held on to one of her hands as he turned and chastely kissed her cheek, not wanting to embarrass George.

'Oh, Harry, it's so good to see you, it really is.' She pulled her coat about her shoulders. 'I'll need to go outside but I won't be long; not many wait for autographs in this weather.' There was a cold blast of air as she opened the door and some of the other performers joined her to stand under the soft blue glow of the stage-door light. He moved to one side as George dealt with dressing-room keys, and then away to the right as someone else wanted to use the payphone. Ten minutes later she came back, her nose red, her eyes watering, and huddled close to him for warmth. He rubbed at her arms until she stopped shivering. 'It's freezing out there,' she said, gazing up at him.

'Only one more night to suffer.' His words were meant to cheer her but had the opposite effect. 'There'll be other nights,' he told her, quickly realising that the end of the show was not something Jessie relished. She gave him a small smile in reply, then clasped his hand and led the way through the pass door and into the auditorium.

There were plenty of uniforms in the bar and he imagined theatres around the country were full every night, the lads wanting to watch real live girls, not the ones far out of reach on the silver screen. They grinned at her when she walked in, and, when he went to get her a drink, swarmed about her. She talked and laughed with them, signed autographs, totally at her ease, a different girl to the one who'd set out on her own to make her way in a business she loved only months before. This was her world and for a split second he felt on the edge of it. An outsider looking in.

He handed her a drink. 'Sorry, chaps.' He placed his arm about her waist, guiding her away to a table.

'You're not sorry at all, you lucky beggar,' one of them called after him. He was right, he wasn't, and he wasn't going to feel bad about it either.

'When did you get here?' She snuggled close and he draped his arm about her shoulder, pulling her to him.

'I caught the second half. You were wonderful.'

She sat up and took a sip from her glass, her eyes sparkling with laughter. 'You always say that.'

'I do,' he agreed. 'But only because it's true. Excited about tomorrow?'

'We are, all of us. It's wonderful to have something to celebrate, and I'm so happy for Frances, so glad it all came right in the end.'

The door from the stalls opened and Ginny came in, Joe close behind.

'Those two together now?' Harry watched them standing at the bar, the slightest of gaps between them. Close, but not quite close enough.

'Just good friends. Apparently.' Jessie beckoned them over. Harry got up, waited for Ginny to take her seat and shook hands with Joe before taking his place next to Jessie. They talked of the wedding, what time they needed to be at the town hall.

'It's an early one, nine o'clock, so we'd best get there for a quarter to,' Harry suggested. 'I can walk with you, Ginny, seeing that I'm staying with George and Olive.' He looked to Joe. 'Unless you two were going to...' Jessie kicked him under the table, and he bit his cheek to stop himself from calling out.

'Joe was coming to call anyway, so all three of us can walk up there. I suppose you'll be leaving with Frances from Barkhouse Lane?' Ginny said, quickly deflecting the conversation to Jessie.

'I will,' Jessie told her. 'It's going to be one heck of a day. It will be a job to pack everything in, what with a matinee in the afternoon and the final show in the evening.'

'Can't be helped, I suppose. They had to take what date they were given.' Harry supped his beer, and wiped the creamy foam from his lip. He'd thought of that first pint a lot while he'd stood in the guard's van as the train made its way in the darkness.

'It's been a bit of a whirlwind for both of them,' Ginny

commented. 'Frances's head must be spinning with all she's had to cope with the past few weeks.'

'I think it is,' Jessie agreed. 'I've hardly seen her lately, she's been so busy at the theatre, and Johnny's been wining and dining her in between. It's hard to believe that tomorrow she'll leave Barkhouse Lane for good.'

'She didn't stay with Johnny?' Harry had been surprised.

Jessie shook her head. 'There was all the bother with Ruby at first. And I think she wanted a little time to herself, to catch her breath.'

'What about you two?' Ginny asked, getting her own back on Harry. 'Are you going to set a date?'

He grinned at her. Touché.

Jessie was quick to answer. 'There's no need for us to rush, is there, Harry. I mean, it's different circumstances.' He was caught out by her swift response, but he shouldn't have been surprised. From the moment he saw her, he knew she was the one for him, but Jessie had held back. She didn't want to get engaged, and then she did, all of a rush. She'd gone off to Cleethorpes and he'd thought he'd lost her, but it had only brought them closer. He'd bought her a ring when they were together before Christmas. She'd been excited. Was she having second thoughts? She must have noticed because she reached out and took his hand in hers, keeping it on her lap. They exchanged smiles.

He sought to change the conversation. 'What's next for you, Joe?'

'I've enjoyed my small stab at stardom but duty calls.'

'You'll be in demand, from what I've experienced.'

Joe placed his glass carefully on the beer mat. 'Really?'

'Really.' Harry was encouraging. 'We've not seen much action. The lads are putting together their own entertainment to stifle the boredom. Must be the same in all the forces. You might not have to give it up, not entirely.'

'Well, that's not bad news at all to end the season on, is it.'

Ginny was staring into her drink.

'Still going to sign up for ENSA, Ginny?'

She looked up. 'Not straight away. I'm here a little while longer. We have a few gigs as Variety Girls. Then I must go back home to Sheffield. I need to sort a few things out.'

'Haven't you thought of joining ENSA, Jessie?' Joe asked innocently. 'It's guaranteed work for six months, and steady pay.'

Jessie shifted uncomfortably. 'I couldn't. I need to stick around to keep an eye on my mum.' She took a little of her drink, and smiled. 'I'm already committed to the solicitor's office. But I'll be all right,' She was trying to sound cheerful, whether for his benefit or hers he didn't know. 'Jack Holland has already got me a few bookings for private parties. Not many, but I'm sure I'll get more when the weather improves.' Her reply made him feel uncomfortable. Jessie had loathed working in an office, absolutely hated it, yet here she was tying herself into it again. It had flummoxed him when she'd written of the failed meeting with the local agent, that she knew it was the right thing to do. He'd been glad she'd not signed the contract. It all sounded underhand, and he wanted to make sure she didn't get into anything she couldn't quickly get out of. But even so...

'I suppose we've all made different choices to what we'd have done if war hadn't come along,' Joe added. 'I'd still be at the bank.'

'And I'd still be at the solicitor's,' Harry agreed.

'Seems I'm the only one going backward and not forwards.' Jessie looked over Joe's head as one of the navy lads came over, holding out his programme for her to sign, then asked Ginny and Joe. Harry noticed how Jessie instantly became more cheerful, as if a switch had been flicked on again. When they'd gone and she sat down, Harry mentioned the lads back at base.

'I didn't realise you weren't going straight away, Ginny. I'd mentioned to the chaps about you.' He smiled to Jessie. 'We wondered if the Variety Girls were available? You'd be paid, of course.'

Jessie perked up. 'Oh, that would be such fun. I'm sure Frances wouldn't object. What about you, Ginny.'

Ginny smiled. 'For our boys. How could I refuse?'

30

The four of them parted at the entrance to the Empire and at last it was just the two of them. Jessie and Harry walked a little further along the road, then he pulled her into a shop doorway, turning his back to shield her from the wind, and kissed her, longing to feel her skin buried beneath the layers of clothing that separated them. Was she as hungry for him as he was for her? She leaned away, catching her breath, then slid her arms about his waist and pulled him close again. He touched his nose to hers. 'Darling, you would tell me if there was anyone else, wouldn't you?' He knew he shouldn't have asked, but something was gnawing away at him, and he couldn't work out what it was.

She slapped the flat of her hand against his chest and tried to pull away. 'How could you even think it!' He put his hand to her face, and she stopped wriggling.

'When I see you onstage, I see how much you love it. How different you are and without it...'

She put her fingers to his lips to stop him from saying any more. 'You're the only man for me, Harry Newman. You're all I'll ever want, and all I'll ever need.' He knew it was a lie. He might be the only man, but he wasn't enough. She was lying to herself if not to him. He kissed her, hoping he was wrong, knowing he was not.

A small welcoming party awaited them in the back room at Barkhouse Lane. They had no sooner walked in than Eddie greeted him with a barrage of questions and proceeded to show him his new Brownie box camera.

Grace chided her son. 'Let him get in the door, for goodness' sake. Are you going to stop for a drink, Harry? I can only offer tea or cocoa.'

'Cocoa would be perfect.' He smiled to Jessie and she returned it as she went through to the small kitchen to help her mother. She had forgiven him his question and the small tiff between them had been forgotten as he walked her home. He was relieved to see Grace in good form and wondered why Jessie worried so about her. All three of the Delaneys looked far happier than he'd ever seen them.

Grace returned shortly after and handed around the mugs. 'Geraldine asked after you. She went to bed not long after Imogen. Babysitting duties have tired her out. She's looked after Imogen each night, while Frances is working and I'm at the theatre,' Grace explained. 'Not that she's complaining. She's loving every minute of it. Do sit down, Harry.' She pulled out a chair. 'How our lives have changed, eh.' He could only agree.

They were all sitting around the table, chatting easily, when Frances came in. He got up to greet her.

'Harry. You're looking damn smart these days – not that you didn't before.' She kissed his cheek.

'Not so bad yourself.' She looked tired. It must have been quite a strain for her, taking over from Ruby. 'All set for the morning?'

She beamed at him. 'It can't come soon enough. Johnny sent his best.' She peered at the mugs. 'Don't suppose there's any left?' Grace immediately got up and returned only moments later, having reheated the milk.

'So, what's the plan?' Harry asked. 'After the town hall service?'

'Back to Lil's. She's putting a spread on.'

'Oh.'

She smiled. 'You're surprised. You thought I'd choose the Royal, or the Cliff. A big hotel. Something swanky?'

'Well, you are marrying Johnny Randolph.' He'd thought exactly that.

'And he's marrying a girl with her feet on the ground,' Frances reminded him. 'It's all too easy to get caught up with the glamour and forget what really matters.' She looked about her. 'Friends. That's what's most important. It always will be.'

Jessie reached for her hand and squeezed it.

'How was the show?' Harry offered Frances his seat and she gratefully took it, kicking off her shoes and pushing them under the table with her feet.

'It's been going really well. Good houses. Great, even. But I'll be glad when the run ends next week. It's been too much, really.'

It prompted thoughts of Ruby. He'd heard what had gone on from Jessie. It was a sad state of affairs. He'd only met her briefly, when he'd been able to help get rid of a slimy creep who'd been blackmailing her. The price of fame didn't seem worth paying to him. Even Frances's wedding would not be the special occasion she deserved. They'd all been careful to be discreet, not wanting to attract any attention that might bring the press heading to their door.

'How's Ruby?' It felt only polite to ask.

'Not much better. Johnny called at the hospital today. They're talking of trying out some electrical treatment on her.'

'He mustn't let them,' Grace said suddenly. 'She needs more time. Oh, that would be dreadful.' They all looked at her. Grace composed herself. 'I've visited her once or twice, Frances. I hope you don't mind.'

'Why would I mind?' She reached across and pressed Grace's arm. 'That's so kind of you. I'm sure that will have helped her.'

'I didn't want to interfere, but I was there as part of my WVS duties – and it was no bother to stay a little longer.'

'Grace, please don't apologise. I know Johnny will only be too grateful. To be honest, we'll both be glad when tomorrow's over. It will be one less thing to think about. I'll feel I can finally relax.'

Harry got up. 'And on that note, soon-to-be Mrs Randolph, I'd best take my leave, so you can all get to bed.'

Jessie went with him to the door.

'At least there's one good thing about leaving tonight?' he said as he put on his coat.

'What's that?' Jessie asked, puzzled.

'I get to say, "See you in the morning."'

She smiled, kissed him and the warmth of her lips lingered on his all the way back to Dolphin Street.

* * *

Jessie had not long been in bed when she heard a quiet tap on the door and Frances stuck her head around it.

'Can I come in?'

Jessie pulled back the blankets and Frances got in close beside her, bending her shoulders and tucking her arms in tight so that her fists came under her chin. 'Can't you sleep?'

'Not really. Too much going around in my head.'

'I can imagine.' She too had found it hard to sleep, her thoughts of Harry and her own future. But it was nothing compared to what Frances had had to contend with these past few weeks. They were quiet for a while until Jessie whispered, 'I'm glad you stayed here with us these last few days. It will be very strange when you and Imogen leave tomorrow.'

'We've been through a lot together, haven't we?'

'Not just us. Not so long ago, Ginny had this bed, when, you know...' It was hard to think of it, let alone speak of it. Ginny had been miscarrying and they'd brought her back to Barkhouse Lane. She'd been terrified but Frances had been so strong, so capable.

'Let's not dwell on the bad things,' Frances interrupted. 'We've had happy times too. Remember the first day when I brought you here? How dire it all was. The state of your room, filthy and neglected, cobwebs hanging from the tatty lampshade.'

The memory warmed her. 'We worked together to get it cosy. *And* my feet were so sore from rehearsing. *And* I was so terrified I'd get the sack before the show opened.' Had it really only been last summer? The months had flown by and now she felt the happy moments would slip away from her when Frances left Barkhouse Lane. 'I'm going to miss you so much, Frances.' To her horror, her voice cracked.

Frances pulled the blankets up to their chins, and huddled close, their breath misting in the cold air. 'I'll still be around.'

But it wouldn't be the same. She felt a little of Frances's strength had brushed off on her while they were together and she worried it might desert her when her friend left. 'Are you nervous?' Jessie asked.

'A little – more excited than anything. I can hardly believe it's happening. That tomorrow I *really* will be Mrs Randolph. Sometimes I have to pinch myself to check it's real.' She got closer to Jessie. 'When I'm in the wings at the Palace, waiting to go on, and Johnny introduces me, and I see him there, in the spotlight, and he turns and looks at me... Oh, Jessie, it's the most wonderful feeling in the world.' She pulled back the blankets. 'Better try and get some beauty sleep or Johnny might change his mind.'

Jessie shook her head, plumped her pillow. 'He'd never do that. He'll never let you go again, not now he's found you.'

Frances tiptoed to the door, turned, and smiled at her. 'Night, Jessie.'

'Goodnight, Frances O'Leary.' It would be the last time she called her by that name. Tomorrow she would be someone else, a Randolph.

31

The lights went on in Barkhouse Lane at 6.30 when Geraldine went down to stir the fire and put on the hot water. Grace emerged soon after, followed by Jessie, who took Frances tea and toast. Imogen sat up, sleepy-eyed, delighted that she could eat in bed, Jessie having also brought milk, and bread and jam.

'Is this the party, Mummy?'

'No, darling, but it's the start of it.'

They dressed in Grace's room, in front of the gas fire, and had the very devil of a time keeping Imogen out of her dress until the last half hour. One of Dolly's sisters was a hairdresser, and she came to fix Frances's hair, pinning the curls to one side only – which managed to look both fashionable and elegant. Imogen stood on a dining chair beside her mother and Jessie brushed her hair, making a good deal of it for the child's benefit, and fastening it with a blue ribbon to match her dress. Jessie lifted her high enough to admire herself in the mirror and, delighted, Imogen ran off into back room to show Geraldine. Flowers arrived soon after eight, for the bride and her companions, small posies of white flowers, myrtle, hyacinth, gardenias, and glossy green leaves of laurel. Very understated and all the more effective because of it.

Five minutes before they were due to leave, Geraldine came into the room, Imogen dressed warmly in her coat and hat.

'My dear, you look...' Geraldine stopped, her voice full of emotion. It was so unlike her, and Frances went to her, and kissed her cheek. 'Quite wonderful.'

'Thank you. I thought this day would never come.' Her own voice began to wobble, and she laughed, blinked back tears, and dabbed at her eyes with the back of her hand.

'You'll spoil your make-up,' Jessie said, passing her a handkerchief then using it herself.

Eddie stuck his head around the door. 'The car's arrived.'

'Oh, I wish Johnny hadn't insisted,' Frances said, nerves getting the better of her. 'It's only a short walk around the corner.'

Grace smiled, held out her coat and Frances put her arms into the sleeves. 'He wants to spoil you and you have to allow him to do so. He feels he has a lot of making up to do.' Her words had the required effect and settled Frances enough to stop her fingers from trembling as she fastened the fur collar at her neck, and bent down to kiss Imogen. Jessie and Grace were leaving in the car with Frances, and Eddie would make the short walk to see Geraldine and Imogen safely to the Fisherman's Arms before joining them at the town hall as the official, and only, photographer.

Johnny was waiting on the town hall steps with Jack Holland, and he rushed down to greet her, embracing her. 'I've never seen you look so beautiful.' She couldn't speak, couldn't find any words to express how she felt, and, smiling, he bent his elbow to her. She slipped her hand through the gap and as Jack opened the door, they walked up the steps together.

* * *

It was a simple ceremony and after it was over, they waited on the town hall steps for Eddie to take their photo. They moved aside for him to take one of Harry and Jessie and another of Joe and Ginny. Anyone passing would have found it hard to tell who had actually got married that fine January morning, which was as they had engineered.

Frances called to him, 'Do you have enough left on the roll to take one of the three of us, Eddie? Me, Jessie and Ginny.'

The boy checked the counter. 'Yes, three more.' He put his hand in his pocket. 'But I've got another film.'

'Save it for later,' Jessie urged. 'It's far too cold for us all to be standing out here.'

Johnny stepped away and Frances held her arms wide so that Jessie and Ginny could tuck themselves beside her. They posed, all eyes and teeth, exaggerated, laughing, arms wide, legs poised just so, while Eddie used the last of the film, then dashed down the steps and made their way to the Fisherman's Arms in Sea View Street. It wasn't even half past nine.

'There'd be a high price on those photos, Eddie, if the press got hold of them,' Johnny said as they walked along. He'd been nervous about having them taken, but they all wanted a record of the day and Eddie seemed the obvious candidate for the job. Everything had had to be stage-managed. He couldn't allow the photographs to get into the wrong hands, not after all the bother with the indiscreet photos of his sister. This was different, but in a way more threatening. The photos of Ruby would never have been published – no newspaper would dare print them; instead they would have been passed around privately for people to leer over. But a photo of Johnny Randolph and his new wife would be a story, a complicated one – and one he wasn't prepared to tell, not yet.

'Not for sale,' Eddie said, placing the camera at his hip. Johnny slapped him gently on the back. He might only be a boy, but he was a good one and Johnny knew he could be trusted.

The door to the Fisherman's Arms was already open but not to customers. Frances had worked there when the theatres had closed at the outbreak of war and today the landlady, Lil, had laid on a small wedding breakfast. The curtains were drawn over and three tables had been pushed together; on them were plates covered with damp tea towels. As Johnny and Frances walked through the doorway, they were showered with rice, and cheers and good wishes were called across to them. Patsy rushed over to her, hugging her so tightly that Frances could scarcely breathe. 'Oh, love. I'm thrilled for you. For both of you.' Frances looked around her, to the happy faces of her friends, friends who had got her through the darkest of times. How lucky she'd been to have them.

Imogen ran to them and took Johnny by the hand. 'Daddy, come and look what I've been doing with Auntie Lil.' Imogen helped Lil remove the tea towels to reveal sandwiches and sausage rolls.

'I asked the butcher down the street to put something nice to one side. No questions asked. And I didn't say what for.'

Johnny swept Imogen into his arms and gave her a kiss.

'Well, you have been a busy little girl.' He and Frances had decided it best that Imogen stay away from the ceremony and the town hall. Like the butcher, the less people knew the better.

'Auntie Lil said she didn't know what she'd do without me. And I looked after Fudge.' The scruffy wire-haired terrier was lying in his usual place, close to the fire, and his ears perked up at the mention of his name.

Lil threw her arms around Frances and planted a kiss on her cheek, then licked her finger and rubbed off the lipstick she'd left there. 'I couldn't be happier for you, lovey. At long last, a ruddy happy ending. Thank the good Lord for that.' She moved on to

Johnny and gave him a hug. 'Look after her, mind, or you'll have me to answer to.'

He laughed. 'Don't worry, Lil. I'll make sure she has everything she deserves from now on.' He had no intention of letting her go again, although he knew his time with her would be shorter than he'd have liked.

He'd been to see Ruby yesterday afternoon and even though he'd wanted to share their news, he wouldn't risk it. She was a little improved, but they had little to say to each other. The doctors were weaning her off her medication. One of them wanted to try a couple of new treatments but after speaking with Frances that morning he'd decided against it. He went over to Grace, who had borrowed a tea urn and set it up on the bar along with cups and saucers, milk and sugar, handing out hot drinks as people came to her.

'Grace?'

She looked up and smiled at him.

'Frances told me you'd been visiting Ruby.'

'I hope you don't think I'm interfering—'

He touched her hand. 'I wanted to thank you. The nurse said that some kind lady from the WVS had been sitting with Ruby, helping her to eat. I had no idea it was you. I should have guessed.'

'It's such a small thing. She reminds me of Davey. He suffered after the war, you know.' She stopped, perhaps not wanting to share more than she felt comfortable with. 'She's starting to talk a little more each time. That's a good sign.'

'Is it?' He had no idea. He'd never known how to handle Ruby, even when they were children. When she blew up it was his cue to go away and leave her. He had left it to his mother to sort her out. He'd left far too many things to his mother. 'I'm very grateful. I'm sure Ruby is too.'

'She's a lovely girl. I liked her enormously when I met her before Christmas. Full of fire.'

'Except the fire's gone out.' He knew what Grace meant, and that she meant it only kindly. Ruby on good form was effervescent.

'It will burn again, you'll see.'

* * *

Lil strode over to Frances. 'Well, I've never known so much ruddy tea to be drunk at a wedding – and in a pub too.'

Frances laughed. 'We've got a show to do, Lil. It's the last night of the panto and there's still another week of the run at the Palace. It wouldn't do if we all rolled up to work the worse for a snifter or two.'

'Aye, well, there's some that wouldn't be so careful.' Was she talking about Ruby, who had been drinking neat vodka before she went onstage? It had given her courage to begin with but then it had taken more of it to get her through her days. As if catching her thoughts, Lil added, 'Shame his sister isn't well enough. Poor lass.' She shook her head. 'These big stars – to read the magazines, you'd think they've got it all. Looks, fame, money but it's a rum old do when they've got all that and it don't make 'em happy.' She twisted to Frances. 'Don't get all caught up in that fame rubbish, Franny. I wouldn't like anything like that to happen to you.'

'I won't, Lil. You'd soon put me right.' It was hard not to get caught up in the whirl of Johnny's generosity and excitement. He'd showered her with gifts – flowers, expensive chocolates, jewellery, and his gifts to Imogen had been too numerous to mention.

'You'd never need it, lovey. You've got your feet firmly on the ground. You've had to.' They watched Imogen climb onto the banquet seating and rub Fudge on his head, chattering away to Patsy's son, Colly, who had followed her like a shadow.

'Have you been to see her?' Lil asked cautiously.

'No. I don't think she'd want me there, not at the moment. She's far too fragile.' She'd been in two minds as to whether it would be helpful. What could she say that would give Ruby any comfort? And Ruby had robbed her of so much: her lover, Imogen's father, but most of all her good name, her reputation – and her relationship with her parents. There was much to mend before she could even consider easing Ruby's hurt feelings. She would leave that to the doctors, for Johnny was paying enough for them.

* * *

Jack Holland helped himself to a sausage roll. His wife, Audrey, tutted as he brushed crumbs of flaky pastry from the front of his jacket. He ignored her and stepped aside as she headed to the other end of the room. It was obvious she was uncomfortable, the small pub not meeting her high standards. But at least she had come, although Johnny knew if he'd been lower down the bill she wouldn't have bothered at all. The two of them watched her walk over to Frances. Lil rolled her eyes, winked at them, then went over and butted into the conversation. The two of them grinned.

'That all went well this morning,' Jack said. 'What's next for you both?'

'I'm taking Frances to London for a couple of days when the show ends next week. That's all I can spare.' He took a piece of paper from his breast pocket and handed it to Jack. His call-up papers had arrived yesterday, but he hadn't the heart to tell Frances.

'Bad luck, old chap.'

'Couldn't be worse timing. I have to report before the ninth of next month.'

Jack handed it back and he returned it to his jacket pocket, all the time keeping his eye on Frances. Jack noticed.

'She doesn't know?'

'I didn't want to mar the day. So many things have been spoiled for her – by me, by Ruby. Our mother. I was hoping to have more time with her and Imogen. I've already missed out on so much.'

Jack commiserated. 'At least she doesn't need to worry financially any more. That will cushion the blow a little. She has Imogen, and today she has her respectability again. A married woman.'

'It's something she should always have had.'

'You made it right as soon as you could. It was not of your doing.' They watched her as she hurried to Imogen, who had lifted Fudge from his seat, the dog's legs moving frantically as he searched for safe ground. Frances stepped forward, lifting up the dog's rear end to support it until Imogen put him down again.

'She looks happy,' Jack said.

'She looks beautiful.'

'How is Ruby doing?'

'It's going to take time. Months. The doctor is an elderly chap. He dealt with men who suffered in the Great War. He says Ruby is fighting a war inside her head. When she's well enough, I'll get her to our aunt in Dorset. Hetty won't put up with any nonsense. I should have taken her there sooner, instead of bringing her here. I thought work would help get her through the bad times, as it did me. I'm beginning to realise that was part of the problem. I'm hoping that this complete rest will perhaps restore her in part.'

'At least in hospital there's no alcohol so that particular habit is being dealt with.'

He nodded and they continued to watch the little show being played out before them with amusement. Lil had joined in and was demonstrating to Imogen how to control Fudge. She sat down, patted the seating and Fudge jumped up, then laid his head on his paws. Lil got up and Imogen climbed beside the dog, rubbed at his head then nuzzled close to him.

Frances came over to them. 'It's time we left. I need to get our things.' They had arranged to go back to the house in Park Drive so that Imogen could get acquainted with her new home. They planned to take her with them to the show that night instead of leaving her alone in a strange house with Mrs Frame, who she'd only met once or twice. She would be comfortable enough in the dressing room. It was no more than his parents had done when they'd been working. He and Ruby had been able to sleep anywhere while their parents went out onstage. He looked around for somewhere to leave his plate. Jack took it from him, and he went over to take his child home.

'Can Fudge see my new house?'

'We'll ask Auntie Lil. She might let us borrow him another day.'

'Aye, he'd like that,' Lil said. 'Now you get off with your mummy and daddy. I'll make sure Fudge knows he can come on a little visit.'

Jack drove them home and wished them the best of luck as they walked up the path to the green front door. They were greeted by Mrs Frame, who had lost some of her reserve now that they were man and wife. It wasn't that she'd been unkind, but Frances had felt her unease at the situation, and could hardly blame her.

'Welcome home, Mr Randolph, Mrs Randolph.' She lowered her head to Imogen. 'Miss Randolph.'

'Hello, Mrs Frame,' Imogen called over her shoulder as she ran excitedly upstairs. They'd spent a little time over the last few days preparing it for her, making sure she had time to get used to the idea of moving again – but this time with both her parents. Frances made to follow her, but Johnny held her back.

'Allow me, Mrs Randolph,' he said, sweeping her into his arms to carry her over the threshold. She kissed him, laughing, her heart full and he set her down in the warmth of the house. The Randolphs were home, a family at last.

32

That evening, when the curtain came down on the final performance of the pantomime, Jessie felt a strange mixture of emptiness and loss. All three of them were subdued while they removed their make-up and packed away their things for the last time. Jack was throwing a small party in the bar for the cast and crew, a final goodbye for the older cast members. The juveniles had been given a small gift of miniature Aladdin's lamps, as had Peggy, and while she appreciated the trouble Jack had gone to it was obvious she was disappointed.

'It don't seem fair that I have to go home with the other juves. I've had a part. I've had lines.'

Jessie and Ginny were sympathetic. 'I agree, Peggy. You've done a sterling job standing in for Frances. The show couldn't have gone on without you.' It was only a small lie but worth it to see the happiness in her face. 'We'll ask Miss Taylor if you can stay with us, if we look after you. I'm sure Harry and Joe won't mind making sure you get home safely.'

'Would you!' She was suddenly animated. 'Would you do that,

for me?' She flung her arms about Jessie's neck with abandon, almost strangling her in the process.

Jessie squirmed to be released. 'We're not promising anything, Peggy, but I agree, it only seems fair, you being one of the stars and all that.' Jessie left her with Ginny to take the costumes up to wardrobe and returned not long after, having squared it with Miss Taylor and then with Jack, who apologised for his oversight.

'She's quite entitled to celebrate with us. She got us out of a hole, after all.' He winked at Jessie. 'Are you sure you're up to being her chaperone for the night?'

Jessie laughed. 'It will probably take all four of us; I'll have to rope in Harry and Joe. Our Peggy is a bit of a handful.'

* * *

When their things were finally cleared and packed away, Jessie, Ginny and Peggy walked through the empty auditorium to the bar. The safety curtain was up and the stage crew were striking the set. Tomorrow it would be on a train heading back to the hire company, along with the costumes and props and many of the cast as they headed home or to other bookings.

They stopped at the doors to the bar. 'It's sad to see the show end like this,' Jessie said. 'Knowing it will be the last one here for a long time.'

'Not necessarily,' Ginny reassured her. 'Jack said the NAAFI will open it for recreational purposes for the troops. They're bound to want shows and when they do, you'll be the first person they call.'

'Then why don't you stay, Ginny? We could be a duo.'

'I could take yer mate Frances's place,' Peggy chirped up.

'You're too young,' Jessie and Ginny said in unison, then laughed. 'Come on, Peggy, the party's starting without you. Let's get a drink.'

'I'll have a gin and tonic,' Peggy said. 'Pink gin, like they have in the films.'

'You'll have a lemonade and like it,' Ginny cautioned, pushing her good-naturedly through the door.

Harry was waiting for them in the bar, along with Joe and the rest of the cast, some who only stayed for one drink then left to pack their belongings, ready to vacate their lodgings at the first opportunity. Sunday would be a day of trains and Harry and Joe would be on them. Jessie didn't want to waste a second.

They were busy sharing plans when Jack came over to them. 'Peggy, your car's waiting.'

Her eyes were wide and she pointed to her breastbone, and looked over her shoulder. 'Me, Mr Holland?'

He smiled. 'Unless we have another star performer called Peggy.'

She got up, unsure of herself for once, a foal trying to find its legs. Jack reached out his hand and led her to the door that opened out onto the street. The girls, Harry and Joe followed her, as did the stragglers in the bar, and they crowded onto the pavement to watch her leave. A taxi was waiting, the driver stood by the open door and Jack ushered the girl forward. She got in and the driver closed the door after her, went round to his own side of the car and got in. Peggy wound down the window and leaned out, grinning and waving. 'Ta ra! Break a leg! *Bon voyage*,' she called out as the car moved down the road.

Jack laughed as they all headed back to the warmth of the bar and said what they were all thinking. 'I doubt that's the last we've heard of Peggy Marshall.'

* * *

Come Sunday afternoon, the station was packed with soldiers and sailors, a few women in their stylish naval uniform. Jessie and Ginny looked at them admiringly. 'If I ever join up, that's the service I'll choose,' Ginny said. 'Blue's my colour and it's a lot smarter than that awful dirty khaki the ATS girls have to put up with.'

The carriages were already full, faces at every window, and it looked very much as though Harry and Joe would be standing for at least part of their journey – Harry back to camp, Joe to visit his mother then on to the army, wherever that might take him. Leave for the BEF had resumed well over a week ago and men were on the move. The little pub under the clock was thick with serge uniforms and men spilled out onto the concourse, bottles and glasses in their hands, kitbags at their feet. Steam billowed out as the trains idled, then one moved off, the whistle shrilling across the crisp afternoon air. The four of them made their way along the platform and when they neared the guard's van, Harry pulled Jessie to one side as Ginny helped Joe load his bags on the train. Jessie was forcing herself to be cheerful, not wanting Harry to remember her red-eyed and snotty-nosed, but no matter how hard she tried, parting was always difficult. They had spent almost every minute of his leave together. He had stayed in the dressing room during the show, or until he needed a break from Peggy's constant questioning. She was thrilled to know 'a real live pilot' and even though Harry had told her he hadn't yet got his wings, she'd only replied, 'Don't mean nothing, does it. You can fly an aeroplane, can't ya?' It had made him laugh but he couldn't argue with her.

'They're setting up coastal command further down the coast in North Coates,' he said to her now. 'It's only a couple of miles away, if that. I'll put in for it when it's up and running. We'd be able to see more of each other.' Men jostled past them and he pulled her further back so they were out of the way.

'I'd like that.' She gripped his hand and squeezed. The platform was thinning out as people boarded the train. She searched for Ginny, saw her talking to Joe, her face glowing with a smile as they chatted. 'Look at the two of them. Just good friends.'

'Joe likes her. A lot.'

'She likes him but she's afraid of getting hurt again.'

Harry lit up a cigarette and tossed his match to the floor. 'Joe wouldn't hurt a fly.'

'Makes me wonder how he'll get on in the army.'

'Perhaps they'll give him a desk job,' Harry suggested.

'Or secret service.' She raised her eyebrows, warming to the idea. 'With all his magic.' She leaned her head on his shoulder. 'Oh, Harry. If he could only magic away the war.'

The guard began striding along the platform, urging people to board, checking the doors, his flag in his hand, whistle to his lips. Harry got into the carriage, pushed down the window and leaned out to Jessie. They held hands for as long as they could.

* * *

'This is it, then.' Ginny was suddenly lost for words and Joe had never been any good at them.

'Can I write to you?'

'I'd like that, Joe. Really, I would.'

He nodded, and smiled. 'How will I know where you are?'

'Send it to George and Olive. They've already said they'll send my post on to me. No matter where I am.' For a moment she wanted him to take her in his arms, but only a moment, afraid of what it might mean, or what Joe might take it to mean. She simply longed to be held.

'We might see each other again,' he shouted as the brakes screamed their release. 'The ENSA shows are everywhere.' He seemed to hesitate, then leaned forward and kissed her cheek. She wanted him to kiss her lips, devour her, but she couldn't turn, couldn't lead him on. He was nice, really nice, but they were friends. Hadn't he said so himself when they were at the wireless station and that priggish neighbour of his had insulted her, insulted both of them?

The guard came up to him. 'If you don't get on now, lad, you'll be waiting for the next one.' It galvanised him and he picked up his bag, stepped up into the carriage, turned, stepped down again and kissed her mouth, so suddenly that she was shocked. She put her hand to her lips and as he turned, blew him a kiss. The train moved off and suddenly her heart felt swollen, as if it was crushing her chest. She could see Jessie in front of her, running down the train after Harry but she was frozen to the spot, full of words she had never found the courage to say.

When the train disappeared out of sight, Jessie walked back to her, her eyes red with tears, and pulled her handkerchief from her sleeve and rubbed it under her nose.

'I know it's silly of me. I try to be brave but I always think it might be the last time I see him.'

Ginny put an arm about her shoulder. 'Not silly at all.'

They walked back along the promenade, the shops' windows boarded over. The tide was in, and waves crashed against the sea wall, sending plumes of water running over the promenade. It was grey and swirling and bitterly cold. Out on the horizon, ships blasted their foghorns. As they made their way towards the Empire, they saw men on ladders removing signs that only yesterday had advertised the panto. Below them, wood panels were being hammered over the glass doors.

'That's the end of the Empire, then,' Jessie said, her voice breaking.

Ginny tugged her close. 'It's only temporary, that's all, Jessie. Temporary. Let's hold on to that.'

33

Mr and Mrs Johnny Randolph arrived in London late on Monday afternoon of 5 February, having caught the early train. They took a taxi from King's Cross, which drew up outside the courtyard entrance to The Savoy. The show at the Palace had ended its run on the Saturday and they had spent the Sunday packing for the three-day trip, a delayed honeymoon. Imogen was going to stay with Patsy and her boys for the time they were away, and when they left her for her little 'holiday', she barely gave them a second glance. Mr and Mrs Frame had moved back home, there being no need for them to sleep at the house while Ruby remained in hospital.

It had been more than four years since she'd last been here with Johnny, and then only to drink in the American Bar to toast her success. She'd been staying in grotty digs, out of town, sharing with three other girls in the chorus. The hotel was much changed; the glass panels in the front hall's swing doors had been painted with blue paint, concealing the interior. Inside, it was quieter than it had been pre-war, the large wooden boards that showed the arrivals and departures of the luxury lines missing from behind the hall porter's desk. There were no wealthy Americans wanting to cross the

Atlantic at present, and who knew when they would return. The staff was depleted and those who remained were older, the younger having already gone off to fight.

They were taken up to their suite and as the door opened, Frances tried not to gasp at the opulence that greeted her. The sitting room had two damask armchairs and a broad sofa, and on the table between them a silver bucket bearing a bottle of champagne on ice, a white napkin knotted about the neck. The porter removed their bags from the trolley, Johnny tipped him, and she waited until they were alone before she dared to relax. While Johnny opened the champagne, she hurried to the window, looked down at the river below, the bridge. Johnny came to stand beside her and handed her a saucer of champagne. They touched the glasses, raised them to each other, sipped. It tasted delicious; she already felt drunk with happiness.

'Will this do?' he asked her.

'Do! I've never seen such luxury.' She rubbed at the fabric of the curtains, moved closer to the French window and looked down onto the Embankment and the river below.

He slipped his arm about her waist. 'Happy?'

She nodded, lost for words.

'As happy as you were that night on Waterloo bridge, the world at your feet?'

'Happier.' Across the water, bells chimed the hour.

'Big Ben,' she teased, echoing his words when he had proposed. 'The real thing.'

'This is the real thing, darling.' He took her hand in his and led her through to the bedroom, where they remained for what was left of the afternoon.

* * *

The following morning, Frances and Johnny left The Savoy by the courtyard entrance and turned left onto the Strand. The Adelphi and the Vaudeville theatres had opened but others remained closed; the offering might have been diminished but the spirit of the city was not.

It was noon on Tuesday morning and people were going about as if nothing much had changed. Barrage balloons floated overhead and ack-ack emplacements were surrounded by sandbags, ready for attack. While they were waiting for something to happen – and hoping it never would – life was carrying on as normal.

Frances linked her arm in Johnny's, happy to wander down the streets they had last walked together over four years ago, inconspicuous among the crowds. Rationing might be beginning to bite, but the Lyons Corner House was busy, as were the other cafés they passed. It was business as usual in the capital. Last night they had crossed to the Savoy Theatre to see C. B. Cochran's *Lights Up!*, with songs by Noel Gay, who'd had a smash hit with 'Me and My Girl' only a few years ago. Evelyn Laye was star billing, the dresses were by Norman Hartnell, with Geraldo's Orchestra making a wonderful job of the score. A note in the programme informed them that if an air raid siren went off, it didn't mean that an air raid was imminent, and advised them to either leave quietly or remain in their seats. The audience around them didn't seem in the slightest bit bothered by the warnings and the two of them had soon relaxed into the show, leaving all thoughts of war firmly outside the theatre. If there *was* a raid, it would take only minutes to get back to the hotel and into the basement, which had been reinforced.

He led her away from the streets around Covent Garden and she smiled when she realised where they were going. She recognised the red gingham half-curtain of the Italian restaurant, the square, small glass panes of the window crossed with tape. Puccini's had been their safe place, away from the usual haunts of the theatre crowd.

He opened the door and let her step ahead of him into the darkness of the restaurant. It was little changed from when she'd been there last, simple and cosy. Bentwood chairs were set around small tables draped in pristine white cloths, the glass and cutlery sparkling in the low lights. On each table was a bottle covered with wax from many candles and she immediately recalled happier times when they'd had plans, plans she'd thought had been forgotten, but realised had only been postponed. They had been little more than children then, with no inkling of the trouble or cares that lay ahead. The silhouette of a short, squat man appeared in the doorway at the end of the room and came forward, squinting as his eyes adjusted from the light of the kitchen to the dimness of his restaurant. He frowned, then as recognition dawned, beamed and hurried towards them. He threw his arms wide, embraced each in turn, kissing them on each cheek. 'Mr Johnny and Miss Frances.'

'Rudi,' Johnny said, smiling at the owner's warm welcome. 'And it's *Mrs* Frances.'

Rudi held her hand, admired her rings, opened his arms and hugged her again, calling over his shoulder, 'Tina, Tina, *rapido*. Come see, come see.'

His wife came out, drying her hands on a tea towel, no doubt wanting to know what was causing the commotion. There was another round of hugs and kisses. 'They married now, Tina. Is wonderful news, no?'

Rudi pulled out two chairs at a table, made them sit down, and hurried behind the small bar that had once been crammed with bottles of Italian wines and was now looking rather bare. He came back with a bottle of wine and poured them a glass, apologising for the quality.

'You back in town for good?'

'Just a couple of days.' They could tell Rudi the truth. He had been discreet when his mother had been most awkward, and he knew of their struggle. His restaurant and its dark corners had been their refuge.

'Is Miss Ruby with you?' They were bound to ask. Johnny's reply was relaxed, his need to gloss over the truth evident only to Frances.

'She stayed in Lincolnshire. To rest. She's not too well.' He smiled, and sipped his wine. She felt his foot rest against hers.

'I sorry to hear. Not serious?'

'No, working too hard, that's all.'

'It makes Jack a dull girl. Too much of it.' His mix-up of the proverb made Frances smile. Too much of everything had made Ruby dull, work and play. If she'd joined them in America, would she and Johnny have been happy – or would Alice have won after all? Suddenly overcome by a feeling of panic, she reached for Johnny's hand.

'Enough of us. How is business? Managing to battle on?'

Rudi's mouth took a downward turn. 'It not easy – but then it same for everyone.' He was uncomfortable. 'Back in Italy things are unsettled; my brother's son was coming over to work in the restaurant. But no more. No. He stay there. My brother.' Tina nudged him. 'No, Tina. I tell them. Is okay. They understand.' Tina looked down at her hands. 'My nephew, he has joined the fascists. My brother angry. Me too.'

The door opened and two men came in, speaking to Rudi in Italian. He got up and went over to them. 'I get you a menu,' Tina said quietly, her expression changing. Johnny watched her, watched Rudi as he leaned toward the men, his voice indistinct. Johnny looked back at Frances.

'What are you thinking?'

She was thinking of children not doing what their parents asked them to – and of the ones who did, even though it was wrong.

'Wondering what would have happened had I come to America. Against your mother's wishes.'

'She would have had to accept it.'

'And if she hadn't?'

'I wouldn't have given her the choice. We were old enough to marry – or I was.' It wouldn't have been as simple as that. At least she couldn't divide them now. 'Don't let's spoil today with what happened yesterday.' It was easier said than done. Keeping ghosts of the past where they firmly belonged was not a skill she had mastered.

They chose from the limited menu and watched the comings and goings of the restaurant while they ate. When Rudi took their plates away, they were in no rush to leave.

'We had some happy times here, didn't we?' Johnny said, reaching across the table for her hand.

'It's where you proposed. The first time.'

He smiled. 'Happier times?'

'No. Now is the happiest of times. Let's just enjoy what we have.' She was well aware that he had something to tell her, something important, but she had to let him do it in his own time.

'While it lasts.' He took a deep breath. 'Frances.' He clasped her hand more tightly and she braced herself for what he was about to say. She could have made it easier but that wasn't fair on him. They had to learn to trust each other, for who else could they trust?

'The day of our wedding...' He stopped, looked over to the window, as if it would give him more courage, then back at her. 'I've got my call-up papers.'

She put his hand to her lips and kissed it. 'I know.'

He sat back, confused.

'When I was hanging up your suit, our first night at home.' Home. It seemed so very odd to know that they had a life together. 'You'd fallen asleep. I went to check on Imogen. And before you awoke, I emptied your pockets before I hung it up. I thought it was a bill for something. When I realised, I put it back again.'

'You didn't say anything.'

'Why spoil a beautiful day? I knew you'd tell me eventually.'

He smiled sadly. 'I'd thought exactly the same.' Of course he had; she knew exactly why he'd held back, wanting one perfect day that no one could take away from them, but life wasn't like that. 'It's all the most dreadful timing. That it arrived that day put the tin lid on it. So many things have been spoiled.'

'That's hardly been your fault. You didn't start the war.'

'If I could have held it all at bay, just a little while longer. I would have moved heaven and earth to do it.'

'Can we make a promise? Don't let's keep things from each other from now on. We share things, good and bad.' She'd had time to think, more than he had, to understand things in a way she hadn't done before. 'Can you imagine how awful it must have been for Ruby all those years, keeping secrets?'

He stiffened. 'I don't want to think of Ruby. She could have told me at any point after Alice died.' She noticed he didn't call her 'Mother' any more. 'She didn't tell me out of spite. I think she liked knowing something I didn't. She's her mother's daughter.'

'At one time I might have agreed with you, but when Ruby discovered Imogen and put two and two together, I only felt pity for her.' The gravity of her deception had been clearly visible on Ruby's face as the truth dawned. Frances would never forget it, as long as she lived. Ruby had been devastated. 'I made things worse by making her wait. I could have told you straight away and spared her. It was selfish of me.'

'You don't have a selfish bone in your body.'

'Oh, I do,' she said, smiling. 'Get the bill, darling. Time we went back to the hotel. I want you all to myself.'

* * *

The light was fading as they strolled back towards The Savoy. They stopped at Trafalgar Square. 'We should call in and see Bernie while we're here,' Johnny suggested. 'I need to let him know how things stand.'

'Well, look who it is.' A man interrupted them.

Johnny looked away from her, his smile disappearing when he saw Mickey Harper, the snake who had caused his sister so much trouble. Harper removed his hat, gave a small bow to Frances and glanced at her wedding ring.

'So, Johnny. It's married women now, is it? You and your little sister do have a liking for a bit of scandal.' He looked Frances up and down. 'Sure you know what you're getting into, Mrs—?' He tilted his head, leering, waiting for her to answer. Johnny bristled, tried to walk on but Mickey stepped in front of him.

'Randolph,' Frances said. Johnny glared at her. 'We've met before, briefly,' she said to Mickey Harper. He screwed his mouth. 'I was at the pub when Ruby got the better of you.' He didn't like that.

'You kept that quiet,' he retorted. 'Unless of course that ring's to make it look respectable. *Mrs* Randolph.'

Frances felt Johnny brace himself, ready to lash out. 'Don't give him the satisfaction,' she said quietly. They began to walk away and Harper called after them.

'Perhaps there's a way to make money out of you after all.'

34

Johnny guided Frances up the steps to Bernie Blackwood's offices in one of the streets running off Whitehall, relieved to find them still open. His personal secretary, Shirley, took them straight through to him and he came from behind his oversized walnut desk to greet them. Bernie recognised her and grinned at Johnny.

'Miss O'Leary.'

'Not quite.' He could see Bernie was puzzled. 'Allow me to introduce you to Mrs Frances Randolph.'

Bernie shook her hand vigorously, removed the cigar from between his teeth, then slapped Johnny on the back. 'Let me get you both a drink.'

Ordinarily he wouldn't have bothered but his encounter with Mickey Harper had shaken him. 'A brandy would be good.'

Bernie looked to Frances.

'And for me, yes, thank you.'

He poured three glasses and handed them over, taking a sip from his own before returning to his chair behind his desk.

'I see you didn't want to let her get away again.' It had been a small joke between them when they'd first arrived in Grimsby. They had been eating fish for supper at the Royal Hotel close to the docks. Bernie had asked if there was a special girl in his life but there had only ever been Frances. The one that got away. He hadn't known then that she was so very near.

'It wasn't something I wanted to put in a letter.' Bernie listened while he told his of his mother's deceit, and Ruby's. 'I wouldn't have wanted it to get in the wrong hands. And it's not something I wanted to say over the phone.' The last thing he wanted was to be the gossip at the telephone exchange. 'We'd managed to keep it quiet so far...'

'Until?'

Johnny drank back brandy, enjoying the warmth as it hit his throat. 'We just bumped into Mickey Harper. The chap who was blackmailing Ruby.'

Bernie leaned back in his chair. 'He's been blacklisted. I put the word round as soon as you let me know. He can't get any stage work, so he'll be looking for ways to get cash.' Bernie leaned across his desk, picked up a match and held it around the end of his cigar to warm it, then light it. He puffed out a cloud of smoke, wafting it away from them with the flat of his hand. 'And Ruby?'

'In hospital. Complete nervous exhaustion.'

'Sheesh!' He shook his head sadly. 'I am sorry, my boy.' He drew again on his cigar. 'Where are you staying?'

Johnny gave a half laugh. 'The Savoy.'

'Oof, bad choice, half of ruddy Fleet Street's decamped there for the duration.'

Frances had only listened to that point. 'I think it's time we stopped hiding. Better that we tell the truth. It's always easiest in the end.'

Bernie rested his cigar on the ashtray and interlaced his fingers, resting them on his belly as he sat back in his chair. 'Beat him to it?'

Frances nodded. 'It gives us a little more control of what comes out and when.'

Johnny didn't want to admit defeat. 'I wanted to hold off doing that as long as possible.' He emptied his glass. He could do with another but when Bernie offered, he asked for water. 'I got my call-up papers. I have to report on the ninth – this Friday. I don't want Frances to have to deal with it all on her own.'

'Then let's make it nothing to deal with. Let me make a call.' Bernie got up. They did too. Bernie rested his hand on Johnny's shoulders. 'Go back to The Savoy and speak with Jean Nicol, the hotel's press officer. She'll make sure it's presented tastefully. "Mr and Mrs Randolph pay a visit to London." No need to say it's your honeymoon or how long you've been married. The next story will be you in your uniform.'

Jean Nicol was waiting for them in her office, and after going over the details of what would be shared, she led them down into the room where the photographer was waiting. When the late edition of the *Evening Standard* arrived, there was a photograph and a small item about their stay at The Savoy. 'It'll be in the *Daily Mail* and *Express* tomorrow morning,' she assured them.

Back in the privacy of their suite, Johnny pulled her into his arms. 'At least that will take the wind out of Mickey Harper's sails. The last thing I wanted was to leave you with more of the Randolph family mess to clear up.'

She slapped her hand gently on his chest in reprimand. 'Hey, I'm a Randolph now. It's my messy business too.'

35

It had been one of those gloomy days when the lights needed to be on to lift the spirits more than to illuminate rooms. The cloud had been low, and a heavy greyness seemed to seep into everything – walls, buildings, people – and the inclination was to hide away until the darkness passed. Grace Delaney knew how important it was to keep moving until one came through the other side of it all. She pulled on the heavy door of the private wing of the hospital and began the long walk down the corridor. She hated hospitals, the smell, the unnatural silence as staff went about their work. It invited too many memories to resurface, of walking through hallways, searching for Davey, the sound of men weeping, sighing, calling out for their mothers as she passed. Too many to care for and not enough people to care. *Dear Lord*, she thought, *let it not happen again*.

Ruby was sitting in the chair at the side of the bed and staring out of the open window when Grace arrived. She removed her gloves and unbuttoned her heavy coat.

'Good to see you up and about, my dear girl. It will make you feel so much better.'

'Will it?' Ruby snapped. She glared at Grace. Clearly something had upset her.

Grace slowly settled herself on the edge of the bed, reached out for her hand but Ruby snatched it away.

'What's happened, Ruby?' There was no answer, Ruby quietly seething. Grace waited then asked again. Ruby took hold of her own wrist and began twisting her hand over it.

'They got married. The nurse took great pleasure in showing me the photograph in the *Daily Express*.' She stared accusingly at Grace. 'Why didn't they tell me? Why didn't you?'

'It wasn't my place.'

'Like it wasn't my place to tell Johnny he had a child?' She pressed her hand to her chest, her face wrought with pain. 'Do you know how much it hurt? To know what I had done. To know the minutes were ticking by, one by one... he had no idea... that little girl had no idea how close her daddy was...' Her sharp shoulders heaved with the burden of it. She sank back into the cushion of the chair and closed her eyes. Grace gently rested a hand to her shoulder.

'Johnny wanted to tell you. The doctor told him not to. They were worried it would set you back. If you want to blame anyone, blame the doctors.'

'Blame is pointless.'

'It is, Ruby. I agree.' Grace waited for her to speak again.

'Everyone lies. I didn't think you would.'

'Ruby...'

But Ruby wasn't ready to listen. 'Mother lied. She didn't tell us she was ill. She came back to England pretending everything was all right. People do that, don't they? Pretend everything is all right when it isn't.'

'Sometimes that's because they don't want to hurt us,' Grace offered. 'She was trying to protect you.'

'You think so?' Ruby let out a small laugh. 'I think she did it out of spite.'

'Of course she didn't,' Grace soothed. 'She did it because she loved you.' There was a tray on the side, the food untouched. Grace opened her bag, and took out a white pottery mug and a flask. She poured broth into it and handed it to Ruby. Ruby ignored her.

'Why do you come?' She examined Grace's face for answers, her eyes full of sorrow, of loss.

'Because I care about you.' She placed the mug in Ruby's hands, trusting her not to throw it.

'You barely know me...'

'I feel we're family. Johnny would want me to look out for you. And Frances.'

Ruby rested the mug in her lap. 'I doubt Frances would want anything to do with me.'

'You weren't to know.' If only they had opened the letters; it would have saved so much distress. Not only to Frances and Imogen, who had been so cruelly wronged, but to her own flesh and blood.

'I came between Johnny and Frances and I robbed that child of her daddy. I know what that feels like.'

Grace nodded, reached out and put her hand on her arm. 'But she has him now.'

Ruby got up, placed the mug on the windowsill and stared out. Grace went to stand beside her. People were heading for the various wards to visit their loved ones, their faces pinched with worry, flowers in their hands, grapes in brown paper bags, magazines and newspapers under their arms. A young man hurried down the road, a nurse held the door open for him and they disappeared into the building together. The pavement was quiet once more, save for a nurse cycling away to the street.

'Your mother did her best when your father died. I did too,

when I lost Davey.' Every thought of him made her chest tighten, her throat constrict. Yet she felt she had lost him long ago, the man he was, before the Great War stole his joy, and ultimately hers. 'Poverty is not a good place. Your mother wanted a better life for you and your brother.' Alice Randolph was a hard woman to defend but she'd had her reasons, even if no one understood what they were. There was enough hatred and confusion in the world without adding to it. Ruby took a sip from the mug.

'You know, your father would want you to embrace life. He wouldn't want you to waste a minute of it. He never did.'

'I can barely remember him. I wasn't very old when he died. Three or four.' She stopped drinking. 'A similar age to Imogen.' Painful as it was, this was progress. Ruby had a long journey ahead of her but at last she was beginning to talk – and to eat.

36

It was dark when Johnny and Frances arrived back in Grimsby on Wednesday night, the train journey arduous and uncomfortable, spoiling any respite they'd gained from their short time away. Every carriage had been full, and there had been lots of stops and starts, giving priority to goods trains. Johnny had to report to the barracks at Doughty Road on Friday, unsure as to where his training would take place, hoping it would be close enough that Frances could be with him for the weekends. She had chosen to remain at the house in Park Drive for as long as the rental was available. It was her preference, Patsy being close by, as well as Lil, Geraldine and the Delaneys. They hadn't planned too far ahead, waiting until they knew more once Johnny had settled in with his unit. There was no rush, healthy finances allowing Frances the luxury to be at home for as long as she wanted, to spend her days with Imogen.

That their time together was limited made each moment more precious than it would have been otherwise. It was no good dwelling on what might have been and planning anything was futile. At the first opportunity he had promised to take her to her family in Ireland and make things right. Frances told him that she very much doubted anything could be made right; it could only be made the best of. The porter placed their bags on the trolley, all the time talking to two chaps from the Royal Naval Reserve who had shared their compartment and were on their way to billets in Cleethorpes. She had told them of the Lil at the Fisherman's Arms and that when the NAAFI opened at the Empire to give their names to George, who was sure to be around. In her hand she carried the new leather vanity case she had chosen in Asprey. It had given him the greatest of pleasure to spoil her and guilt flared again, that she had struggled so much and for so long. And yet there was no bitterness for what she had suffered, only a gratefulness in her heart that she had Imogen, and that they had found each other again.

She slipped her arm through his as they waited and snuggled close.

'Cold?'

'A little.' How different she was to Ruby, who complained about everything, the lighting, the dressing rooms, that drinks were either too cold or too hot. He bit back his irritation at his sister. After their encounter with Mickey Harper, they had talked long into the night, neither of them wanting to hide from the truth, to embrace the difficult things and deal with them as they arose. They couldn't change the past, but they could make a better future for all of them – and that had to include Ruby. He had to find a way to build a relationship with her again and make a start before he left for the barracks in two days' time.

The porter led the way to the taxi rank, his torch shining a faint path ahead of them and they followed him to a waiting car. They would have the night alone at Park Drive, having phoned ahead to Patsy from one of the stations to warn her of the delays. It hadn't even elicited a whimper of disappointment from Imogen, who was delighted to have an extra day with her 'brothers', as she called Patsy's two boys. That she saw them as such must have both gladdened and saddened Frances, the relief that she lived as part of a warm family while her mother worked a blessing. It was something she would never have to do again; he had made certain of that.

* * *

Ruby was sitting by the window but there was nothing to see, just the odd nurse or orderly as they moved from one part of the hospital grounds to another, the same brick wall, the same entrance door to the emergency service maternity home. Day and night she saw heavily pregnant women arrive, and in time she saw them leave, the lucky ones with their husband beside them, as the nurse pushed them in the wheelchair and carried the babies, fearful that they might drop their child. As if there had been the slightest chance that something so precious could not be carried by the two people that had made it. She had thought it the cruellest of places to give her, facing that door, but then she knew it was no more than she deserved, to spend her days looking at what she would never have. Her thoughts flitted to Imogen, so like Johnny. She closed her eyes, longing to shut out the world and everything in it. Men had wanted to be with her, had showered her with gifts, taken her to expensive dinners – then to bed, their payment. Then they had left. Had that been her fault too?

A nurse came into her room carrying a breakfast tray and placed it on the table over her bed. It was the cheery-faced girl with the greenest of eyes and the mass of freckles. 'No more news, Miss Randolph, but I'm sure they'll allow visitors again soon. It's just a precaution.' The girl chattered on, but Ruby had learned to let it drift over her head. She didn't have to respond; she didn't have to do anything. And when Grace wasn't here, she didn't have to eat.

* * *

Early that same morning, Johnny and Frances made their way down the long road that led to the hospital. Frances had persuaded him that telling Ruby the truth was for the best, no matter what the doctors said.

'You can't leave without letting her know that you've been called up and then send her off like a package to your aunt Hetty. It's not fair.'

He had been exasperated. 'What's fair got to do with it? She's hardly been fair to you.'

'Right, then. It's not right.'

'I'm beginning to hate that ruddy word.'

'Well, you know I'm *right*,' she had teased as she helped him on with his coat and kissed him. He had smiled and his frustration with Ruby lessened. He had worked out what he was going to say to her as they walked, but as they arrived at the entrance door, they were greeted by a sign that said *No Visitors – Scarlet Fever Isolation*.

Johnny threw up his hands. 'That's it. I'll have to write to her. I can't risk you or Imogen getting it. I'd be worried sick.'

'Ruby might already have it. Isn't it best if we find out? Someone will have some information.' Without waiting for an answer, Frances hurried towards a nurse walking ahead of them. They were directed to take another route about the building and called in at a small office where they were told that the isolation would last eight weeks.

'I had scarlet fever as a child,' Frances implored. 'Can't I at least go in?'

There was no persuading the receptionist. Johnny was relieved but Frances wasn't going to give up.

'What's wrong with a letter?' he asked her.

Frances twisted. 'A letter. One that might not get delivered? The state your sister is in, and you think a letter will do?' She dug in her heels. 'We're not going until we've seen her.'

'Frances, for God's sake, you heard what they said.'

'You give up too easily,' she said quietly. 'Perhaps you always have.'

Her remark shook him. 'Now, look here…'

'No, you look.' Her cheeks were red; whether it was heat or anger, he wasn't sure. 'If you think you can go away and leave it to your aunt Hetty, or me, to drop the bombshells on Ruby that one, we're married, and two, that you've been called up, and heaven knows what other news we… might have to impart, then you're mistaken, Johnny Randolph. You're not leaving until you've spoken to her yourself. Do your own dirty work and start making things… right!' She marched ahead of him, looking up and down the length of the building. She walked over the grass verge, counting the windows until she cautiously came close and peered into one. 'Your sister is right there. You can tell her yourself.' She tapped gently on the glass. Johnny remained on the pathway, all the things he had worked out he was going to say a jumble. Frances tapped again, and beckoned to the person inside. A figure come forward. Frances stood back as Ruby pushed the sash a little.

He was shocked when he saw her. She looked so frail and vulnerable. Frances spoke gently to her. 'We have to keep our distance, Ruby, but Johnny… has news.' Frances looked to him. She wasn't going to let him get away with anything, was she, and he was suddenly glad. He came beside her.

'Ruby. I'm sorry I haven't been to see you. I… We…' He turned to Frances, but it was clear she was leaving this to him. 'We got married, Ruby; we've been in London a couple of days. Bernie Blackwood sent his regards for your speedy recovery.'

Her eyes were blank, her skin and hair dull and Rudi's words came back to him, about too much work and too much play.

'I heard. It was in the *Express*. I'm happy for you, both of you. Imogen most of all. You're a lucky man.' Her voice was thin, a whisper, but he knew she meant every word and his heart suddenly ached for her to be as she was when they were young. He wanted to reach out and take hold of her hand but knew he couldn't.

'I've got my call-up papers. I couldn't hold things off any longer. I tried.' Time had slipped away from both of them. He had brought her away from London to help her, setting up a show she could carry without him, to give her a purpose, something to distract from her self-destructive path. It had only made things worse. 'Frances will be here if you need anything. Just concentrate on getting well. I've arranged for you to stay with Aunt Hetty. I know how much you love her – how much she loves you, Ruby. And you'll enjoy Dorset. The fresh air will be wonderful for you.'

The movement of her head was barely perceptible but he knew she'd understood.

She lifted her hand, remembered, and placed it on the sill. 'Be safe, Johnny boy. Be safe and came back home.'

He nodded, his throat thick with emotion, unable to speak any more lest his voice betray him. He had to be strong for them all, just as he always had, the man of the family. He had promised his mother he would take care of her. What a poor job he'd done so far.

Ruby blew him a kiss and closed the window, and he went to Frances, who held out her hand to him. As they turned to walk away, the door to the building opposite opened and a nurse came out carrying a child. He saw the words 'Maternity Home' and his heart went out to his sister. He would get her moved to another room, another view. He turned back, wanting to comfort her, but Ruby had gone.

37

Two days after Johnny left, Frances was on the bus travelling to RAF Grantham with Jessie and Ginny. Young Peggy had invited herself when she got wind of the show, and they had managed to persuade a couple of local entertainers to add a little variety: a ventriloquist and an elderly comedian, who had been more than happy to contribute. Eddie's boss, Mr Coombes, had provided the bus and driver at his own expense as it was 'for the boys'.

Jessie twisted in her seat and looked down the length of the bus to where they had banished Peggy, who was now bending Eddie's ear.

'I told her to save her voice. She'll be hoarse by the time we get to the camp.'

Frances checked over her shoulder and grinned. 'She's excited. She'll be fine. That girl has leather lungs.'

Ginny was in the seat across the aisle and leaned forward. 'Have you heard where Johnny is going to be doing his training?'

'Kettering.' The last time she'd seen Ginny and Jessie had been at the wedding. There had been a lot for them to catch up on. She'd spent every last minute with Johnny and the rest of her time being with Imogen, settling into the house and making home – or as much as she could.

'And Imogen?'

'Taking it in her stride. To be fair, she's used to him not being around. Me too, when it comes to it. These past few weeks have been quite odd for both of us.' There was no need to tell them that Imogen was as unsettled as she was. 'There's been a lot of change in her little life, let alone mine. Coming to Barkhouse Lane, then, well, meeting her dad for the first time.' Imogen had thought her dad was a trawlerman like Patsy's husband, Colin. Patsy's kids were used to their father's long absences but at least they had their mother with them all the time. Imogen had sometimes had neither.

'At least you have that lovely house,' Ginny commiserated.

'Yes, and Mrs Frame to do for you,' Jessie added. 'What a luxury.'

Frances smiled, agreeing with them, and stared out into the blackness of the countryside. How could she complain that the days already seemed too long, the nights longer? Her entire adult life had been spent working and now that she didn't have to, she was lost. She'd tried to help Mrs Frame with little bits about the house but if she picked up so much as a duster, the housekeeper thought she might lose her job. So Frances stepped back and tried to fill her days with long walks with Imogen and keeping up with her exercise routine. The discipline of it helped.

'Will you stay there?' Jessie asked.

'For the time being. I didn't want to live in London. I don't know anyone, not really, and my true friends are here, Patsy, you, and you, Ginny. You'll keep in touch, won't you?'

'Try stopping me.'

Jessie lost her smile at the reminder that Ginny would be leaving. As soon as her audition date had come through, she'd booked her train ticket. She would be leaving in two days.

'I suppose this show is the best way for the Variety Girls to bow out,' Ginny said, smiling at Frances and Jessie.

'Yes. Time for us all to move on,' Frances replied. Jessie did not answer.

* * *

The bus pulled to a halt at the gates to the camp and after a quick conversation with the driver it was waved through. The chatter on the bus quietened as they leaned against the windows and peered out. A small group of men in uniform were lingering outside a long brick building, their breath fogging about them. Jessie checked her hair and make-up in her compact. She wanted to look her best for Harry. It was silly, really, how quickly her heart had started beating at the thought of seeing him. The doors opened, letting in a blast of cold air and to her delight he stepped onto the bus, searching for her. She put away her compact and got up and he caught her in his arms, kissing her nose. 'Oh, it's so good to see you. All of you,' he said, greeting Ginny and Frances with handshakes and kisses on cheeks. He didn't take his eyes off Jessie, and she didn't want him to, so glad to see him, wanting to be alone with him and yet excited to see where they would be performing. Would she always be pulled in two directions like this?

They were helped off with their bags and cases and led down a cinder path, into the back of the building where there was a low platform for a stage. Someone had painted the most marvellous backdrop that looked like Piccadilly Circus, the statue of Eros in plain sight. The real thing had been removed for safety and the fountain covered with sandbags and boarded over. It was nice reminder of how things had been – and how they would be one day again, or so they hoped. Eddie soon disappeared in search of someone with whom to talk engine capacity and Peggy followed him, eager to look around.

It was warmer inside, chairs and benches set in rows facing the stage, and a thrill of excitement exploded inside Jessie at the thought of being able to sing again. After the panto ended there had only been a couple of gigs, nothing regular, and nothing imminent.

Harry led the way to the back of the room where three wooden panels had been fixed together. A sheet of paper with the words 'Star Dressing Room' had been stuck on one of them; a couple of standard-issue blankets had been hung over a cord to make a doorway and accord them a dramatic entrance. 'The lads put it together. It's a bit cramped but I told them you were used to sharing.' There was a small posy of flowers and she knew that he had left them for her. 'I'd better leave you to get ready,' he said to them all, and then to Jessie, 'I'll be at the back, same as always.' He spoke to the ventriloquist and comedian. 'If you'd like to come with me, chaps, you can get changed in the gents.'

Behind the screens there was a trestle table set out with a mirror and chairs for the girls. They had done a sterling job and the three of them were touched that they had gone to so much trouble. They hung up their costumes on a line of rope that had been strung along the back wall for that purpose and took it in turns to use the mirror. The curtain was thumped, and someone said, 'Knock, knock.' Ginny pulled it back a little as Frances was still dressing.

'Have you got your dots, girls?'

'I recognise that voice!' Frances said. 'Dickie Daniels.' The blanket was pulled back and a grinning face loomed around it.

'Frances O'Leary. How the devil are you!'

'O'Leary no more.' She held out her hand to show her wedding ring, pulled her dress on over her slip and adjusted the waistband.

'Who's the lucky blighter? I thought you were waiting for me.'

Frances laughed. 'Huh, I'd have been in a long line. Girls, this is Dickie. He was in the band for a show I was in a few years ago.'

He smiled and shook their hands as Jessie and Ginny introduced themselves. 'So, you're the girls they've all been excited about.'

'And you haven't?' Frances teased.

'I came for your music.' He raised his eyebrows. 'First drinks on me after the show, girls.' Jessie handed him their music and he flicked through it. 'That looks great to me. Do you want to have a quick run-through?' He directed his question to Frances.

'Jessie will talk you through it. She's the musician.'

He winked at her and Jessie blushed.

'And her fiancé's the chap who got us here.'

'Ah, well, you can't win them all.' He looked expectantly at Ginny.

'A drink will be lovely. Thank you.'

Satisfied, he withdrew and Jessie followed him out onto the stage where the piano was set. The other chaps were already there, a drummer and bass, lead guitar, trumpet player and trombone.

'Gosh, I thought we'd be lucky to have a pianist. I didn't expect this.'

'Half of Ambrose's orchestra are in the RAF or the army. Most of the lads signed up in the first few weeks.' He took a seat at the piano and Jessie talked them through the running order. It was so very easy working with professional musicians, especially of this calibre, and any excitement she'd felt at performing doubled. Harry was at the back of the room with a couple of friends, and she gave him a little wave, then got on with her job, thrilled to be able to do so.

They opened with three upbeat numbers then brought Peggy on to do a couple of impressions. Jessie had helped her put together a short medley of songs where she switched from Jessie Matthews to Marlene Dietrich, on to Judy Garland and finished off with

Gracie Fields. Her three minutes went down a storm, the lads loving her cheek and bravado as she bounced joyously about the stage, throwing winks to them. Ginny was in stitches just watching her. 'Cor, what I wouldn't give for an ounce of her confidence.' She was followed by the ventriloquist, then Jessie sang a couple of solos. The comedian was next and it was wonderful to hear the swell of laughter as it built with each joke. After he had taken his applause, the girls were greeted with whoops and cheers as they stepped out to finish the show. The lads were an appreciative audience, the officers taking the front row seats. Jessie searched and found Harry at the back of the room, his back against the wall, and didn't think she could ever be happier. Each song was greeted with a round of applause and after it ended the crowd were on their feet, whistling and shouting. The three of them stood there, holding hands, smiling out to the audience and to each other as the rest of the performers joined them.

Peggy gripped hold of Jessie's hand. 'We blew their bloody socks off, didn't we?'

Jessie could only laugh and agree. 'We did, Peggy. We did.'

Peggy didn't possess a change of clothing and she stepped off the platform in search of Eddie. In the changing room, Ginny and Frances stood back, giving Jessie space to get changed quickly so that she could rush off to be with Harry.

'Thanks, you two. Oh, didn't it go well? I'm so glad we came. We should do this more often.'

'This was our last hurrah,' Frances said quietly, but Jessie pretended she hadn't heard.

* * *

A few minutes later, Frances and Ginny joined Jessie, and Harry got them drinks as men crowded around. They handed out publicity photos of themselves and the remainder of the ones they'd had printed as the Variety Girls. Jessie signed it and handed it to Ginny along with the pen. It couldn't end; it just couldn't. Harry noticed her change in mood. 'Everything all right?'

She gave him her biggest smile. 'Perfect. Just perfect, being with you, singing... being with you...' He took her hand, but she was pulled away by one of the ground crew who had a camera and wanted to take a photo of them.

'Fair's fair, Harry old chap; you've got her for the rest of your life.'

It was hours later when they piled back on the bus to leave. She'd barely seen Harry all night, although he was always close by, somewhere she could see him but just out of reach. Jessie was the last to get on, the sound of the engine labouring behind her and Harry as they said goodbye, fumes swirling out from the exhaust and into the inky blackness of the night. 'There's never enough time, is there, darling,' she said, pulling up the collar of her coat. It was beginning to freeze and although she didn't want to leave, she longed to be in the warmth. 'I've hardly seen you.'

He placed a warm hand to her cheek. 'Seems I'm always going to have to share you.'

'Not always.' But as she said the words, she saw the look in his eyes. It didn't matter how much she lied to herself, he could see right through her; he always had. She loved him with every bone in her body, but she never felt as alive as she did when she sang, when there was music. It was as if there was something missing, a part of her that only fell into place when she was onstage. A part that Harry alone could not fill.

38

The girls were gathered around their favourite table by the window in Joyce's café, a habit they'd formed last summer when they'd first got together, before the show opened, before war came and upset their plans, their hopes and dreams. Ginny's bags were already at the station, ready to be loaded onto the Sheffield train. She was calling home for a few days before going down to London. The three of them had walked back up the sloping pathway that ran between the railway and Victoria Terrace for a farewell cuppa. The café was on the corner of Dolphin Street, only a few steps away from the stage door of the Empire, and the wall behind the counter was decorated with signed publicity photos of stars who had played the theatre and been guaranteed a warm welcome from Joyce and her staff.

There were few other customers that Sunday afternoon and Joyce was on her own, cooking, serving and cleaning the tables, knowing she could call on Dolly if she needed any help. She cleared the table of empty mugs and plates behind them and came back with a cloth to wipe it down.

Jessie was glum. While Ginny remained in Cleethorpes, she'd

always held out hope that they could keep the act going but her leaving had squashed any chance of that happening. 'This is the last time we'll be here together. Sad to think that it's all come to an end.'

'As all good things must.' Frances twisted and drew a smiley face in the condensation that had crept up the glass behind her. Jessie smiled but it didn't cheer her.

'Our paths will cross again,' Dolly reassured her. 'The Empire will open after all this is over. Jack will make sure of that. It's a pity it was requisitioned when it was starting to do so well. The war has interrupted so many things.'

'Yes,' Ginny agreed. 'Not an end, an interruption.'

'Are you lasses calling me?' Joyce teased.

'No, but we could have been.' Jessie grinned.

Joyce stopped her wiping and rested her fist on the table, the cloth still in it.

'What time's your train, lovey? Eeh, Dolly will miss you staying at her house, won't you, petal, and her mam and dad, bet they've loved having the extra company, used to a house of lasses, they are.' Dolly didn't even bother to answer a question until Joyce had run her course. Joyce folded her arms. 'Gawd, it wa'n't so long ago we was all tickety-boo, knowing what was coming next. Easter, Whit bank holiday...'

'We'll still have Easter and Whitsun,' Jessie said.

'Yes, but not the holidaymakers with money to chuck about.' She bustled back behind the counter.

Jessie hadn't thought that far ahead. 'I suppose the lack of holidaymakers will make a huge difference this summer. I don't suppose many people will venture to the coast with all this going on.'

Frances turned to Dolly. 'How's your sister getting on? With her guesthouse being a billet. Is it all working out for her?'

'It seems to be, although I think she'd prefer it as it was, getting different people each week. But it's regular money and it's every week, no quiet months like there is in the winter. Although I think she misses that. It gave her a chance to put her feet up for a bit instead of running around after everyone.'

'Perhaps I should contact the billeting officer,' Frances said. 'There are empty rooms at Park Drive. I might as well put Imogen in with me and let them to good use. It's not as if I won't be able to cope with Mrs Frame on hand if I need her. I'll have to run it past Johnny but I'm sure he'll be agreeable. It would make me feel I was doing my bit.'

Jessie put her elbows on the table, her hands to her cheeks. 'I don't feel I'm doing mine. Not at the solicitor's.'

'There are many ways to fight the good fight. Keeping things ticking along is just as important,' Joyce called from the counter, turning to check the clock on the wall behind her. 'What time did you say your train was, Ginny?'

'I didn't,' Ginny said, getting to her feet. 'But we'd best be leaving anyway; we can take a slow walk down to the station.'

Joyce returned, minus the cloth and plates, and gave her a quick hug. 'Mind how you go, lovey. And if you ever need anything, there'll always be a welcome for you here.'

'Thanks, Joyce.'

'And that goes for all of ya.' She rubbed her hand under her nose and hurried through to the kitchen.

They stayed with Ginny until her train left, then made their way back to the main road, Jessie feeling the sharp pang of being left behind. A lorry had parked in front of the Empire and soldiers were unloading wood from the back of it. The three of them leaned against the wall on the opposite side of the road. Jessie was curious. 'I wonder what they're doing?'

'Dad might know,' Dolly said as she hugged them in turn and then left them to go home. 'I'll see what I can find out.'

As they walked along Alexandra Road, Jessie was reminded of her first day of rehearsals, when she'd arrived all adrift, full of passion and bravado. Where had it gone?

As if catching her thoughts, Frances said, 'What next?'

'Next?' Jessie paused.

'For you.'

'Work on Monday.'

'Is it enough?'

'I don't know what you're talking about.' She started walking again, feeling her shoulders hunch to protect herself from Frances's interrogation.

'You're not the girl you were, Jessie Delaney. It's less than a year since we walked along here, and you were ready to do anything to make your name. This was just the beginning, you told me. And what of London, of Bernie and Vernon Leroy? You can't keep turning things down.'

'Mum needs me.'

'That's an excuse and you know it. Grace is thriving – and that's thanks to you, bringing her here, taking a risk. You need to risk again.'

It was an excuse; she'd known that for a long time, long before the panto ended, only she didn't want it to be true.

'It's nothing to do with risk. It's... it's Harry.' There, she had blurted it out, but doing so made her miserable. She should be happy; she had everything – Harry, her mum, Eddie. She was loved, not like poor Ginny, who had no one to stay home for. Frances didn't understand so Jessie tried to explain how he felt.

'He won't want me travelling around the country, will he, trying to make a name for myself. After the war's over he'll go back to being a solicitor... and even if I could find work locally, he would be coming in from the office and I'd be going out. That's not what he wants.' She had tried so many times to imagine their home, their furnishings, how they would live but the more she thought about it the worse it seemed. She loved him, but could she settle to a life without performing? 'I don't want to reach for a dream then have it snatched away. It seems pointless to try.' It sounded so petty. 'I love Harry, I really do.'

'Have you talked to him about it?'

'I didn't get a chance. There's always so much to say, and so little time, and I don't want to make him miserable, not when...' She didn't need to say any more; Frances knew what she was thinking. Why cause upset when the future was so uncertain?

'Oh, Jessie. I'm sure if the two of you talked it over you would work it out.'

Jessie shook her head. 'I can't seem to find the words when we're on the telephone. It doesn't seem right – and I don't know when we'll get the chance to be together again.'

Frances put her arm about her shoulder. 'Could you tell him in a letter?'

Jessie was close to tears. 'We need to talk about it face to face; a letter will prolong the agony. I'll have to wait. And until then I'll just have to stick at what I'm doing. He didn't want me to go away in the first place.'

'He wouldn't want you to be unhappy.'

'I'm not unhappy...'

'Who are you trying to convince? Me? Or you?'

Jessie couldn't answer and they walked along in silence until Jessie said, 'What about you?'

Frances let out a heavy sigh. 'I need a rest. To pause and give myself time to think before I do anything. So much has happened these last few months and it's been hard to take it all in. I don't know what I want to do. But *you* can't keep making excuses.' Jessie quickened her pace, wanting to put distance between Frances and her questions but her friend was having none of it. She pulled at Jessie's arm. 'Don't walk away; face up to what you want, Jessie. Is it going to be enough, for the rest of your life, working in an office, running a home?' Was she talking about herself or Jessie? She looked into Frances's dark eyes; the answer wasn't there.

'I don't know, do I?' She leaned against the wall at the top of Barkhouse Lane. 'I'm just having to pause, aren't I. Like you.'

39

March came in with a roar and went out like a lamb. The trees in the park across the road from the house were beginning to green and Frances took Imogen there every day. Early that April, Germany had invaded Denmark and Norway and the so-called phoney war was over. Activity around the docks in Immingham and Grimsby increased and the navy presence became more visible as the number of ratings added to their numbers. Johnny telephoned as often as he could, always asking of Ruby and it saddened her, this rift between siblings that she had no idea how to heal. On his leave she had travelled down to him, spending the weekend in a hotel near to his camp. It meant they had longer together, and time was precious. It didn't matter how long it took her, or how many trains, for she felt redundant most of the time, Mrs Frame more than capable of running a battalion let alone a house.

As the situation in Europe deteriorated, Frances put the empty rooms at the house to good use, with Johnny's full agreement. The billeting officer had made sure that only officers and messengers came to the house so there was always a steady stream of people, but none stayed long, and she preferred it that way, not wanting to make a deeper connection. She had tried to visit Ruby but Ruby would not allow it. To cheer her she'd sent a basket planted up with daffodils, fruit if she could get hold of it. The naval officers often came with extra rations, which they generously shared, and she was overwhelmed by her good fortune. But it didn't matter how many people came and went; she was lonely, more so than before because her heart ached for Johnny when previously it had been filled with anger towards him. There was no anger any more, not for him, or Ruby, or even for Alice Randolph. The slate had been wiped clean and a new chapter had begun.

Imogen skipped ahead of her, along the path that wound around the lake. Two boys were on their knees, pushing wooden boats with sticks. One was lying on his belly, his arm stretched out, his coat on the floor beside him, his sailboat out of reach, while another ran about looking for a long stick. Any further out and he would have to paddle. The water would be freezing cold. A fleeting thought of Ruby came to her, knowing she had walked into it on New Year's Eve. Had she meant to do something so drastic, or was she, as Johnny had convinced himself, numb of all feeling?

'Here, Mummy?' Imogen stopped at a bench. Frances nodded and, as she caught up with her, handed over the paper bag she was carrying. Imogen peered into it and smiled approvingly, walking close to the edge of the lake as ducks swam frantically to be the first to greet her. Mrs Frame saved what she could for the ducks, crumbs from the biscuit tin and crackers – every little scrap that could be spared for the child's happiness. Frances took a seat. At the other side of the lake, a group of soldiers jogged along the path, bulky rucksacks on their backs, the noise of their heavy boots thunderous. Imogen watched them, distracted momentarily, and turned her attention back to the ducks, giggling as they dived for crumbs, bottoms wiggling in the air. Frances smiled. It was what she had wanted all along, time with Imogen, no money worries, love. Then why was she so restless?

'Oi, git out of it. Shoo! Off with ya!'

Imogen turned away from the ducks and Frances looked over her shoulder. The park keeper was shaking his stick at a dog that had been there the last couple of days. They had seen it in different areas in the park and outside of it, trotting up pathways and pavements. Rationing was beginning to bite, the lack of supplies leading to queues that Frances was secretly glad of, because it gave her something to do, people to talk to. The dog, a scruffy grey and white mongrel with brown patches about its mouth, ignored him and left a message on the grass. Frances bit back a smile. The park keeper ran after it, shaking his fist, his stick, and the dog ran into a bush. Imogen watched until the dog disappeared then upturned the bag to shake any fragments hiding in the corners. Satisfied she had fed her feathery friends the last of them, she handed the bag back to her mother, who folded it neatly and added it to her pocket.

'Where does the dog live?' Imogen asked. 'Does it live in the park?'

'It might do.' There was no 'might' about it. It wasn't the only stray she'd seen lately. If people struggled to feed themselves then a dog would be considered a luxury. Hundreds of cats and dogs had been either put down or abandoned long before war was declared.

'Hasn't it got a mummy to look after it? Or a daddy?'

'I'm sure it has. It's probably just run off. It will find its way back. Dogs do that.'

Imogen climbed onto the bench next to her and the two of them watched the boys. As Frances had suspected, one of them, the taller of the two, had taken off his socks and shoes and was wading out to rescue his craft. Their shouts and laughter drifted over the water.

Imogen said, 'I wonder what Colly and Bobby are doing.'

Frances reached out and placed her hand on Imogen's leg.

'They'll be at school.'

'I miss them. I miss having someone to play with.'

'You'll be at school soon. You'll have friends then.' Imogen was quiet and Frances knew that she was not the only one who was lonely. Imogen had spent a lot of time with Patsy and her boys, a boisterous, noisy lot they were too. Frances got up. 'Come on, let's go and see the boats.'

They walked around the pond and as they did so the dog appeared and came into step behind them. Frances ignored it, but Imogen kept turning back. Imogen slipped her hand from her mother's and stopped. The dog stopped too.

'Here, boy,' she said, bobbing down a little, rubbing her finger-tips together to entice him. The dog came forward, cautious.

Frances caught hold of her hand. 'Don't encourage him, Immi. He might bite.'

She began to walk but Imogen wouldn't move. The dog sat on his hindquarters and tilted his head to one side. Frances sighed. Why did he have to do that? He looked so damn cute. Imogen dragged her towards the dog. 'Poor thing. Are you lost?' The dog held out his paw. Imogen took hold if it. 'Good boy. He's a good boy, isn't he, Mummy?'

Frances reluctantly agreed. 'Come on, Immi. We need to get back; Mrs Frame will have dinner ready.' She guided her away, walking towards the boys, who had now rescued their boats and were shaking the water off them. By the time they reached them they were walking away.

Imogen didn't seem in the least bothered, too entranced by the dog. 'I think he's lost his mummy. We should look after him.' She looked up at her mother, her brown eyes pleading.

Frances laughed. 'We can't just take a dog. He belongs to someone.'

Imogen jutted out her stubborn little chin. 'But we could look after him until we find them.'

'It's not as simple as that. He could—'

'We could look after him like Auntie Patsy looks after me, and then, when his mummy's not busy, she can have him back.'

It stopped her in her tracks. Was that how Imogen saw it? That she was too busy for her?

'Oh, darling.' She squatted down on her haunches, and took hold of Imogen's hands. 'I wasn't too busy. Never. But I had to go to work. To look after us.'

'But now Daddy looks after us. And Mrs Frame.'

'Yes, and that means I can look after you and spend time with you. Like we've done today. In the park.'

'But we have lots of people to stay all the time.' She couldn't argue with that. They'd both had to adjust to the comings and goings as people arrived at all hours. It was quite normal to come down to breakfast and find another stranger at the table. 'Please, Mummy? Please.' Imogen looked at the dog and then to her mother. 'He looks like Mr Brown.'

Frances didn't understand. 'Mr Brown lives near Auntie Patsy. Mrs Brown has gone to heaven. Mr Brown is sad. The dog is sad. I'm sad.'

Frances looked again. He did look sad but that didn't mean she could give in.

She started walking. Imogen dragged her heels; the dog followed. Frances tried to ignore him. They crossed over the road and Frances quickly closed the gate behind them, placed her hand on the small of Imogen's back to hurry her along. The dog sat by the gate. Imogen loitered on the doorstep. 'Auntie Patsy takes Mr Brown food. She says he doesn't eat properly.'

'Auntie Patsy is very kind.'

'I want to be kind.' She looked up at her mother. 'We could feed Mr Brown.'

'We could.'

Imogen's face brightened. 'Can we?' Frances nodded and Imogen, suddenly delighted, ran to the gate and lifted the latch.

'Immi, what are you doing?'

'Getting Mr Brown,' she called. Child and dog arrived at the porch, side by side.

'But I meant...' Two pairs of brown eyes looked up at her.

'He's sad, like Mr Brown.' Imogen folded her arms. 'I want to be kind.' Her bottom lip trembled and tears filled her eyes.

Frances couldn't bear it. 'Take him around the back. Mrs Frame might have some bones for him. I'll go and ask.'

She hurried through the house and into the kitchen. Mrs Frame was reading the local newspaper and looked up as she came in. 'Is something wrong?'

'Not yet.' She leaned at the window and beckoned Mrs Frame to do the same. In the garden, Imogen was talking to the dog, the dog close at heel.

'What on earth?'

'It's the dog from the park. It's been there a few days.' He was scrawny and scraggy. Probably hadn't eaten for days. 'Have you got any bones left? Just a few scraps for it.'

Mrs Frame pursed her lips. 'You know if you feed it, you'll never get rid of it?'

She didn't need telling, but Immi, out in the garden with the dog, was transformed. She was chattering away as she led the dog about the garden, pointing out the vegetable patch and the swing that hung from the chestnut tree. They'd both had a lot to contend with these past months. It wasn't just herself who'd had to adjust; Immi had to too, and seeing the boys in the park had brought it into sharp relief.

'I know that. But it's made Immi so happy.'

Mrs Frame shook her head, but went to the pantry all the same, muttering to herself as she did so, and came back with a hock bone. She handed it to Frances, who was still at the window. Mrs Frame stood with her. Could she see the change too? Why hadn't she noticed how lonely Immi was before?

'It'll likely have fleas,' Mrs Frame said. 'There's a tin bath in yon shed. I'll find an old towel.'

Frances gripped her shoulder. 'Thanks, Mrs Frame, that'll be grand.'

She went out into the garden to tell Immi, who threw her arms about her, and Frances knew it was worth any trouble having a dog would cause. Together they went to fetch the bath while the dog made short work of the bone. Mrs Frame and Frances ferried the water and she and Imogen got the dog into the tin bath and gave him a good scrub with a bar of Sunlight and a scrap of old flannel. The dog was passive throughout and as Frances looked into his old brown eyes, she knew she'd done the right thing.

'We're only looking after him, Immi. His owner might be looking for him.' It was highly unlikely, but she had to make sure Immi was prepared for it. Just in case. There had already been too many goodbyes.

'Well, I will tell them off. They should look after you, shouldn't they, Mr Brown.'

'You can't call him Mr Brown,' Frances said, smiling.

'Why?'

Frances had no answer. Immi could call the dog what she wanted for the time they had him. It had made her happy and for that she was grateful. They rinsed the dog with the help of the watering can, the dog shaking himself and wetting them both, which brought about much laughter. When Mr Brown was dry, he sat at Immi's feet and she reached down and ruffled his fur. 'Colly will be so jealous when he knows we have a dog. I can't wait to tell him.'

40

Jessie got up from her desk and as soon as she did so, Beaky Bird was on the alert, peering down her imperious nose and giving her a glacial stare. Jessie lifted her hands, wiggling her fingers to show the black ink from changing her typewriter ribbon. Miss Bird tutted.

'You should take more care, Miss Delaney. Anyone would think you get into a mess on purpose.' Jessie didn't blink. How well Miss Bird could see through her. With a flick of her head, she gave her permission to go wash her hands.

It was a relief to escape the stuffy room, the endless clatter of typewriter keys – a life to be endured, not enjoyed, and she spent the days thinking of ways to break the monotony of it. She looked forward to three things: lunch break, home time and Fridays.

Back at her desk, she glanced at the clock. Another hour until lunch. She placed a sheet of carbon between two sheets of paper and squinted at the shorthand notes given to her by Miss Bird, glanced up to see her watching her, smiled, and began to click away at her barely acceptable forty words per minute.

As soon as she was free to go, she dragged her cardigan from the back of her chair, collected her coat and bag and hurried around to the bus station in the marketplace. Her mood brightened when she spied Eddie in his blue overalls, sitting on an upturned crate, his brown hair as unruly as always. His sandwich tin was open at his side and, seeing her, he placed it on his lap to make space for her.

She sank beside him, her shoulders sagging, unwrapped her sandwiches and stared at them.

'Another lovely morning, Jess?' He nudged her playfully with his elbow.

'Don't,' she said. 'It was grim.'

'Miss Bird no better?'

She shook her head. 'It's not Miss Bird, it's me.'

'Not got any shows this weekend?' He unscrewed the top from the flask at his feet and poured a cup of milky tea, handing it to her.

'Nothing until next month. A twenty-first over in Grimsby.' She sipped; the tea was hot and sweet and it soothed. The party was almost six weeks away. Since Ginny had left in February she'd managed to get to sing at a couple of parties, birthdays and anniversaries, mostly because of Jack and Audrey Holland's connections. She'd put a small advert in the local paper but there was a lot of competition from established locals and until she got herself known it was difficult. Her endeavours to get work in the clubs had been fruitless. She had traipsed in and out of so many of them, plucking up courage each time to ask, only to be told that Frank Parker handled all the bookings. He had it all wrapped up and she wondered now whether to go back and sign the contract.

'It takes time to get known. I suppose people haven't got spare cash.' He grinned. 'You can sing for Harry and his chaps when you go to celebrate him getting his wings. There's bound to be a party.'

'He's still worried he won't pass.'

'Harry will walk it. You know he will.'

A part of her didn't want him to. She'd rather he be safe on the ground than in the air, being shot at. There had been fighting over the sea, reports of planes coming down off the coast – of accidents. Oh, Harry. She hadn't been able to pluck up the courage to talk to him and the more she thought about it the more she realised she couldn't put a damper on his celebrations. She had arranged to take the Friday off, without pay, much to Miss Bird's annoyance, to celebrate with him. She was so proud of him. It seemed everyone was making something of their lives and she was stuck in a hole.

'Wish I could come with you,' Eddie said. 'Ask him if he's been up in a Bristol Beaufort yet. I know he was hoping to get into Coastal Command. Wouldn't it be smashing luck if he was posted to North Coates? You won't forget to ask, will you, Jess?'

'I wouldn't dare.' She returned his cup and began rewrapping her half-eaten sandwich.

'Aren't you going to eat that?'

'Do you want it?'

He grinned and she handed it over. He made short work of it. He pulled out a folded sheet of paper from his pocket. 'A letter. For Harry. Will you put it in with yours to save on a stamp?'

She stared at the greasy marks left by his fingers and looked at him. He drew his hand across his mouth, wiping away the crumbs. 'What? Harry will know it's from me.'

She gave a small laugh as she walked away. With the ink from her fingers and the grease from Eddie, Harry was certain to know who they were from. As she turned onto St Peter's Avenue, someone called her name and she turned, delighted to see Jack Holland. He was smiling broadly, and she felt her spirits lift. A booking? She stopped and he came towards her. 'I was hoping to bump into you or your mother. How is she, by the way?'

'Busy.' She told him of her mother's WVS work, which she slotted around her dressmaking – or was it the other way around? It was hard to tell these days.

'And her health?' His concern was genuine. He had known her father when they were in France during the Great War and since making her acquaintance had kept a watchful eye on her progress.

'Much improved. Her cold was just that, a cold. It didn't go to her chest. The sea air agrees with her.'

'And you? How are you getting on at Foster and Fox?'

'Oh, I'm hardly their star secretary.'

Jack grinned. 'But then there's not where your star is meant to shine.' She nodded, checking her watch, conscious that she would be late and give Beaky something else to moan about. Understanding, he said, 'Let me walk with you.' They got into step, and he talked as they walked.

'I wanted to let you know the Empire will be opening again.'

She stopped, her eyes wide with excitement.

'No, not like that, Jessie. More's the pity.' Deflated, she continued walking. 'The NAAFI are about ready to open it up for the forces. They've removed the seats and rearranged things to suit them. The chappie in charge told me that the WVS are going to take over the refreshments and I suggested they should perhaps put on some entertainment.' She stopped again and he placed his hand to her back and moved her forward. 'I don't want to be responsible for you getting a black mark.'

She grinned. 'A black mark and a black look.'

'That's the spirit. Things are never as bad as they seem.' They stopped at the kerb and crossed the road. There was a queue outside the butcher's and one of the cleaners from the Empire called hello, which they acknowledged as they passed, Jessie tapping her watch and miming her hurry.

'I also suggested that a singalong on Sunday evenings would go down well. It was something your father and I organised in the Great War. Always a morale booster for the lads.' He was suddenly quiet, and she didn't interrupt, but waited for him to break the spell of his own thoughts. Her father had been the same, given to sudden bouts of reflection, paralysed until the memory had run its course. He smiled at her, back in the moment. 'They're planning to open up on 6 May. I put you forward to start things off for the first few Sundays. I hope you don't mind?'

'Mind!' Delighted, she clenched her fists to stop herself from hugging him. 'Oh, Jack. Thank you so much. Thank you, thank you.' She stopped at the front door of the office and checked her watch. Two minutes late. Beaky would be on the warpath, but suddenly Miss Bird didn't seem so bad, the day not so long. There was finally something good to look forward to.

41

Frances replaced the telephone handset on the cradle after talking with Johnny, her mouth suddenly dry. 'Everything all right?' Mrs Frame asked as she walked into the kitchen.

She processed Mrs Frame's words, wondering how to answer. Imogen was sitting on a rug by the range reading a story to Mr Brown, who rested his head on her lap. Neither paid any attention to her. 'You look troubled.' Mrs Frame stopped scraping potatoes, and wiped her hands on her apron. 'Is Mr Johnny well?'

The question confused her and then, realising that Mrs Frame had an idea that something awful had happened, she nodded. 'Yes, he's well. It's his aunt.' She pulled out a chair from the kitchen table and sank down onto it.

'Let me brew a cuppa. You look like you need one. The leaves will run to another pot.' Mrs Frame filled the teapot and put a cup and saucer in front of her, took one for herself, sat down beside her and poured the tea. Frances blew over her cup. 'Is there a problem? With Mr Johnny's aunt?'

Frances sipped the hot tea and leaned against the chair back. 'There is. Aunt Hetty has taken in refugees from the low countries.

She has a house full of Belgians, a family sleeping in her sitting room until something else can be found for them.'

'I heard. On the wireless. Poor devils, leaving with what they can carry. The German forces are very close.'

Frances nodded; what were her difficulties when compared to theirs? Leaving home and not knowing when they could go back, or if there was anything to go back to. She looked Mrs Frame in the eye. 'Ruby leaves hospital tomorrow.'

Mrs Frame took a sip of her tea and nodded, understanding. Frances went on. 'I've packed her belongings and sent them on.'

'Can you get them back?'

'I doubt it. They'll have to arrive in Dorset and be sent back again. Heaven knows how long that will take.'

'You're a similar size,' Mrs Frame offered.

'We are.' They could share, and she didn't mind that at all, in the circumstances, but she doubted Ruby would be agreeable. By the look on her face, Mrs Frame was of the same opinion.

'Dearie me, what a to-do. And we have a Wren arriving tonight. I don't rightly know how long she'll be here for and I've put her in Miss Ruby's room.'

Frances drank her tea. She could cope with one night of drama but the thought of living with Ruby, even if she were fully well, would undoubtedly be a challenge. She thought again of the refugees. They were the lucky ones; she would make Ruby have no doubt as to that.

The following morning, Frances waited in the hospital corridor for Ruby, having already talked with the consultant. He was apologetic at discharging her, but the hospital was short-staffed, and every bed needed. The Randolphs' money was no cushion in war and much of it had been spent on Ruby's care in the past few months. 'It's time Miss Randolph went out into the real world and stopped hiding. I think it best.' Best for who he didn't say.

A door further down the corridor opened and Ruby stepped out, a nurse beside her carrying a suitcase, which she handed to Frances with a smile heavy with sympathy. Ruby had not endeared herself to the staff while she was in their care. She was much improved, but she was still dull and grey, her eyes bereft of any sparkle they might once have possessed. The two of them walked out to the waiting car that Grace had organised through the WVS. One of its members had petrol for such occasions and she smiled warmly and got out to open the back door for Ruby. Ruby didn't return it and Frances was already irritated as she fastened Ruby's case to the parcel shelf at the back and got in beside her.

As the car pulled up outside the house, Ruby got out and went inside, without a word of thanks to the driver. Frances unfastened the suitcase, apologising for her sister-in-law's bad manners. 'Not your fault,' the woman replied kindly. 'We all have our cross to bear.'

Ruby was already at the top of the stairs when Frances walked through the front door. 'Wait, Ruby. There have been some changes since you've been away.'

She twisted, giving her a withering stare. 'I haven't been away. I've been *ill*.'

Frances shot up the stairs after her, but not fast enough to stop her. Ruby had already opened the door to reveal the Wren stretched out on the bed, reading a map.

'Who the hell are you?'

The girl swung her legs over the bed but didn't get up. 'I might ask the same question.'

Frances bit her cheek. Good for her; that was exactly the way to respond to Ruby. 'I'm sorry, Rachel. This is Ruby's room, but she's been... ill.' Ruby glared at her. 'We weren't expecting you,' Frances told her, 'and it was too late to inform the billeting officer.'

The girl got to her feet. 'Should I move?'

'No, get some rest. I'm sorry we disturbed you.' She forced Ruby out onto the landing and closed the door behind them. 'Why couldn't you have waited?'

'Where are my things?' Ruby demanded. 'You can put them all back when that girl has gone.'

Frances was incensed. '*That girl* has travelled over a hundred and fifty miles on a motorbike to deliver important documents for the admiralty; she had to ride in pouring rain and didn't get here until the early hours. She needs rest before she starts the journey back. And we are going to let her get that rest. You can have my room for tonight. I'll get Mrs Frame to make up the small bed in the box room and Imogen and I can sleep there.' At the mention of Imogen, Ruby lost some of her fire.

'Doesn't Imogen have a bed of her own?'

'She gave it up. She sleeps with me. Natalie has that room. Another girl who works in the naval offices. It's our way of doing our bit.'

Mrs Frame was waiting at the bottom of the stairs. Frances saw her reach for Ruby's case.

'I'll do that, Mrs Frame. If it's not too much trouble, I'm sure we could all benefit from something to eat and a hot drink. Ruby?'

Frances went down the stairs and fetched the case while Ruby waited on the landing for her return. Frances opened the door to what had been Johnny's room and was now hers and Imogen's and placed the case on the floor beside the chest of drawers. She opened the window. It was almost the end of April and the blossom on the cherry trees in the park quite beautiful. On some days it was hard to remember there was a war on. 'Mrs Frame has changed the sheets. I've taken what Imogen and I need to see us over until your room is free. We'll be downstairs when you're ready.'

In the kitchen, Mrs Frame picked up the teapot and poured

Frances a cup then one for herself. 'Should I take one up to Miss Ruby?'

'No, she'll come down soon enough.' Mrs Frame looked uncomfortable. 'Believe me, Mrs Frame, I know Ruby of old. It's no good being weak; she'll walk all over us.'

They heard Ruby come downstairs and go into the sitting room, opening doors and closing them. She eventually joined them in the kitchen. 'Where are my things? Surely not in my room, with that girl.'

'Your things are quite safe, and you'll have them tomorrow,' Frances said calmly, then kindly, 'Sit down, Ruby. Have something to eat with us.'

She remained in the doorway. 'I want them now.'

Frances pushed a sandwich in front of an empty chair. 'If I could get them for you I would.' She looked at Ruby and wondered how best to help her. It was going to be difficult for both of them, learning to live with each other after so much had divided them. But there was enough conflict in the world without her adding to it and no matter how much Ruby irritated, with her demands and dramas, it must have been a shock to come home and find all her belongings missing, someone else in her room. Replaced. 'We put them on a train to Dorset,' Frances explained, 'so that they would be there when you arrived. We had no idea that Aunt Hetty would not be able to take you.'

'Take me! Like a parcel. Why not just stick me in a trunk and be done with it!'

Frances let out a long sigh. 'We weren't to know. I called the station as soon as I knew you were coming home. They've intercepted them at King's Cross. Mr Frame will arrange for them to be collected in the morning.' Frances poured a cup of tea and set it beside the sandwich.

Ruby pulled out the chair and sat down. 'You've made yourself very comfortable here by the looks of things.'

'I've tried to, Ruby.'

'Oh, I bet you have. First you take Johnny, then you take my place in the show – and now you've taken over the house. I saw you gloating when he came to tell me you were married.'

'Now listen here.' Frances could barely conceal her irritation. Mrs Frame got up to leave. She didn't want to make the woman uncomfortable for the world but if she let Ruby get away with it once there'd be no end to it. Mrs Frame went into the back garden. 'I did no such thing. I was the one who made Johnny come to tell you. He should have told you sooner. As for the show, Jack wanted to keep the cast in work. They were thinking of others, unlike you.' She took a deep breath. 'If you don't like it, go somewhere else with your self-pity. I don't want it in my house.'

'It's not *your* house.'

'Our house. My home. Imogen's home.' She softened her tone. 'If anyone should feel aggrieved, it's her.' She could scarcely keep her temper, and if the house had been empty she doubted she would have. But she would not allow Ruby to derail her. Her stance seemed to have worked for Ruby didn't say any more and, looking at her, Frances felt a sliver of shame for speaking to her so harshly. But pandering to her wouldn't work; it never had. She had talked it over with Grace, who had been in full agreement. Frances had to be strong and firm but not without kindness. Ruby's outburst had been nothing more than a tantrum a child would have at not getting their own way. They ate in silence, Ruby nibbling at the soft edges of the sandwich, and presently Mrs Frame came inside, followed by Imogen and Mr Brown.

The child stopped, and scrutinised Ruby. 'You're the lady with the sparkly brooch. I've seen you before.' She walked towards her. 'You're my auntie Ruby, aren't you? Are you better now? Mummy said you've been very poorly.' Ruby looked at the dog and Imogen followed her gaze. 'Say hello, Mr Brown. Paw.'

The dog held up his paw and Ruby gingerly took hold of it with two fingers, shook it up and down, then rubbed her fingers on her dress. Imogen climbed onto a chair to sit at the table and the dog lay at her feet. Mrs Frame placed a slice of bread and jam in front of her and Imogen took it and began to eat.

'Mr Brown's an odd name for a dog,' Ruby said, peering at the animal under the table.

'It's because he's sad. Like the man who lives next door to Auntie Patsy.' She looked at Ruby, tilting her head to one side. 'You're sad too, aren't you?' Ruby sat upright. 'Because Daddy went away again. It made everyone sad. But I've got Mr Brown now because I haven't got Colly.'

'Who's Colly?'

Mrs Frame gave Imogen a glass of squash and she took a long gulp before answering. 'He's in my other family. I stay with them when Mummy goes to work but she doesn't have to do that any more, do you, Mummy?' Frances shook her head. 'Did you and Daddy have a dog when you were little?'

'We didn't have any pets.' They didn't have any friends either. Always on the road, hanging around theatres and boarding houses, their friends the other acts in the show, most of them older, resentful of two kids getting above them on the bill. She missed him. Her time in hospital had been the longest they'd ever been apart, and it had made her more aware of the enormous gulf that lay between them, not just in distance, but in their relationship. There were bridges to build but she had no idea how to start, how to find her way back. 'We were working.' There had been no time for love or affection. And, sitting at the table, Ruby saw what she had missed, and all that she would never have. But what had the child meant? 'Who is your other family?'

'Auntie Patsy, and Bobby, and Colly. She's not my real auntie, not like you. When Mummy went away, I lived at their house. I had my own bed and Mummy came to see me on Sundays but now she doesn't have to go away again.'

'That's a lot better.' It was increasingly difficult to keep talking. The child didn't mean to make her feel uncomfortable, she knew that, her questions so innocent. It was Frances who had suffered, and Ruby could not look at her, or at Mrs Frame. Shame rushed over her in a huge wave, and she felt she might drown.

'It is,' Imogen said happily. She had jam in the corner of her mouth and her little tongue wiggled about to lick it away. In the end she pushed it in with her finger and took another bite. She rushed to eat, obviously wanting to say something else but her mother told her to empty her mouth of food first. Mrs Frame got up from the table and left them alone.

'Daddy was sad when he went away.'

'Was he?'

'I was sad too.' She went very quiet.

'He will come back again soon,' Frances reassured her. Ruby prayed with all her heart that he would. That he would be safe for however long this war lasted. She couldn't bear that little girl to have to live a life without him.

That night, Frances tucked Imogen up in bed and Mr Brown settled on the floor at her feet. She listened as Imogen said her prayers, her eyes shut, hands pressed together. She asked for God to watch over them all and added, 'And God bless Auntie Ruby and make her not sad any more. Amen.' She opened her eyes and sat up, reaching down to give the dog one last rub. 'Do you think Mr Brown can make Auntie Ruby happy like he makes me?'

'Let's hope so.' Frances leaned forward and kissed her, doubting very much the dog would make any difference. She got up and the animal let out a low groan as it settled itself. 'Don't let Mr Brown on the bed, Immi. You know how cross it makes Mrs Frame.' Imogen closed her eyes to avoid answering, and when Frances came upstairs later Mr Brown was lying on top of the bed, just where she'd expected him to be. The dog grumbled when she nudged him onto the floor, and she pulled back the blankets and got into bed beside her daughter. She leaned over her and whispered into her ear, 'Daddy sends kisses and says "Sweet dreams, darling." And so do I.'

Across the hall, Ruby lay fully clothed on top of Frances's bed. On the ottoman set in front of the bay window there was a doll with long brown hair, a small selection of story books and a game of snakes and ladders. A childhood. Images floated into her head, of untying a red ribbon from a big white box, lifting the lid to find a doll, much bigger than the one in front of her. Of happiness and delight. The window was open a little and she heard an owl hoot across in the park. The house was different to when she had left it, that night when she went to the Palace, angry that Frances had taken everything from her – her brother and her career – not even considering what she had taken from Frances. She wasn't quite sure what it was. It was just a feeling, something she couldn't quite identify. It felt calm and still. It felt like a home.

42

They had taken out the seats from the stalls of the Empire, but they hadn't removed the heart of it. Jessie could still feel it beating, albeit faintly. The boxes were still there, the gold ornate carving about them perhaps a little shabbier, but the curved seating of the dress circle was intact. She stood up there, peering down below at the tables and chairs that now filled the space, where only last summer the audience had roared with laughter at the comedian Billy Lane, had marvelled at the acrobatics of the Duo D'Or and been enchanted by songstress Madeleine Moore. Ghosts, now, that slipped through the cracks of the days, much as her dreams had. She pushed down the red plush seat and leaned on the rail. It had been on the stage below that she'd taken her first steps at a solo career less than a year ago. The presence of her father about her was almost as strong as it had been when he was alive, encouraging her as he'd always done. Had she let him down? Below her milled a hundred or more lads in army serge, playing cards and dominoes, reading newspapers, writing letters to their girl. Was Harry writing to her too? She heard footsteps on the bare boards behind her and turned to see Jack Holland, who took a seat next to her.

'Nervous?'

'Always.'

'That's how it's meant to be. You wouldn't give of your best otherwise.'

Her father had said the same. Nerves were fear and excitement intermingled.

'Bernie was asking about you.' Bernie Blackwood was in business with Jack and Johnny Randolph. The two older men, realising that war was imminent, had invested in three theatres, knowing that people would want to forget their troubles and worries and search for something to get them through the bad times.

'Was he?' She didn't want to sound excited, lest Jack push her forward, and she wasn't ready, not until she had spoken to Harry. It was a conversation she'd had in her head so many times since speaking with Frances but not one she'd had with him. She'd tried to write, erasing word after word in an effort to express herself, failing miserably.

'There's work for you, Jessie – you only have to say the word.' He placed his arm on the back of his seat and twisted to face her. 'You know, Jessie. There are many ways to play our part in war and conflict. Music soothes the savage beast, and all that.'

She peered over the brass rail and grinned at him. 'They don't look too beastly.'

Jack smiled at her small attempt at levity. 'They will be, when their time comes. Now, they're just bored, waiting for something to happen.'

'Like me?'

He sat back in his seat again, folding his hands. 'You're not waiting, though, are you? More holding back.'

She felt her cheeks burn. Was it so obvious? Unsure of how to reply, she kept quiet.

Jack leaned forward. 'Don't worry. It's not noticeable to every-one, only the people who love and care for you.'

'Has Mum been talking?'

'She didn't have to.' Below them there were shouts and slapping of the table as the cardplayers finished their game, chairs being pushed back on the wooden floor, doors banging shut as they made their way to the bar that was now a place where refreshments of the non-alcoholic kind were served. Her mother was there, with other women from the WVS. The bar had been emptied of alcohol and they now served hot meals and hot drinks.

'Your mother is playing her part. I know serving tea and soup might not seem to be an important part of winning this war, but it is. Keeping spirits up with food, a kind word, a song...' She looked to him, hoping to draw from his confidence in her. If she could only talk to her father, but she couldn't – and Jack was the nearest thing she had.

'I'm struggling. What I want seems so... frivolous. It's not a time for dreaming any more, is it, when so much is at stake?' It had been a sobering week. Mr Chamberlain had resigned, and Mr Churchill had become prime minister. The British had failed to liberate Norway and the Germans were advancing on Belgium, Holland and Luxembourg. Closer to France, closer to the Channel, to England. The mood in the offices of Foster and Fox had changed, as they had everywhere else; people talked of nothing else.

'Don't underestimate how important entertainment is, Jessie. How much it means to these boys. Your father and I felt the differ-ence, actually felt it.' He was remembering and she watched his expression change as he did so, his jaw setting hard. 'When you're knee deep in mud, and God knows what else, cold and wet, and far from home, then anything that transports you back there, helps you forget, even for a short while, is so precious. So very welcome.' His face changed again, and he smiled at her, his eyes expressing his warmth, his support for her. It had been a wonderful day when he walked into her life – or rather she had walked into his, when she'd got work at the Empire. Anger had got her there: anger at her aunt Iris, who wanted them all to fit into a life that wasn't suited, like a straitjacket. She understood that stability was what her mother needed, to catch her breath after Dad died, but that way of living was so wrong for them. Grace was much happier here, as was Eddie – so why did she feel like she was in a straitjacket again?

Jack looked over his shoulder as the approaching sound of childish chatter grew louder. Miss Taylor's juveniles came up the stone stairs and assembled along the rear of the dress circle, outdoor coats covering their costumes, the froth of yellow tulle skirts bursting out at the bottom. Peggy was at the back, keeping the younger girls in order and she grinned when she saw Jessie and gave her a small wave. Jessie was pleased to see her. You couldn't stay glum while Peggy was around. 'Ah, the cavalry has arrived,' Jack said, getting to his feet. Jessie followed him. Miss Taylor's juveniles were instructed to settle down in the seats of the back row and wait. There was much pushing and shoving as they fought to sit next to their friends and Jessie bit back a smile as Peggy took charge.

'Control yourselves. This is a *theatre*. You're not here to play and be silly.' She lifted her chin to Jessie, proud at how quickly they had settled, and walked along the row in front of them like a sergeant major inspecting her troops.

Jack shook Miss Taylor's hand and Jessie introduced herself again in case Miss Taylor needed reminding that she had been in the panto.

'I must apologise again for asking the children to come along in their costumes,' Jack explained. 'All the dressing rooms are being used for storage and the WVS ladies are using the larger ones for donations.'

'No need, Mr Holland. It's worked out rather well. Most of the children don't live too far away. And there's less for them to lose. There's always a shoe or a sock missing.'

'Is there anything you need? We've managed to bring in a few local musicians who are too old for service this time and are happy to play for you.'

'That won't be necessary. Miss Evans, our pianist, will be along shortly.'

'Then if you don't mind the children waiting up here, I'll get Jessie here to come and get them when it's their turn to go on.' His remark elicited an eruption of excited chatter, which Miss Taylor silenced with a glare. 'We have a couple of other local acts, a magician, a couple of boys who do a Flanagan and Allen act. They're very good. I think the lads will enjoy it.' Jessie remembered the Lister Brothers winning the talent show last autumn. At least they were still working towards their stab at stardom.

While they were talking, Frances joined them, slipping off her coat and draping it over the seats in front. Jessie hadn't seen much of her these last weeks, both of them busy with their own lives now, but it was so good to see her friend again. Jack ended his conversation with Miss Taylor and came over to Frances, kissed her cheek, asked how she was. As Johnny's wife, her relationship with Jack had changed. She was no longer an employee; her husband was Jack's partner and Jessie felt a gap between them that hadn't been there before. Frances had moved on and she was still treading water.

'I've just seen your mum. I said I'd pop down again once I'd said hello.'

'I'll come with you.' Jessie checked with Jack that she wasn't needed.

'I'm sure we can rely on Peggy to keep order,' he said, loud enough for the girl to hear and she seemed to grow an inch or two at his words.

Grace was at the tea urn, her back to them as they walked into the bar. Some of the boys cheered when they walked in, one or two whistled, one stepped forward, fancying his chances. 'Down, boy,' Frances said as his mate dragged him back. Grace turned at the commotion.

'I might have guessed,' she said, smiling. 'Do you want a drink, girls?'

She filled two white mugs from an oversized metal teapot and pushed them forward. Frances sipped. 'Oh, that's grand, Grace. It actually tastes like tea.'

Grace had a word with her colleague, who took over, then she came the other side of the counter and joined them at a table. 'How are you, Frances? And Imogen? Is she more settled?'

She told them of the dog. 'I doubt anyone will claim him.'

Grace agreed.

'I was rather hoping they would, to begin with, but she's so attached to him, it would be dreadful if they did.' She told them how unsettled Imogen had been at the house before the dog's arrival. 'I knew she'd miss Patsy's boys and everyone at Barkhouse Lane; I just didn't realise how much.'

'Are there no little friends about?' Jessie asked. Barkhouse Lane was always full of kids, playing hopscotch and skipping with ropes, the lads kicking a ball up and down.

'Not that I know of. It's her birthday next week. I'm having a little party for her. Patsy's bringing her boys and Mrs Frame is going to bring three of her younger grandchildren.' She couldn't hold back her smile. 'And Johnny has three days' leave. I'm hoping that he'll arrive in time for it.'

'Oh, that will be marvellous for you all,' Jessie said.

'I haven't told Imogen. Anything could happen and I'd hate for her to be disappointed.'

'Very wise,' Grace added, then, smiling, said, 'The fates must be smiling upon you all at last.'

Frances agreed. 'I'm hoping that he and Ruby will be able to do a little fence mending while he's home.'

'She's not causing you any problems?' Grace ventured.

'Not as such.' Frances told them how morose she was, how she sat in the chair or the garden watching, not joining in, kept out of the away if any of the lodgers were around. 'She hasn't left the house.'

'What, not even for a walk?' Jessie was amazed.

Frances shook her head.

'It's possibly very frightening, to be back in the middle of life's comings and goings after being shut away from it so long,' Grace suggested.

Frances agreed. 'It'll take time. And she's got plenty of that.' She checked her watch. 'Which you haven't, Miss Delaney. You'd best go and get yourself ready. These boys will be waiting for you.'

Miss Taylor's juveniles opened the show and were greeted with polite applause. The lads loved the Lister Brothers' Flanagan and Allen routine and roared with laughter at the comedian. Jessie waited in the wings with Jack.

'Don't hold anything back, Jessie. Give them everything you've got – and enjoy yourself.' He stepped out onto the stage and introduced her. The band played the first few bars of her opening song and she took a deep breath and stepped out to take centre stage.

Her nerves melted away as soon as she opened her mouth to sing, as she knew they would. The spotlight fell on her and she was suddenly aware of that missing piece of her sliding into place. She sang to the boys, boys who would be on the front soon enough, fighting for girls like her, for their sweethearts and wives, their sisters and mothers. Her heart soared, and she stared beyond the lights and up into the dress circle where she felt her father was looking down on her. She sang song after song, and as she held the last note, the boys were on their feet, applauding, whistling; Jack brought her back on, announcing that Jessie would lead the singalong and for them to join in. The house lights were switched on and she could see their faces, all the way to the back of the auditorium. Some of them were on their feet to see her better and she stepped down from the stage and walked among them, singing the whole time, touching a hand, an arm here and there. Their smiles were the greatest of rewards and at last she understood that this was what she must do. She made her way back to the steps and, unbidden, Peggy stepped up with her. Jessie shared the microphone then stood to one side for Peggy to have it alone. The lads laughed and whistled as she winked and blew kisses their way. When Jessie stepped beside her, she whispered, 'Cheers, Jessie. I loved every bit of that.'

The tempo changed and Jessie began the first line of 'Keep the Home Fires Burning'. The room quietened, the lads hushing each other as she sang, then they joined in, voices low so that they could still hear her clear voice ringing out, over their heads and up into the gods. She had the strangest sensation of her father being with her, beside her, above her, around her, and she knew, just knew that this was what she had to do. To sing. To entertain. Jack was still in the wings, watching, and he smiled and nodded, knowing that at last she had realised that what he'd said was true. That he believed in the power of music, and he believed in her. What had he said earlier? That he had *felt* it, that her dad had felt it – just as she was feeling it now. The doors at the back of the stalls opened and Grace came through, followed by Eddie. She'd wanted so much more for them all, a home of their own, their own front door, a garden. She would never get it staying here. And even though there would be difficult conversations ahead, finally she knew what she needed to say to Harry.

43

Frances, Ruby and Imogen were in the sitting room at the front of the house listening to the Forces Programme and Mrs Frame was in the kitchen making fruit jellies. Patsy had phoned that morning to say that she'd managed to get fresh cream from the local farm in Waltham and had enough sugar to make some ice cream for tomorrow's party, which had been met with whoops of delight from the birthday girl. Frances was on her knees, wrapping a whip and top in multiple sheets of newspaper ready for a game of pass the parcel, and Imogen was beside her ready with her index finger to hold the string in place while her mother tied a bow. Mr Brown's ears pricked up at the click of the garden gate. He gave a long growl, then ran to the window and barked. Imogen followed, standing on her tiptoes to look out.

'It's a man,' she said, then quickly turned, her voice high with excitement, her eyes wide. 'It's Daddy!' She ran out of the room, Mr Brown at her heels, and Frances got up from the floor.

'I'm glad he made it,' Ruby said. 'For Imogen.'

'For all of us, Ruby. It's wonderful to have him home.'

Outside, Johnny held Imogen in his arms, his bag at his feet, Mr Brown barking and jumping up at him, Johnny trying to push him away from his leg, father and daughter laughing. Imogen leaned down to the dog.

'Stop it, Mr Brown. This is my daddy. He's come home for my birthday.'

Frances rushed towards him and Johnny opened his free arm to bring her into his embrace. She looked up at him and touched his face. It was so glorious to feel his skin, taste his kisses. She stole another. 'God, Frances. I can't tell you what a sight for sore eyes you are.'

'Have you got sore eyes, Daddy? Mrs Frame will make them better.'

Johnny smiled. 'I think Mummy can do that all by herself. Later.' He kissed her again, looked towards the house and smiled. Frances followed his gaze and saw Ruby at the window, watching them, Johnny between his wife and child, together again.

'You two been getting along?' he asked as he picked up his bag and they walked to the front door.

'Well enough,' Frances told him. 'It's been two weeks since she arrived, early days, but I think she's improved a little. Slow progress – but it's progress in the right direction.'

He put Imogen down and she ran into the house shouting for Mrs Frame. 'Daddy's home and he's got poorly eyes.'

They smiled at her excitement, then at each other as they stepped up onto the porch and the open door. He put his bag just inside the hall, then took her in his arms and kissed her, and she wanted to hold on to that moment forever and never let it end. She could hear Imogen running from the kitchen to hall, the dog's claws on the tiles as he followed her, then into the sitting room, chattering to Auntie Ruby.

He gave her a small kiss, squeezing her. 'We'd better go in.' And, reluctantly, she let him release her and they went into the house. Frances let him go ahead of her, into the sitting room, and waited by the door as he went over to Ruby, slowly at first, cautious, then more quickly and took her hand, kissing her cheek. Frances could see that she was sullen again and she put her hand out to take Imogen away into the kitchen to talk to Mrs Frame about Daddy's eyes.

* * *

Ruby looked little improved since the last time he'd seen her, at the hospital. She'd been there almost four months. He felt guilty that he'd been away and left her care to Frances but there'd been no alternative. Aunt Hetty had been most apologetic, but she had also been firm. 'Ruby will not solve her problems by running away from them, and neither will you.' But he hadn't been running away, had he? He'd been called away, to fight, and yet he'd rather be here fighting. It couldn't be easy for Frances, finding herself nursemaid to Ruby. Although in her letters Frances had said that Ruby did little other than drift about the house.

'How are you, Ruby? Feeling better?'

'Glad to be out of that hateful hospital.' She dropped down into a chair. Her fingers were long and thin, with little flesh on them, like the rest of her. 'I suppose it suited you, having me just where you wanted me. Locked up.'

'You weren't locked up, Ruby.' She so easily could have been; if it hadn't been for Grace's intervention and guidance, they might have gone down a different path altogether.

'It might have been better if I had.'

* * *

They went to bed early, and remained there as long as they could but not as long as they wanted. At seven o'clock, Imogen rushed excitedly into the bedroom and jumped on the bed, Mr Brown following suit. 'It's my birthday. And I'm four! I'm a big girl now.' They wished her happy birthday, and while she snuggled next to her daddy, tucked inside his arm, Frances got out of bed and brought the presents from under it. Imogen unwrapped a post office set and a Mr Bull printing outfit. Simple pleasures, with none of the extravagance that her father would have succumbed to, and she sat between them, admiring the miniature stamps and envelopes, the writing paper with the fairies in the corner and flowers around the edge. 'I'll be able to write lovely letters to you now, Daddy. I've even got stamps.'

Frances smiled at him. 'I'll make sure I post them myself.'

* * *

The invites were for one o'clock and when Mrs Frame and three of her younger grandchildren arrived at the front door, Ruby thought it time to disappear – yet Imogen had other ideas. 'This is my auntie Ruby,' the child announced as the children huddled shyly by Mrs Frame, their eyes taking in the grandness of their surroundings.

'And this is Ann, Betty and Sidney.' Mrs Frame nudged the children further into the hall as other guests started to arrive.

'Pleased to meet you,' Ruby said kindly. Mrs Frame gave the tallest one a nudge and they wished Imogen a happy birthday in unison and handed their gift over to her. She gave them her grateful thanks and showed them into the sitting room, the perfect hostess. It made Ruby smile and she lost some of the apprehension she'd felt since she'd known of the party. Patsy arrived soon after with her two boys, Colly and Bobby, and Imogen hardly gave them time to get through the door before she dragged them off to meet Mr

Brown, who was under strict instruction to remain in the kitchen for the duration. Grace and Jessie arrived with their landlady, Geraldine, and greeted Ruby fondly, then went to find the birthday girl. Grace had made her a dress for her dolly and Olive had knitted an outfit for her doll. Grace gave Ruby a small hug and plenty of encouragement.

'Lovely to see you, Ruby. You look well, doesn't she, Johnny, much improved. Good to see you looking so well too. All that square-bashing not too much on the feet?'

'To tell you the truth, Grace, I'd rather dance day and night than do an hour of marching.'

In the dining room, the table had been pushed along one wall and the chairs placed around the other three. The children sat on the floor and Jessie played the piano as the children passed the parcel, the adults overseeing that no one held on to the parcel too long. It was quickly followed by musical statues, then musical chairs and Simon Says. After the games were over, the table was restored to its place in the centre of the room, the chairs too, and the children sat up to eat paste sandwiches and gasped at the treat of jelly and ice cream. Rations had been pooled and Mrs Frame had produced a small cake filled with jam. The adults drifted between the dining room and the kitchen, Ruby in and out of both, feeling uncomfortable wherever she was. Frances was at the sink washing cups while Patsy dried, Mrs Frame refilling a jug of squash, which she gave to Jessie. In the end Ruby took a chair in the window and watched the children as they ate, Jessie going between them, refilling their glasses. Johnny came in the room, looked about and, seeing her, came and sat beside her, and handed her a drink.

'Grace thought you might want a lemonade. It's hot in here – and noisy.'

She took a sip and they watched the children, chattering ten to the dozen, Mr Brown under the table alert for scraps, having sneaked out of the kitchen. Ruby smiled when she saw Imogen duck under the tablecloth and feed him a sliver of bread.

'We never had this,' she said to Johnny. 'Parties. Friends. We never had a childhood, did we, always moving around. Surrounded by grown-ups who probably hated us and thought we were spoiled.'

'We had parties. It was just different.'

'Daddy liked parties. Mother didn't, did she?'

'She was practical. Mother was different when Father was alive. She didn't have to think about earning money, only what she could spend it on. Father was the same. He wanted to spread it around. They'd come from nothing, got to the top through hard graft and Mother wanted to stay there when Father died.'

'She could have made it better. She could have made it fun. At least some of the time.'

'Can't you remember any good times, Ruby?' He wasn't angry with her, just confused. She could tell he recalled things differently to her.

'Vaguely. Mostly I remember the work. Rehearsing. Travelling.' That was what stuck out most in her mind. Work, not fun. Not like this. Mrs Frame's grandchildren had soon forgotten their inhibitions and all six children were delighting in each other's company, enjoying the party. 'Look at Imogen, how happy she is.' She looked to Frances. 'Frances is a wonderful mother. She's strong; she put her child first. And that's what makes the difference. Mother put fame and money before us.'

Johnny leaned forward, his hands resting on his knees. 'I used to think that, Ruby. But being away from everything gives a man plenty of time to think. I'm not a soldier; I'm out of my depth. The only thing I've ever had to fight for is a place higher up the bill and a better dressing room. Mother had had a taste of luxury and she didn't want to lose it. She didn't squander the money we earned, or use it for herself. She invested it. She made sure we wouldn't suffer from financial instability. They'd lived through one war, remember, and the Depression.'

Ruby watched the children, so at ease with each other. 'We might never suffer financial hardship, Johnny, but she made us suffer in other ways. Mother divided us.'

He nodded his agreement. 'But only if we let her.'

44

Music drifted out through the open windows of the sitting room at the house at Park Drive. The sofa and chairs had been moved to one side, along with the occasional tables, and the rug rolled up to the end of the room, Mr Brown on top of it. Imogen and Frances were dancing to the gramophone, performing pliés and jetés, Imogen a sprite as she threw her arms wide and skipped about. Frances went through her ballet movements, using the back of a dining chair as a barre. It felt good to stretch and move, and the rhythm and routine of it helped when her head was a muddle. Johnny's leave had been all too brief, and she lived with the very real fear that he would be posted to France, to join the troops trying valiantly to hold back the German advance.

Ruby came through the door and Imogen invited her to join in but she wouldn't. She slumped in a chair, her back to the window. When the record came to an end, Imogen flopped onto the floor beside her aunt. They were all feeling a bit deflated. When Johnny left, he took some of their joy with him.

'Care to join me, Ruby?' Frances bent forward, sweeping her

arm low then raising it as she pulled her torso long and lean, pointing her leg forward, her toes a perfect line.

'I don't know why you bother,' Ruby responded. 'You have no need to work any more.' Frances didn't stop, didn't feel the need to bite back. Ruby was unhappy and only Ruby could remedy that.

'I enjoy the discipline of it – and it makes me feel better in my mind as well as my body. And I've always done it.' None of them knew what the fates had in store, and she had to keep dancing whether there was an audience or not. She wanted to be prepared – just in case. Imogen chose another record and wound the handle with her mother's help, rested the needle in the groove, then picked up her doll and danced about with it. Shortly after, Mrs Frame came in, talking over the music and Frances stopped, removed the needle and swung back the arm.

'Mr Frame would like you to come and check what he's done so far.' She rolled her eyes. 'Gawd, men do like to have a bit o' praise when they've done a job, don't they? It's a good job I don't expect you to come and check the laundry while I'm doing it. We'd never get anything done.'

Frances laughed, agreeing, put the music back on for Imogen and followed Mrs Frame outside.

At the bottom of the garden, Ted Frame was finishing the floor of the Anderson shelter. They had delayed building one as the Randolphs hadn't planned to stay after the show was over but with Johnny called up, things had changed, and Frances thought it better late than never. When the shelters had first been distributed, not everyone had taken them, and those that had were teased as being windy. They had proved to be the sensible ones. The structure had been erected, the roof covered with turf to make it look part of the garden. Frances had given instructions for the lawn to be dug up when she moved in and the vegetable patch extended. They were growing as much as they could, sharing what they didn't need.

Tendrils of green beans were curling up the sticks Ted had placed along the back of the fence and the green leaves of the carrot tops and potatoes were leading the charge. Ted was standing by the open door, his cap pushed on the back of his head, his large hands covered with dried mud. He stood to one side to allow for her inspection.

'I put a couple of layers of bricks on the soil and then laid planks on the top. It's all right now, while the weather's good, but when it turns it'll be like a bog in there.'

'Good thinking, Mr Frame. It looks grand, so it does.'

He had made benches either side of the door and she placed her hand on them to test for stability, and stamped on the floor a couple of times to make a show for him. Mrs Frame smiled at her performance. 'We could add a few bottles of water, a tin of biscuits,' he said to his wife. 'Best to take cushions and pillows as you need 'em, otherwise they'll be cold and damp and neither use nor ornament.'

'I've already sorted that, Ted Frame. You stick to your job, and I'll keep to mine.'

He raised his eyebrows to Frances, who grinned at his wife's reprimand.

'It's grand, Mr Frame,' Frances said, interrupting what might turn into a minor battle. 'Let's hope we don't have cause to use it.'

Mr Frame grunted. 'Oh, I don't doubt you will. We all will. I heard on yon wireless that it's not looking good. Troops are on the march, trying to hold the lines in France. A young lad down our street copped it last week. God rest his poor soul.'

Frances shivered, despite the warmth of the day. It was as well to be prepared but she didn't want to dwell too long on what was happening overseas.

'I'm sure Imogen will want to come and look at the little tin house, as she calls it.' They'd all tried to make it sound fun and exciting, not wanting to frighten her if they had to hurry out to it in the night. But who knew how any of them would react when the time came. Frances prayed it never would.

Back in the house, the music was still playing, only this time it was 'Teddy Bears' Picnic'. Hearing Ruby's voice, Frances held back, peered around the door but didn't go in. Imogen was dancing and Ruby was clapping her hands, making twirling movements with her finger, directing Imogen to pirouette at certain points. Imogen obliged, was dizzy, fell down and the two of them burst into laughter. She couldn't remember hearing Ruby laugh, not ever. Imogen got up, ran over to Ruby and grabbed her hand, tugging her to her feet.

'Dance with me till Mummy comes back, Auntie Ruby,' Imogen insisted. Ruby hesitated but with a little more pestering from her niece, she went over to the gramophone and wound the handle, replaced the needle, took Imogen's hand and began to dance. Frances withdrew to the kitchen. She would leave them to it. Imogen had achieved what no one else had been able to do and for that she was thankful. Let Ruby enjoy it while she could.

45

Harry's blue Austin 7 was parked a little way from the bus stop in Grantham and Jessie's heart began to flutter when she spotted it. He was leaning against the door, pulling on a cigarette and as the bus came to a stop in front of him, he took one last drag, threw it onto the path and ground it out with his heel. He adjusted his cap, craned his neck, peering in the windows until he saw her, then grinned. Oh, his smile was everything; she had forgotten how wonderful it was and she wanted to barge through the line of people waiting to get off the bus. Instead, she tried her best to wait patiently for her turn, irritated when the old man in front chatted to the bus driver, holding them all up. Every minute was precious, and she wanted to spend it with him. As her turn came, Harry stepped in front of the door and reached out for her hand to guide her down.

She leaned forward and kissed his cheek, adjusting the basket on her arm, conscious of the other passengers about them. The old man went up to Harry and shook his hand. 'Good luck, son.' Harry thanked him and the man doffed his hat and went on his way. Jessie's heart twisted with a mixture of pride and fear at what his uniform represented. He took her basket from her and placed it on the back seat of his car. The passengers dispersed and the bus drove off, leaving them alone, and he put his arms about her waist and pulled her close. How she'd missed him, how she'd longed for him. He kissed her mouth, his lips warm, the familiar tang of tobacco on his tongue. She'd missed the smell of him, the feel of him.

'Oh, Harry.'

'Pilot Officer Harry, if you don't mind.' He flicked his hand over the wings that were sewn on his sleeve and she smiled and ran her hand over it, loving the touch of him; she put her hand to his dear face.

'Oh, darling Harry, well done. Well done. Although I knew you would pass. Didn't ever doubt it. Did you celebrate? Oh, of course you did. How's your head?'

'My head will be fine when you stop asking so many questions.'

He held the car door open for her as she got into the passenger seat then closed it behind her. Once he was in the driver's seat, he leaned over and kissed her away from prying eyes.

When he drew back as they came up for breath, she gripped his hand. 'It's like old times, isn't it, just you and I.' She thought back to when he'd driven her home from Uncle Norman's office on Wednesdays, when he came to help Eddie with his entrance exams after school. She felt another piercing shaft of guilt. As their only male relative, Eddie would likely have taken over Uncle Norman's practice, perhaps with Harry as senior partner, the two of them together. She could easily paint that picture in her mind, of the life she had robbed them of. 'Can we pretend the war never started – just for today?'

He turned the ignition and smiled at her. 'We can do anything we want – just for today.' It made her feel ashamed. How could she make him so unhappy when she loved him so much? Was she doing the right thing, choosing to do her bit by singing. She had thought about nothing else on the bus journey. She leaned across and kissed him again and as he drove off, leaving the market town behind, she held on to his hand, putting hers over his when he changed gear, not wanting to lose one second of touching him. Those carefree days before the war, before Harry signed up, before she left Holt, were so very far away and she longed for them now. Looking back, it had seemed so complicated, making the decision to leave, to try and make her way in the theatre, to provide a home for her mother and Eddie. The simplicity of it was now like a dream as she thought of what lay ahead.

'I know a smashing place where we can eat,' Harry said cheerfully. 'The landlord's a pal. Afterwards we can go for a little drive, as much as the petrol will stretch to.'

They drove down the high street of a small village, passing the post office, the petrol station, a butcher's, greengrocer's and newsagent. Entirely self-contained, it was the kind of place that appeared in books and magazines, that everyone dreamed of living in. It made her stomach flip, reminding her of The Beeches where she'd lived with her aunt and uncle. This way of life was not for her, and, in an odd way, it reassured her. At least she knew what she didn't want. Harry pulled the car to a stop outside a pub on the edge of the village and led her inside, the pair of them ducking beneath the low oak beams. There was a large stone fire opposite the bar, logs stacked inside the grate that would burn in winter, but not today when the sun was shining and all the windows flung open to let in the warmth. Harry introduced her to the landlord and his wife, a cheery couple who had heard all about her from Harry. Good things, she hoped. They enjoyed a lovely meal, seated by a low window, looking out into the gardens where ducks waddled freely, a pond beyond, a weeping willow dripping its branches to drink. It was all truly lovely but she was glad when they left and it was just the two of them again. Harry drove down country lanes and she wound down the window, loving the feel of the breeze in her hair and the sun on her face until he pulled up on the verge and they got out. He took her basket and a rug from the back of the car and led her into a field, up onto the higher ground. He pointed out the airfield in the distance and she squinted against the sun, her hands to her eyes, shielding until she could make out the planes, large and small. 'What type are they? I promised Eddie I'd ask.'

'And will you remember any of it?'

She grinned. 'You'll have to write it down.' She asked him about his days, and he told her as they spread out the blanket together. He removed his jacket, making it into a pillow for her.

'Things are hotting up, since Holland and Belgium fell. France will be next, unless the BEF can hold them off. Then they'll need air support. They can't get chaps like me through fast enough.' She tried not to look afraid. He rubbed his thumb down her jaw, and held her chin. 'Don't worry. You know I'd never take a risk. Not that kind, anyway.' It didn't make her feel any better.

They lay down, side by side, holding hands, faces warmed by the sun, talking about their lives, what had been happening back home in Cleethorpes. She tried to summon up the courage to tell him that she wanted to leave, to go to London, but she didn't want to spoil their one precious afternoon. He leaned over and kissed her, softly then greedily and she responded, loving the warmth of him, the weight of him. He put his hand inside her blouse, touched her breast, lowered his head and kissed her there and she didn't want to enjoy it as much as she did, but she loved him so much and it felt so good. He moved his hand further down and it shocked her. She pushed him away and sat up, flustered, her eyes beginning to water. She couldn't look at him. 'I can't, Harry. I can't.'

He sat up beside her, knees bent as she fastened her buttons. 'Forgive me, Jessie. I got carried away.'

She nodded. 'It's easy to get carried away.' She thought of Ginny, of Frances. 'It's not that I don't love you – I do...'

He reached for her hand. 'I'm sorry.'

How could she talk to him now, about her longing to sing, to entertain? How could she talk about morale when she had withdrawn from him?

'I want to wait. Until we're married. I don't want to be like...'

'I know,' he said, understanding, leaning across and kissing her gently on the mouth. 'God, Jessie Delaney, what you do to me.' His eyes were full of love, and she felt her own brim with tears, then fall on her cheeks. For a while they remained where they were, holding hands, neither of them knowing what to say to each other. Over in the airfield, a plane took off and soared with the birds and Jessie watched it come closer.

'Hurricane?'

'Lysander.' He grinned and it seemed to break the awkwardness between them. 'You'll never make a plane-spotter.' He put his arm about her and after a while she took out the flask and poured a tea.

'It's still hot.'

He took a sip, then handed it back to her. 'Save some for your journey home.'

'I will.'

He looked out over the landscape. 'About getting married?'

She lowered the cup.

Harry shifted uneasily. 'This is all going to sound so wrong now, after... well.' He sighed, shrugged and took a deep breath. 'What I'm going to say has nothing to do with what just happened between us.' He took her hand again and she felt panic rise in her chest. 'I know you're unhappy.'

'I'm not,' she protested.

He stopped her from saying any more. 'Darling, Jessie. It doesn't matter what you say; your letters tell me otherwise. When you went to Cleethorpes in the summer you were so excited, the words just spilled from the page, your happiness in every line. And though I missed you, yearned for you, I was so happy for you. You were passionate about what you were doing. You're not now. Your letters have lost their sparkle – and so have you.'

'I don't have much to talk about.' It was true, her life was not what it was, but that was the same for everyone.

'Let me speak, Jess.' He leaned back and put his arm about her. He looked so sad, and she was the cause of it. How could she do this to him? She loved him. She leaned her head on his shoulder.

'I didn't know what it was at first, what had changed. But when you came here with the girls, I watched you singing, and then I understood.' He paused. 'That's when you're fully you, Jessie, when you're singing. When you're not, it's as if a part of you is lost somewhere, and I don't have the power to find it. I wish I could.'

How well he knew her. 'It's been a lot of change, that's all.'

He put his fingers to her mouth. 'I don't want you to stop doing what you love. I don't want us to live our lives with you always wondering "what if". I'll know I stopped you.'

She took hold of his hand and kissed it. 'But you haven't...'

He shook his head. 'Let's hold things off a little. Follow your dreams, Jessie. Give it a year. If it's a mistake, you'll know.'

'And if it's not?'

'We'll know that too.' He lifted her hand to his lips, still clasped in his, and kissed her fingers. 'And we'll work something out.' He checked his watch. 'I need to get you back for your bus.' He got up, pulled her to her feet and they folded the blanket, and packed the basket. He slid his arms about her waist and pulled her to him. The sun was in her eyes and she put her hand up as a shield so she could see him.

'Jess, don't be mad at me for saying what I did. I've got my wings; I want you to soar too.'

'But, Harry...' Tears began to fall. She couldn't help it. This wasn't how she had expected it to be, not at all and yet... and yet here he was, setting her free. It was what she'd wanted.

He was chatty in the car going back to the bus station, but she hardly noticed how green the trees were, how full and heavy the May blossom was. He reached across for her hand. 'Sing to me. Like you did when we went to Cromer last summer, remember? "Grab your coat..."'

She couldn't find a song, couldn't sing a note; her throat felt tight with misery. He shook her hand, encouraging her, and she began to sing to him, only for him. He was the only man on earth who understood her enough to let her go and she loved him then more than she ever thought she could. He stopped the car, and they waited inside it for the bus to arrive. He twisted in his seat to her.

'You know, when you came here and sang to the lads, it wasn't only you who was transformed; they were too. For that time, what was it, an hour or so, and after, when you were chatting to the chaps, they forgot they were fighting a war, forgot they were tired. For days afterwards it was all they talked about.' He looked up as the bus pulled up to the stop. 'Don't stop singing, promise me?'

She couldn't speak, couldn't find the words to say all she had wanted to say – and she had no idea when they would be together again. He tapped his pocket. 'I have your picture here with me, at all times, close to my heart, Jess. That's where you always are.'

He kissed her full and hard on the mouth and she threw her arms about his neck, not caring if the passengers could see her. It didn't matter any more. He pulled away and got out and went around and opened her door. It was with a leaden heart that she got out and took one last kiss.

He waited while she got on the bus and found a seat, and ran along by it as it drew off, making scribbling movements with his hands, urging her to write. And she smiled and nodded as the tears fell. The bus picked up speed – and then he was gone.

The old lady next to her patted her arm. 'Parting is hard, but the heart is strong. God willing you will see him again soon.' The words were well meant but only made her more fearful. *God willing.*

When she arrived home, Grace was in her room, sewing and mending, small repairs she did for some of the lads who turned up and the NAAFI. Grace was mother to them all and she loved it. She was more of her old self; they all were. Eddie was stretched out on his mother's bed, reading a comic. For all he contributed to the household he was still only a boy – but they were happy here. Happier than they'd been in Holt. She flopped down in the chair beside her mother.

'How was Harry?'

'He wants to slow things down a little.'

Grace stopped sewing. Jessie explained about her year of grace.

'He hasn't clipped your wings as some men would.' Her mother handed over a button tin and a shirt and asked Jessie to find a match for the one that was missing. 'I always knew he was a wonderful young man; I never realised how wonderful.' She pushed the needle through the fabric and patted Jessie's knee. 'How unselfish of him. That's true love, darling. You couldn't ask for more.'

'Then why do I feel so rotten?'

Grace picked up her needle and concentrated. 'Because now there are no more excuses.'

46

When news came of the Dunkirk evacuation, Jessie couldn't sleep, couldn't concentrate and Miss Bird was cutting her no slack, even though she knew Harry was part of the defence. It was the final push she needed. On 1 June she walked out, glad to see the back of Miss Bird, certain the feeling was mutual. She made a long overdue phone call to Bernie. Within twenty-four hours she was part of a concert party and by the end of the week on an old bus bound for somewhere in Lincolnshire. Over the next few weeks they played camps and bases, factories and hospitals, and every song she sang for Harry. She didn't need Frank Parker after all. She'd made the right decision then and she concentrated or making more. If she was free on Sundays, she led the singalong at the Empire, wanting to squeeze every drop from the year Harry had given to her. She joined the local defence volunteers, laughing when she found out that the comedian Tommy Trinder had joked that the initials LDV stood for Look, Duck and Vanish. They needed laughter as never before as the news from over the Channel became ever darker. Mussolini declared war on France and Britain and all Italian men in Great Britain were rounded up and sent to internment camps; there was also news of Italian owned businesses being attacked in London, Manchester, and elsewhere, their windows smashed, the buildings ransacked – some set alight. France surrendered and by the end of June the Channel Islands had been occupied by the Germans. Harry and his colleagues were fighting along the coast, and over southern England, outnumbered but defending the country and all they stood for. His calls were brief and she made sure to keep her tone light and upbeat; she wouldn't grumble and she wouldn't have him worry about her for one fraction of a second. Jessie refused to be afraid; she was home in her bed each night. She was lucky. As Plymouth and Cardiff were bombed, more and more children were evacuated and at the end of July Frances wondered whether to send Imogen back to Patsy's.

Jessie sat across from Frances at the kitchen table. She had more time to visit now that her days were free and being with Frances gave her courage. The two women could speak of their fears for their men and distract each other if their spirits were low.

'She might be safer there.'

'But so far, any trouble here has been over the water, by the docks.' She knew Frances was torn, having to yet again decide whether it was the right thing to keep Imogen with her.

'And if they come inland?'

'I've stopped thinking, Frances. I stopped thinking when the men were stranded at Dunkirk. I nearly drove myself to a standstill worrying about Harry. I couldn't eat, couldn't sleep and it didn't help Harry, or me. I'm taking each day as it comes.'

An enormous bluebottle came in through the open window and buzzed around them. Frances batted at it with her hand. 'It's hard, isn't it?'

Jessie nodded; she didn't want to speak lest her voice betrayed her.

'Keeping busy helps.' Frances got up and swatted the fly with a tea towel. 'Still up on the roof of the Empire on fire watch?'

'Yes. Up there with George, a bucket of water and a stirrup pump – though what help the pair of us will be if we come under attack, I don't know.' She quite enjoyed her shifts; the two of them had taken old chairs from the stalls to sit on and Olive sent George with a flask of Bovril and anything she could rustle up for the two of them as a small treat. It was calming looking up at the stars and chatting, George telling her stories of the acts he'd seen at the Empire over the years. They had a fine view of the promenade and ornamental gardens, of the ships moving along the Humber estuary, and she enjoyed the stillness of the night, the old man's company.

The back door opened and Ruby came in and washed her hands at the sink. She'd been in the garden all morning with Imogen, who came in shortly afterwards, Mr Brown's nose covered in soil. Frances got up. 'Oh, Imogen, what has Mr Brown been doing?' The dog sat on his hindquarters and cocked his head to one side for sympathy. She rubbed the tea towel over his snout. The dog shook his head in protest and slunk under the table. Jessie laughed.

'He was helping us find the potatoes; he was good at it, wasn't he, Auntie Ruby?'

'He was.' Ruby drank a glass of water. Jessie hadn't seen her for a couple of weeks, and she looked much improved. Her skin had taken on a healthier colour and her hair was beginning to regain some of its lustre. She was still thin but that didn't mean she was weak and it was clear that she responded to Imogen in a way that she couldn't with anyone else. Imogen crawled under the table with Mr Brown, pulling the tablecloth to conceal them.

'Mum asked after you,' Jessie said, hoping to draw Ruby into the conversation.

Ruby turned away from the sink. 'How is she?'

'She's well. Busy with her own work and out with the WVS most days. She enjoys it. She wondered if you'd like to join her now and again? They're always looking for volunteers.'

Ruby didn't look at her, staring down at Mr Brown. 'Tell her thank you, but no.' Jessie knew Ruby still hadn't left the house. Between them they had concocted all manner of things to entice her, but nothing worked, and Jessie knew Frances found it wearing. When Ruby came into the room it was like a cloud covering the sun. Their relationship wasn't easy, but Frances was trying her best – and it appeared she would be doing so a while longer. Aunt Hetty's Belgian refugees had been found homes, but their places had been taken by Channel Islanders. Their need was far greater than Ruby's. Grace had told Jessie to be persistent and, knowing how much happier she was herself, now that she was doing something she loved, she suggested something else, having already talked it over with Frances.

'Mum told me that the WVS are wanting to put something together for the YMCA in Heneage Road. As it's not too far away, I thought you might join me, Frances. It would only be a couple of hours and the lads would appreciate it.'

'That would be fun,' Frances responded, knowing full well what Jessie was up to. 'When is it?'

'Next week. The eleventh. Mum said she'd look after Imogen; she'll bring her to see the show.'

Hearing her name, Imogen pushed back the tablecloth and leaned out. 'Can Mr Brown come too?'

Frances shook her head, and the tablecloth came down again.

'Ruby?'

Ruby didn't reply. Jessie looked to Frances, who simply shrugged.

Jessie put her elbow on the table and rested her chin in her hand, tracing the pattern of the tablecloth with her finger. 'I'm so glad to be performing again. Harry knew me better than I did myself.'

'He didn't,' Frances corrected her. 'You didn't want to listen to what your heart was telling you.'

Was Ruby listening to them? Could she open her heart? There was no life to her, no joy; she was just existing and not living. The doctor had said it would take time but how long? It saddened Jessie, for in the fleeting moments she had seen Ruby before Christmas she had been kind and generous. Too generous.

Imogen got out from under the table. 'Can we go in the little tin house now?'

Frances said that they could. 'Shall we let Jessie come too? See how fast she can be?'

Imogen clapped her hands in delight. 'Ooh, will you, Auntie Jessie? We're having rehearsals, like Mummy does in her shows. You have to practise and practise to make it look easy.'

Jessie was puzzled.

'The tin house is the Anderson shelter,' Frances explained. She lowered her voice. 'I want it to seem normal. In case...'

Jessie nodded; there was no need for her to say any more. Shortly before midnight on Midsummer's Day, three bombs had dropped in fields near Hewitt's Circus, causing little damage, but it was a wake-up call and shook them all. Three weeks ago, the anti-aircraft battery at Cleethorpes Boating Lake had chased off a lone enemy aircraft who fancied his chances in broad daylight. They could no longer be complacent.

'That sounds *really* interesting. What do I have to do?' She squatted down in front of Imogen.

'When Mummy says, "Go!", we have to run to the little tin house as fast as we can.'

'I'll bet I'm faster than you,' Jessie said, straightening up.

'Bet you're not.' She turned to her aunt. 'She won't be, will she,

Auntie Ruby? I'm the fastest. Mr Brown is next fastest. Mummy is *always* last.'

Jessie stood up and looked to Frances, who was trying so hard to make light of a grim situation.

'Yes, Imogen is always fastest,' Ruby confirmed.

'Right!' said Jessie, bobbing slightly and bending her arms as if ready to run.

Imogen moved further to the back door and copied her. The two of them looked to Frances.

'Ready. Steady...' Jessie bobbed lower; Imogen wobbled. 'Go!' The child was out of the door, Mr Brown bounding after her. Jessie followed as slow as she could and ran into the shelter after Imogen, shortly followed by Ruby and Frances, pretending to be out of breath.

'Told you. Told you.'

Jessie tickled Imogen as she climbed up onto the bench that Frances had made up with a pillow and blanket. Jessie sat opposite and folded her arms.

'S'not fair, you've had more practice than me.'

Imogen giggled at her.

'What do we do now?'

'You can read.' Imogen pointed to the books. 'Or we can tell stories.'

'Or we can sing,' Jessie suggested.

Frances nodded. 'Good idea.'

'What shall we sing?' Jessie tapped her index finger on her chin. 'How about "I'm Forever Blowing Bubbles"? I like that one. Do you know it, Immi?'

'Yes.' Imogen began to sing, her voice so sweet and lovely that Jessie wanted to pick her up and squeeze her. She joined in, Frances too and then to her surprise so did Ruby, quietly at first but when

Imogen turned to her, smiling, Ruby smiled back, still singing until they came to the end of the song.

'I used to sing that with my mummy too,' Ruby said, quietly. 'It made her happy.'

'Why was she sad?'

Ruby glanced at Frances. 'Sometimes she was frightened and lonely. And singing cheered her up. Just like your singing has made us all smile.'

Imogen looked to her mother and Jessie, who nodded vigorously. 'Did Daddy sing too?'

'Not really, your daddy was usually doing other things. He worked hard learning all his dance steps, like you do with Mummy.'

'And you,' Imogen said.

'And me,' Ruby replied, suddenly embarrassed. But Frances knew; she'd told Jessie that after the first time she saw Ruby dance with Imogen, she'd left the carpet rolled up, the furniture to one side. No one ever used that room; they all preferred sitting in the kitchen. They'd used it every day since. Frances went through her routine then would leave, knowing Ruby would lose her inhibitions once she was alone with Imogen. She'd heard their laughter often, Imogen's delight as her aunt joined in the fun, dancing as fairies, sprites, elves – and Mr Brown standing guard at the door.

'I miss my daddy,' Imogen said thoughtfully.

'I miss him too,' Ruby said. 'And I think your mummy misses him most of all.' Her words took Frances by surprise. Things were beginning to change. Ruby was thinking of other people's sorrows, not just her own.

47

When Jessie left, Ruby went up to her room and Imogen sat at the table with her magic painting book. Frances wrote a letter to Johnny. He had been posted somewhere down south and she had been able to work out where he was headed despite the lines being redacted by the man with the blue pencil. They had all got so much better at letting each other know things in a roundabout way. It was what Ruby was doing, she realised, in the shelter, sharing little snippets of her life, working it all out with Imogen's help, not hers. She glanced across to Immi, who was engrossed in her book, washing the water over the page with a paintbrush and smiling with delight as the colours appeared. She looked up and sat back expectantly. Frances admired the picture. 'It's magic.'

'It is,' Frances said. 'Would you like to send one to Daddy? I think he'd like that.'

'Oh, yes, please.'

Frances gently removed the page and placed it in the sun, on the windowsill. 'When it's dry, we'll put it in an envelope, and when we take Mr Brown for a walk we'll post it.'

* * *

When Ruby came downstairs, Frances and Imogen were in the hall, putting Mr Brown on his lead. She handed over an envelope. 'Would you post this for me?' Frances glanced at the address, then looked at her. 'There are things I need to say to Johnny that I haven't been able to say before. Some things didn't make sense – and now, perhaps they do. Or more than they did.'

'I've painted a picture for Daddy,' Imogen said excitedly. 'I've got an envelope too. With my very own stamps.'

'Have you?'

Imogen nodded. 'Let's go together. You can put your envelope in, and I'll put mine and Mummy's in, and then they'll all get to Daddy at the same time.'

'Oh, I'm not sure...'

'The fresh air would do you good.' Frances opened the door and sunlight streamed into the hallway. 'It's such a lovely day.' Imogen ran out, stopped on the path and waited for them, holding out her hand for Ruby to take. She stepped forward, the child's small hand warm in her own and she suddenly felt connected to the earth again. At last, she had someone to hold on to.

* * *

It had only been a short distance to the postbox, a mere hundred yards, but it had been like walking across a continent. Her legs had been shaking, her heart pounding so hard in her chest that she thought she was having a heart attack, but she couldn't let Imogen see how afraid she was when Frances worked so hard to keep her confident. Images of her mother came to her, distraught when their father died, lying across the bed, crying, her open purse and a few coppers on the counterpane. She'd been terrified but Johnny had told her it would be all right; he was the man of the house, and he would take care of them. Was that why he worked so hard? Her mother had not stopped crying and she'd climbed beside her and started to sing. 'I'm Forever Blowing Bubbles', just as Imogen had sung in the shelter. She saw now that that was the start of it, wanting to please her mother.

'You look exhausted,' Frances said, handing her a mug of tea. 'But then you've taken a huge step forward today.' She went to the window to check on Imogen and Mr Brown, then took a seat beside her.

'It was a few paltry yards.'

'We both know it wasn't.'

She was filled with shame for the way she had treated this strong woman, who had struggled alone with a young child because of her. 'I'm so sorry, Frances. I don't know where to begin, to try to...'

'There's nothing to be sorry for.'

'Oh, but there is.'

Once she had felt helpless, that nothing she could do would ever right her wrongs, but today had been like a door opening on a world that she might once more step into. She couldn't let it close in on her again.

48

For the next few nights, Ruby's sleep was broken by dreams and she woke, her skin glistening with sweat, then fell back to sleep again, staying in bed late. During the day, scenes from long ago played out in her head, the past more real than the present. Her mother's fear and her own, intermingled, being left alone, with no one to care for her. She hadn't thought of the consequences of intercepting Johnny's letters; how could she have known? If Mother had been alive and the truth had come out – what then?

She lay down and closed her eyes. Would she ever be free of these nightmares? Johnny was onstage; she was next to him. Their mother was shouting at her. She had forgotten the lines to a song – what was the song? She started to cry. She heard her mother's voice as clear as if she was standing over her. 'Don't you dare cry, or I'll give you something to cry about.' Johnny reached for her hand, whispering to her. 'You can do it.' Could she? She tried to remember the words; she could hear the tune, da, da, da-da, da, de, da, de, da-da. Her mother shouted again, but it wasn't her mother, was it? She sat up. It was Frances shouting for them to 'Go! Go!'

She threw off the sheet, heard the siren, the rumble of planes overhead and rushed after them, into the garden, into the little tin hut. Imogen was sleepy, Frances holding her on her lap, smiling, being calm, being brave. Ruby had to be brave too, for Imogen. She lit the lamp with shaking hands, the match burning too quickly.

'Who was fastest?' Ruby asked her. Her feet were bare and she was glad Mrs Frame had thought to add an old rug to the floor. There was a crunching sound in the distance, like something having the air crushed out of it and she shuddered with fear.

Frances looked at her and mouthed, 'All right?'

She nodded; she was shivering, though she wasn't cold, but she didn't know how to stop. The sounds outside got louder; they could hear people shouting, the sound of the air warden's rattle, a whistle. The planes droned above. Frances began to sing to Imogen, quiet lullabies as planes roared overhead, getting closer.

Mr Brown growled at something outside. Ruby's heart felt it would burst from her chest, it hurt so much, and she gasped for air. The noise came closer; she couldn't bear it. There was a high-pitched whistling sound. It made her teeth chatter. She leaned forward to open the door.

'Ruby, close it,' Frances called through gritted teeth.

'I can't... I can't breathe.'

There was a huge explosion, followed by the noise of breaking glass, then shouting; was it a tree falling? The sound of alarm bells as a fire engine raced to where it was needed. Mr Brown barked furiously and burst forward, pushing open the door, and ran off. Imogen sat up, struggling to get off Frances's knee. 'Mr Brown, Mr Brown!' Frances closed her eyes, couldn't look at Ruby. Imogen started to cry, to wail and Frances tried to console her.

'He'll be all right. He was chasing a cat. I saw it. He'll be in the park.'

'He won't, he won't.' Imogen wriggled frantically, pulling at her mother's hands, trying to escape her grip. Ruby watched helplessly.

Frances wouldn't let her little girl go; she was strong – she would hold on to her no matter what. Imogen was sobbing.

'Don't cry, Immi, please don't cry.' Ruby couldn't bear it. 'Shall we sing?'

Imogen screwed her fists to her eyes. 'I can't sing, I can't! I can't!'

If only she hadn't opened the door. But that was who she was. Ruby Randolph was selfish; she thought only of herself. She'd heard them all talk. All of them. She had to find Mr Brown. It was her fault.

'Don't worry, Immi.' Ruby was distraught. 'I'll get him back for you. I promise.'

Frances called after her as she dashed out, but she wasn't going to stop. She would show them that she could think of others; she loved Imogen, loved her. She had been kind and sweet and gentle—

She had to find Mr Brown. She ran down the path and out over the road, along the edge of the park, holding on to the railings, her eyes adjusting to the light cast from huge fires that were a few streets away. In the distance she could hear the sounds of the ack-ack guns, the thrum of heavy engines, alarm bells. So much noise! She put her hands over her ears. She had to go into the park. Had to. She hadn't meant to go into the water, she hadn't realised what she was doing, Johnny had got it all wrong, they had all got it wrong. She didn't want to die; she'd wanted to put things right but she didn't know how. Couldn't find the way. Finding Mr Brown would be a good thing – for Imogen, it was for Imogen. She ran in through the gates and along the path, calling, calling, ignoring the pain that hurt her bare feet, the noise around her. All she had to think of was Mr Brown, and when she found him they would go home. A bomb dropped, shook the ground, and the sky lit up with flames. Smoke pooled up to the sky and for a second she watched it, mesmerised, and saw the enemy plane overhead, flying over her. She couldn't move. The sky was red, lighting up the park, the trees, reflecting on the water, and as her eyes adjusted, she saw Mr Brown, barking furiously at the plane as it flew over them. Was she still dreaming? She shouted his name, but he would not be distracted, barking, barking, and she had to make him stop. She ran to him, grabbed hold of his collar, dragged him into a bush, sank down to the ground and threw her arms about his neck. She rubbed her face into his fur, and finally, after all those years, the tears fell. She had done something good.

49

The stench of cordite and burning wood filled the summer air and when the all-clear sounded they'd picked their way carefully through the garden and back into the house, avoiding the broken tiles that had been jettisoned from the roof, and bits of glass and wood that had fallen from heaven knows where. The windows at the back of the house were intact but the front was a different story – every single one of them had gone, the curtains flapping in the breeze. Frances had been shocked at how far the devastation had reached, fire and smoke visible from the other side of the park. The bombs had landed streets away, but the damage was far-reaching, not just to buildings, but to their peace of mind. It was too close for comfort and she was afraid the planes might be back again, and closer next time. Thankfully, all three of them were safe and sound but it made her reconsider her decisions so far. Perhaps Imogen would be better out in the countryside with Patsy after all. She poured hot milk into two mugs and handed one to Ruby, who was at the kitchen table, her feet soaking in a bowl of hot water, and checked on Imogen, who had fallen asleep in the dog bed, her head resting on Mr Brown's belly.

'How does it feel now?' Ruby's feet had been cut and bleeding and Frances had extracted numerous small slivers of glass from them with a pair of tweezers.

'Much better. Thank you.'

It had been a strange night, frightening, but strange. Frances had been angry when Ruby opened the door of the shelter but beside herself with worry when her sister-in-law ran out of it. Imogen had cried endlessly, eventually falling asleep with exhaustion, and Frances had found herself praying more earnestly than she'd done in years for Ruby's safe return. And now here was Ruby, saying thank you.

'I can't believe you didn't feel it.'

Ruby closed her eyes. 'It's been a long time since I've felt anything.'

Frances rubbed her shoulder and took a seat beside her. 'I'd rather it hadn't been so painful for you, or so frightening, but thank you for what you did.'

Ruby opened her eyes. 'I didn't do anything. I only tried to put right the wrong I'd done.'

'It was an accident.'

Ruby shook her head, and took a sip from her drink. 'It wasn't. I was thinking of myself. As usual.'

'That's just it, you weren't thinking; you were afraid – you needed air.'

'I didn't think of the dog.'

'Why would you? We were all safe inside. You weren't to know he would run out.'

'You wouldn't have made that mistake.'

'How can you be so certain?'

Ruby looked down into her mug. 'Because you put Imogen's happiness above your own.'

'Isn't that what every mother does?'

Ruby didn't answer; she didn't have to.

'That was clumsy of me,' Frances said.

Ruby shook her head. 'You knew my mother. I used to think she was putting us first, me and Johnny. I was so afraid of being alone. He was the clever one, the one with talent. He could easily have gone on his own. I was just holding him back.'

'Ruby, you know that's not true.'

Ruby shrugged. 'When I was a child, he looked after me. We were inseparable. I didn't know how I could function without him, and Mother played on that, on my fears.'

'They were her fears too.'

Ruby nodded. 'She was afraid of being on her own.' Tears began to fall, and, lifting her head proudly, she brushed them away. 'I don't know what's the matter with me. I can't seem to stop.' She gave a small, embarrassed laugh. Her pain was visible, and Frances's heart ached for her.

'It's shock. You've had quite an ordeal.' Poor girl, her whole life had been an ordeal. 'But, Ruby...' She reached out and clasped her hand. 'You went out, on your own. And you went in the park. That's another good thing to come out of it.'

Ruby tried to smile. She didn't think it a victory, not yet, but it was something to build on.

* * *

For the first time in many months, Ruby slept – deep uninterrupted sleep – and woke to discover it was eleven o'clock. Her feet were not as sore as she'd expected, the cuts mostly superficial, and she pulled on her dressing gown, pushed her feet into her slippers and went downstairs. In the kitchen, Jessie was leaning against the sink, waving to Imogen, who was in the garden with Mr Frame, the pair of them checking for damage. Grace got up to greet her.

Ruby pushed at her hair. 'I must look an awful sight.'

Grace wrapped her in an embrace then stood back and held her by the shoulders. 'Oh, Ruby, what a silly thing to do – and what a brave one. You could have been killed.'

'Someone was,' Jessie told them. 'By flying shrapnel. Four bombs were dropped...' Frances went to the window to check Imogen was well out of earshot. 'There's a massive crater in Abbey Park Road. Lots of damage, but thankfully few casualties.'

'A few more yards and it might have been us.' Ruby shuddered and they fell silent. War had finally arrived on their doorstep – or almost.

Mrs Frame came in for a bucket, found some old newspapers and went back out front to gather up broken glass. She and Mr Frame had come to the house an hour after the all-clear, having checked that their own family were accounted for. They had distracted Imogen and roped her in on their 'treasure hunt' and she'd been tasked with checking the vegetable patch for snails that might have gone to hide there. Normality. It was what her own parents would have done to lessen the child's fear, and in their absence the Frames were substitute grandparents.

'Have you been up all night too, Grace?' Frances asked.

'No, we were safe enough in Cleethorpes, but I heard from one of my colleagues that the bomb fell only streets away from you. I wanted to make sure you were all okay, and if there was anything I could do.'

'I suppose they'll cancel the show,' Frances said. 'What with all the damage hereabouts.'

'The show will always go on,' Jessie said defiantly. 'It's more important than ever. We can't let old Adolf think he's winning.' Grace smiled and rubbed at Jessie's shoulder and Jessie rested her hand on her mother's. It had been difficult to acknowledge her own frustrations, her own yearnings, but once she had learned to do so, any difficulties she faced were easier to overcome. She took a seat at the table. 'Why don't you come with us, Ruby?'

Ruby pulled her dressing gown about her. 'Oh, no, I couldn't.'

'Yes, you can,' Frances said firmly. 'You've already shown how brave you are. The more you put it off, the harder it will be.'

* * *

At six o'clock, Frances got Imogen ready and the two of them came to say goodbye to Ruby, who was stretched out on the sofa listening to the wireless.

'You could leave Imogen with me,' Ruby offered. 'I'll take care of her.'

'I know you would. I know how much you love her.'

Imogen came and sat beside her. 'I love you too, Auntie Ruby. So does Mr Brown. He's not sad any more. He'll look after you when we go out.'

'Why don't you go and say goodbye to him,' Frances said, 'while I talk to Auntie Ruby.' Imogen leaned across and threw her arms about Ruby's neck, kissed her cheek and went to find Mr Brown.

'I'm not leaving Imogen here, because I'm afraid. But not of leaving her with you. I've left her so many times and if anything happened, and I wasn't there... I already thought I was selfish for keeping her here with me when she could be safer with Patsy. So many parents have already made that sacrifice and sent their children away. But I made a promise to Jessie, and to the lads that I would do the show. I can't break that promise.' She checked that Imogen was still out of the way. 'Life is full of compromise, Ruby. I find it hard to forget what your mother did, to me, to you, to Johnny. Most of all to Imogen. She robbed her of her father – and her aunt.

Imogen adores you and she will never know what went before. It won't make her happier and I don't want to make her sad, like Mr Brown.' They shared a smile, but Ruby knew she meant it for her. 'The only way to make sense of it is to know your mother was doing what she thought best.'

50

After they'd gone, the house seemed to close in on her and the wireless irritated. Ruby thought on what Frances had said, that she had to go out again or it would be harder. She didn't want it to be harder. She didn't want to be afraid any more, of life, of anything. Upstairs, in her room, she switched on the light even though it was still only late afternoon. The front windows had blown out in the blast last night and Mr Frame and some men from the ARP had boarded them over. She could no longer see the park or the lake; there was nothing to see at all. She sat down at her dressing table, picked up the brush and ran it over her hair. Her mother had been doing what she thought best. Had she? She thought of Frances, how she had coped with a small child, but Frances had friends; she had people around her who supported her. She wasn't alone. There was a knock on her door and Mrs Frame came in.

'Your dress.' She hung it on the wardrobe door. Ruby hadn't worn it in months. She hadn't gone anywhere to warrant it, had worn the same skirt and blouse over and over. There were so many clothes in her wardrobe, but she hadn't touched them. Such a waste when Frances had gone to so much trouble to retrieve them for her. 'Mrs Randolph, Frances, asked me to press it for you.'

Ruby placed the brush on the dressing table. 'Did she ask you to do anything else?'

'Only to tell you that the show starts at 7.00.'

Ruby stared at her reflection. It had been a long time since she'd looked properly. She had turned away from the mirror, hating the sight of herself. How could anyone else bear to look at her?

'I may be speaking out of turn, but Mrs Randolph thinks a lot of you. She's a good woman.'

Ruby couldn't argue with that. 'She is, Mrs Frame. She is.'

Mrs Frame went back downstairs, and Ruby sat for a long time, forcing herself to look in the mirror. Her head was a jumble of thoughts and her heart was beating so hard in her chest that it hurt. With shaking hands, she opened her powder box and picked up the puff, dabbed some on her forehead, her nose and her chin. It was easier after that and she slowly made up her eyes, added rouge, and finished it with a slick of lipstick. Make-up was such a wonderful disguise.

She put on her dress. It hung off her a little more than it had before, but it didn't look too shabby, Frances had a good eye. She chose flatter shoes, easing them onto her feet and winced a little at the pain. The pain felt good; it kept her focused on something other than her fear. Opening her jewellery box, she took out her brooch, her mother's brooch. One day she would give it to Imogen – once she had almost sold it. Frances and her friends had rescued her then – and Frances was rescuing her now. She couldn't let her down. Couldn't let the boys down who would be going off to fight, for people like her. Was she still worth fighting for? She picked up her bag, deciding she was.

She called out to Mrs Frame before she left, hesitating at the front door. Mrs Frame came and stood beside her. Ruby put her hand on the knob, pulled it open and took a deep breath. 'Would you like me to walk with you?' Mrs Frame asked, as she stepped out into the small porch.

'No,' Ruby replied. 'I can do this.'

She didn't look back.

* * *

As she walked, she concentrated on looking straight ahead, not at the buildings that were damaged, didn't look left towards the area that had caught the brunt of the blast. Her brooch glinted in the sunlight and her feet hurt as she carried on down Hainton Avenue. She could feel the wetness of blood in her shoes. A couple walked towards her, and she bent down to avoid looking them in the eye, adjusting her shoe, her heart hammering as they came closer. On Heneage Road, she began to give in to the panic, her legs leaden. Only a few more yards, that's all it was, another street to cross and she was almost there. Someone was coming up behind her and she waited for them to pass, the long shadow looming in front of her. As she moved aside, the man made a grab for her bag. She shouted out, in shock more than surprise, and as he tugged, she gripped tighter, suddenly furious. How dare he! How dare he! She lashed out with her hands, with her fists. He loosened his grip and somehow she managed to swing out and hit him hard with the bag, over and over again and he put his hands up to shield his face. Stunned, he ran off. A whistle was blowing, someone was shouting and when the ARP warden came to her aid with his tin hat and his rattle, she was leaning against a wall, catching her breath.

'Are you all right, love? Did he take anything?'

'No,' Ruby managed to say. 'He took nothing at all.'

The man was kindly; he put a hand to her arm and steadied her until she could steady herself. 'Where are you heading? I'll go with you. See you safe.' He was old, his grey curly hair peeping out from his hat, perhaps the age her father would be, had he lived. Such kindness – it was all around her, and she hadn't let it in. But now she would. She had fought off the bad, and she would do it again.

She pulled herself erect, threw back her shoulders and ran her hand over her hair. 'There's no need, but thank you. I'll be quite safe from now on.'

She found the YMCA building and went in. Grace and Imogen were seated on the back row of the room where the concert was being held. Row upon row of men waited for the show to start, and those not lucky enough to get a seat leaned against the walls. In front of them, just below the stage, the band was waiting for their cue. On seeing her, Grace got up and rushed to her side. 'Ruby, what happened?'

'Happened?'

'Your hair, your stockings.'

Ruby looked down at her laddered stockings, and her dress torn at the hem. 'I had a little altercation.'

Grace took hold of her elbow and guided her into the entrance hall. 'Altercation?'

She explained what had happened.

'Oh, Lord, Ruby – and you didn't turn back?'

'I couldn't.' It was the truth. 'I knew I had to keep going forward.' She found she could smile. She felt happy; it was an odd feeling.

'Oh, Ruby. That's wonderful.' Grace embraced her and Ruby could feel the warmth of her body, the strength in her arms as she held her close.

'I saved you a seat, just in case.'

Ruby smiled again. 'You're as thick as thieves, you and Jessie. And Frances.'

As they took their places, the lights dimmed and the band

started to play. A rapturous round of applause erupted, and a cheer went up as the curtain opened and Jessie began to sing.

Ruby admired her, going out on her own, just as Frances had done – only with a child to care for. If they could do it, then so could she.

The kids from a local dancing school came on and then a comedian, followed by Frances, who had a magic of her own. She walked down into the audience and sang to the boys, boys just like Johnny, boys who might already have seen more than their fair share of horror. Were they afraid of what might lie ahead, like she was? She watched their faces change as Frances sang to them in turn, how they reached out for her hand as she passed, walking to the back, in search of Imogen. She smiled when she saw Ruby, blew Imogen a kiss and returned her attention to the boys as she made her way back onto the stage. Jessie joined her and when the music stopped, Jessie stepped to the centre of the microphone. The lights went up in the room.

'That's enough of us, lads.'

There was a loud 'No' in response and she laughed. Frances slipped her arm about Jessie's waist. 'It's your turn now. Join in if you know it.' The band started up with 'We're Going to Hang Out the Washing on the Siegfried Line' and straight into 'Run, Rabbit, Run'. Frances leaned across and said something to Jessie, and while Frances held the chorus, Jessie put her hand to shield her eyes and beckoned to Ruby.

Ruby shook her head. It was too much, far too much but as the songs went on and she looked around her, she knew she had to do her bit too. Slowly she found the courage to get to her feet. Could she? Grace took hold of her hand and whispered to her, 'Enjoy it.' As she walked down the aisle, Frances met her halfway, and together they walked up onto the stage. Jessie reached out for her hand and pulled her forward as the song came to an end. There were nudges and whispers as the boys recognised Ruby. Jessie stepped forward again.

'Yes, boys, some of you already know but we have star of the West End Ruby Randolph here tonight.' The applause was thunderous. Ruby wanted to run but as she looked out she saw that they were just boys, boys like Johnny – brothers, and sons, and fathers – and there was nothing to fear at all. Jessie stood back from the microphone and Ruby stepped forward.

'Hello, boys,' she said, and they stamped their feet and whistled. She couldn't help but smile and she looked to the girls and mouthed, 'What now?'

Jessie told the band to play 'It's A Long Way To Tipperary' and Ruby led them, the lads on their feet, joining in, regardless of how tuneful they were. They went straight into 'Pack Up Your Troubles', Jessie and Frances taking the stage either side, leaving Ruby to hold the centre. When they finished, the rest of the cast came onstage to take the applause and they left them with one last song. 'Goodnight Sweetheart'. It was one of the songs her mother had taught her, but this time she remembered the words, and the memories of this evening would replace the ones that had given her nightmares.

Jessie slipped her arm about her waist and Frances did the same and there was no barrier between them any more. Frances had held out her hand and helped Ruby across a no-man's land of her own making. She couldn't blame her mother, or herself for that matter; she knew that now, understood it. Forgiving other people was the easy part; forgiving herself was more difficult, but she had made a start and that was what mattered. They were all just doing their best, each and every one of them.

ACKNOWLEDGMENTS

It's been fun coming back to the Variety Girls – it seems a long time ago when I wrote 'The End' in the second book in the series, and so much has happened since then. A name change for one – but I have to say the Seaside Girls suits them so well.

Thanks to the wonderful team at Boldwood, I've been able to discover what Jessie, Frances and Ginny did next. I have to say, Ruby is a particular favourite, so I'm glad I got to tell her story and I hope she finds happiness and love in the future. I hope we all do. It's been a difficult time for so many, and continues to be so, but like it is in my books, it's family and friends who get you through the bad times. I've been very blessed with mine.

As always, any mistakes are my own.

Thanks to Vivien, Gaia, Margaret and Helen, who metaphorically hold my hand. Knowing they're there for me makes the difficult days less so.

As with any show, there is always a huge team behind the scenes to get a production ready to roll and this is mine:

Thanks to my fabulous editor, Caroline Ridding, who finds all the holes in the story and helps me patch them so seamlessly. Nia and Claire, who work so hard to let readers know of my books, likewise to Jenna, Megan, Marcela and Ben. Copy editor Becca Allen, who catches my inconsistencies so brilliantly and keeps track of the cast of characters as I move from one book to another. To Sue and Shirley, who pick up those final errors before the Seaside Girls face the audience. And to Amanda Ridout, who most certainly would have been giving the great producers like C. B. Cochran a run for their money.

Susan Scott, the archivist at The Savoy hotel, London, for recommending *Meet Me at the Savoy* by Jean Nicol, the press officer during the war period and after. It provided a fantastic insight to behind the scenes as well as the stars who stayed there over the years.

Help came from unexpected quarters when the Variety Girls first stepped out onstage, so huge thanks to Neil Sean, Liz Green, David Pogson, Andy Howells and Lucy Ambache, who have been so generous with their support.

To local historians and enthusiasts who have kept me supplied with plenty of press cuttings and photographs: Trevor Ekins, Paul Fenwick, Pete Spilman. Tracey and Adrian at Grimsby Archives. Dave Smith who keeps me fed with factual information of the Empire in its heyday. To Mavis Newman for sharing her Harmony Sisters stories, and Patricia Dickens for memories of the Empire when her father, Jack Webster, was stage manager there.

Wonderful bloggers and Facebook friends who've been amazingly supportive.

Most of all, to you the reader. Thanks for picking up the books and continuing to enjoy them. It makes writing them very special.

And as always, to my family. I won life's jackpot with them all.

MORE FROM TRACY BAINES

We hope you enjoyed reading *A New Year for the Seaside Girls*. If you did, please leave a review.

If you'd like to gift a copy, this book is also available as an ebook, hardback, large print, digital audio download and audiobook CD.

Sign up to Tracy Baines's mailing list for news, competitions and updates on future books.

https://bit.ly/TracyBainesNews

Why not explore the rest of the Seaside Girls series?

 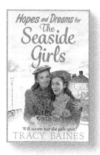

ABOUT THE AUTHOR

Tracy Baines is the bestselling saga writer of *The Seaside Girls* series, originally published by Ebury, which Boldwood will continue with. She was born and brought up in Cleethorpes and spent her early years in the theatre world which inspired her writing. Her new saga series for Boldwood is set amongst the fisherfolk of Grimsby.

Follow Tracy on social media:

 twitter.com/tracyfbaines

facebook.com/tracybainesauthor

 instagram.com/tracyfbaines

Sixpence Stories

Introducing Sixpence Stories!

Discover page-turning historical novels from your favourite authors, meet new friends and be transported back in time.

Join our book club Facebook group

https://bit.ly/SixpenceGroup

Sign up to our newsletter

https://bit.ly/SixpenceNews

Boldw∞d

Boldwood Books is an award-winning fiction publishing company seeking out the best stories from around the world.

Find out more at www.boldwoodbooks.com

Join our reader community for brilliant books, competitions and offers!

Follow us
@BoldwoodBooks
@BookandTonic

Sign up to our weekly deals newsletter

https://bit.ly/BoldwoodBNewsletter

Printed in Great Britain
by Amazon

29437051R00169